Fractured Ever After

A Collection of Fairy Tale Retellings

The display type was set in Goudy Bookletter 1911.
The text type was set in Garamond.

Published by Rowanwood Publishing, LLC.
www.rowanwoodpublishing.com

First Edition

Introduction

We are the Just-Us League, an international group of friends dedicated to the craft of telling stories.

Though we come from diverse backgrounds and have different styles of writing, we share a common passion for storytelling.

In our seventh anthology, we have ventured off the beaten track to explore our favorite fairy tales in a new way--by fracturing them. Fractured fairy tales twist the original much in the way a shattered mirror warps a reflection, and in doing so, they offer new and unexpected viewpoints, whether from the best friend of Prince Charming or the eldest of a trio of porcine carpenters. What happened after Rapunzel left her tower? What did the emperor's new clothes really look like? Did Cinderella want to marry her prince? The answers to these questions—and many others—can be found among the pages of this fantastical collection.

Without further ado, we present to you the *Just-Us League Anthology: Volume Seven*. Please enjoy.

Sincerely,
The Just-Us League

Table of Contents

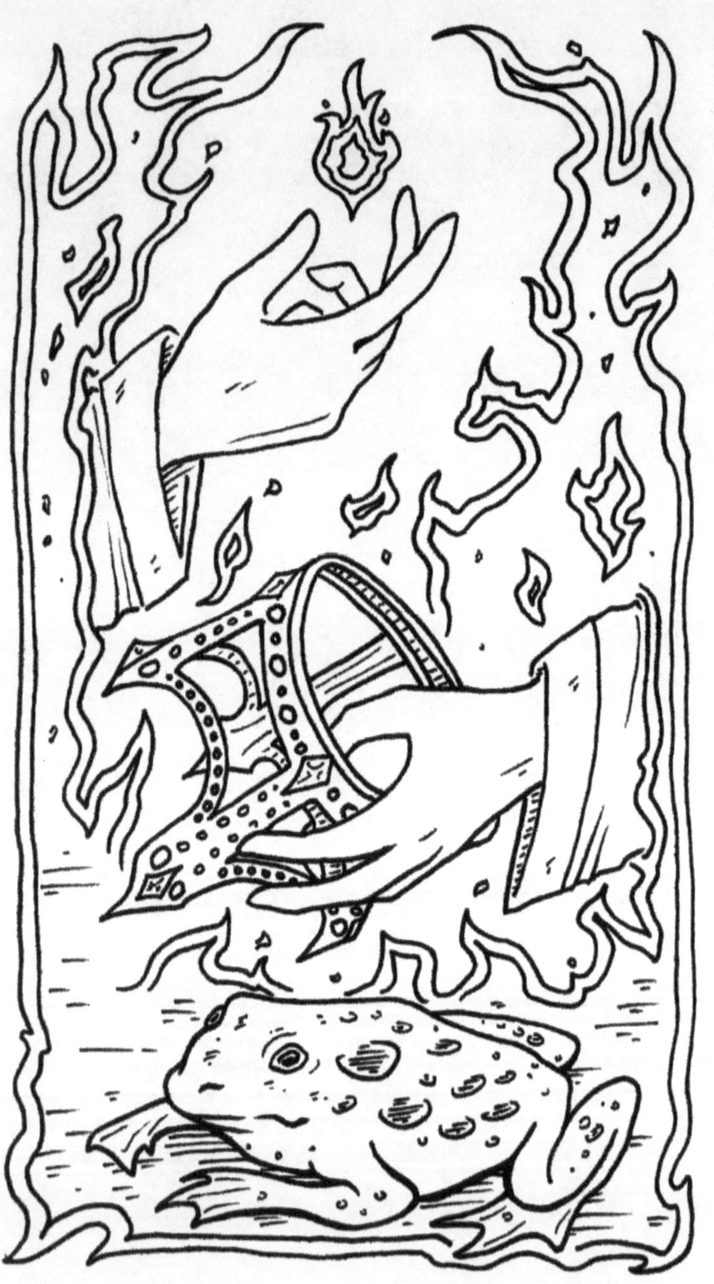

The Frog Prince

Heather Hayden

"So you want me to turn you into a human?" The mage tilted her head, curls the color of sunshine tumbling over her shoulder. "I've had humans ask the reverse of me, including a princess trying to escape an arranged marriage, but I've never had a frog ask to be transformed before."

"I'm not an ordinary frog." Gil stood as tall as he could, his croaking voice as bold as he could make it. Though aided by the tall pondside stone beneath his feet, his efforts did not even bring him to eye level with the sitting human. It cricked his neck to lean back and meet her gaze, but he held it firmly. *This might be my only chance.*

She pondered for a moment, blue eyes flickering from him to a vague distance and back again. "If what you've told me is true, then it may be possible, but it might not be reversible. Are you certain this is the path through life you wish to take?"

He didn't even need a moment to consider. "Yes."

"Very well." The mage closed her eyes for a moment before looking down at him again, her expression as flat as the stone he perched upon. "I shall do my best. Come." She held out her hand.

Gil's skin twitched as he stepped into her warm, dry palm. A fluttering began in his stomach, as though he'd eaten a prickle fly. "Are you transforming me now?"

"Not quite yet." Standing, the mage carried him away from the shore of the pond. "I don't want you falling into the water mid-transformation." She knelt and rested her hand in the grass. "Stand here."

With a quick hop, he leapt into the cool blades of grass. A breeze stirred them, tickling his sides until he flinched away. This far from the pond, his instinct kicked in, urging him to retreat to the safety of the murky waters. A different, deeper compulsion held him in place.

"This will hurt." There was a hint of apology in the mage's gentle voice as she rose to her feet, her shadow blocking the warm sun. "I cannot prevent that."

"I understand." Gil drew in a deep breath and held it. As the human began to move her hands through the air, he closed his eyes.

For a moment, he felt nothing but the quiet shifting of grass stems and the rough dirt beneath his webbed toes.

Then agony squeezed the breath from him, twisting and pulling and crushing. If he'd had air to speak, he would have screamed, but the cry caught in his chest and burned like a summer-high sun.

The pain lasted for an eternity before it faded away, leaving him limp and panting in the grass. Every part of him felt heavy, an unfamiliar weight holding him anchored. Yet his senses were on fire. Strange scents, strange sensations, strange sounds. Gil cracked his eyelids and winced at the brightness. The toes of his front feet curled, making him flinch at the odd limberness of the joints. Though he tried to raise one foot—no, hand, he corrected himself—to see it, his leg—arm—would not comply.

"It will take a moment for your body to adjust." Something rested on his shoulder, and he started. "Easy there, it's only me."

Gil tilted his head to find the mage kneeling beside him, much smaller than he remembered. Smaller than him now, in fact, as far as he could tell. Her hand still felt warm, though damper now, and beads of sweat dotted her forehead. Her voice held an undercurrent of exhaustion. "If it weren't for your heritage, I'm not certain the spell would have succeeded."

A bitter laugh rattled out of Gil's chest, deeper and louder than he expected. "I suppose I have my father to thank for it, although this wouldn't have been necessary if it weren't for him."

She said nothing, merely remained beside him until strength seeped into his muscles. As he began to move, the mage rose to her feet and walked over to the leather bag she'd left near the pond.

"Magic can do many things, but creating clothes from thin air is not a trick I'm capable of." She dug through the bag, pulling out a few items similar to what she wore. "We're lucky you're small for a male, or I might not have had anything that would fit." Her steps were a little unsteady as she returned to his side, and she sank to her knees with an exhausted sigh. "I doubt your father would want you turning up in a dress, so let's hope these trousers work."

***

Half an hour later, Gil could walk several paces at a time without wobbling. The urge to hop along on all four limbs had faded after his first flailing attempts sent the mage into gales of laughter. Gil chuckled as well, guessing he looked as graceful as a tadpole with brand-new legs. She helped him stand and taught him to balance on two legs instead of four. The clothing chafed against his skin and made him twitch, but she explained that it was a requirement among humans.

"It's a foolish custom," Gil muttered, plucking at the shirt.

The mage chuckled. "Don't be too upset. It'll help keep the sun from burning your pale skin." She touched his arm. "I guess frogs don't tan the way humans do. You had best limit your time outdoors."

He nodded and took a few more steps, awed by how small his world seemed now. The clearing, which would have taken a hundred leaps to cross as a frog, could be traversed in no more than a few long strides. He was pretty sure he could even hop over the small pond in one leap, though something told him it would be a bad idea to try that before he had grown used to his new body.

"I've done all I can." The mage patted his shoulder then went to pick up her bag. "I will show you the way to the castle gates, but after that, I must be off."

The fluttering returned to his stomach. "So soon?"

A faraway look clouded her eyes, and she gazed off into the distance. "I never stay in one place for long." Without another word, she headed into the trees, her slow pace allowing him to keep up.

Gil followed, marveling at each new sight and sound, wincing when he stepped on a sharp stone or twig. The mage had explained shoes, but his feet were too large for her spare pair of boots, so he picked his path carefully, leaning on tree trunks for support.

By the time they reached the edge of the forest, he was walking with relative ease. The mage paused at the edge of a flat expanse of dirt and glanced at him. "Let's rest here a moment."

He sank gratefully to the ground, but rather than join him, the human poked around in the underbrush until she found a long fallen branch. After breaking off a few protruding twigs, she brought the stick to Gil.

"Here. You can use this for support. The castle isn't far, but I don't want you falling flat on your face on the way. Healing isn't a strong suit of mine."

Gil stood and grasped the branch. The flexibility of his fingers still startled him, but he wrapped them tightly around the hard wood and raised his chin. "I'm ready."

She cast an unreadable gaze over him, nodded, and headed left down the long stretch of dirt. He fell in behind her, each thump of the stick and his bare feet a solemn reminder of how far he'd already come, and how far he had to go.

Father, I'm coming to see you. You will answer for what you did.

***

Gil became more and more fidgety as the day dragged on. Although the road had been empty at first, the longer they walked, the more travelers came into view. Some cast curious glances at Gil and his companion, while others ignored him, focused on their own destination. Even the few glances they received were more than he wanted; he couldn't help but wonder if they could tell he was a fake, a creation of magic.

As though reading his thoughts, the mage rested a comforting hand on his arm. "You have as much right to be here as they do."

Be that as it may, Gil chose to watch his feet shuffling through the dust rather than risk catching the eye of yet another curious onlooker. His toes looked so odd. So did his feet. And legs. *Everything* seemed strange; the world was larger and smaller all at once. Even with his view limited, the sounds of rolling carts and stamping horses and snorting oxen—to say nothing of shouted greetings and loud conversations—almost overwhelmed him. And the smells—Gil's nose almost burned from the effort of processing every scent that reached it, whether foul or fair.

Any normal frog would have turned tail and fled by

now. Muscles twitched in his legs, part of him yearning to do so even now, but Gil pressed on. *I will not turn back.*

The mage touched his arm again. "You're doing well." She lifted her hand and pointed ahead of them. "There's the castle."

Gil raised his eyes from the unending dirt path and stopped in his tracks. "It's...huge."

"Huge" didn't do the building justice. Brilliant white stone rose almost above the treetops, sparkling in the sunshine. Behind the impressive walls, sharper spires of the same pale material reached for the sky. Long banners flapped in the breeze, and Gil stared at the pale green shape upon the darker green background.

"Is that...a frog?"

The mage followed his line of sight. "Yes. Perhaps I should have warned you." Her calm tone held a note of sympathy, echoed by her slight frown. "I believe the king had the kingdom's crest changed upon his...return."

Gil's hand tightened on his staff until his knuckles turned the same white of the castle's stone. "How dare he make a mockery of us."

"I must leave you here." The mage turned to face him directly, her expression as impassive as it had been when they first met. "But please, Gil, remember to listen before you condemn. Everyone makes mistakes." Sadness flickered in her eyes before she turned away. "Even me."

Gil caught her arm as she took a step back the way they'd come. "Can't you go in with me?" His stomach twisted at the thought of proceeding on his own.

"This is a path you must walk alone." She pulled gently away.

He clutched his staff for support and took a deep breath. "Thank you for everything you have done."

Sorrow tugged at the corners of her mouth. "Don't thank me yet." She turned again.

"Wait!" Gil reached after her, not quite daring to grab her arm again. "I don't even know your name."

The mage looked over her shoulder and smiled. "It's Eveline."

***

Gil wanted to scream in frustration. It had taken almost an hour of waiting in line to reach the castle gates, and the guards had turned him away because he didn't have "papers." His attempt to explain who his father was fell short—the guards even laughed at him as they waved him aside.

Glaring at the two blond men in armor as they inspected the next in line—a farmer with a cart of cabbages—Gil debated what to do. He had to get inside, but the walls were impassible, and the gate was guarded both inside and out.

With a sigh, he settled against the wall, its stones warm against his back. Weariness tugged at him, but he forced his eyes to stay open. Perhaps he'd spy a way in if he watched for a while.

Some time later, a gentle hand shook Gil out of his doze. "Are you the one claiming to be the king's bastard son?"

Blinking, Gil looked up at a boy—too slim and gangly to be fully grown, but nearly as tall as Gil was. "Huh?"

The boy repeated the question, his green eyes brimming with curiosity.

"I don't know what 'bastard' means, but I am the king's son," Gil insisted. "I need to speak with him."

"Well, you don't look like an assassin." The boy pinched Gil's arm.

"Ouch!" He jerked away and rubbed the sore spot.

"What was that for?"

"Come on. You can go in with me." Straightening, the boy beckoned. "I can take you straight to the king."

"You can?" Gil studied the human more closely. Nothing unusual, as far as he could tell. The boy's clothes seemed fancier than most of what he'd seen so far, with intricate, pale green vines edging his shirt and vest. His expression was open, and though a hint of mischief sparkled in his eyes, Gil didn't get a sense of malicious intent. "Why would you help me?"

The boy shrugged. "I'm bored, I guess." He grinned. "Besides, if you are who you say you are, then that makes us brothers."

"What?"

***

Gil's thoughts were still swimming about like a mess of tadpoles by the time Prince Emyr stopped in front of a massive pair of gilded doors. His father had another son—a human son. That knowledge clawed at his heart. Not only had he and his mother been abandoned, he'd been replaced. *She'd* been replaced. If she hadn't already died of heartbreak when Gil had barely grown his legs, this would have crushed her.

Father has a lot to answer for.

"You ready?" Prince Emyr smiled at Gil. "It's after three so all the petitioners should be gone for the day, but Father should still be in the throne room."

Gil straightened his shoulders. "Yes."

The guards at the door glanced from the prince to Gil as they approached. "Your highness, who is this?"

"A friend of mine who wants to meet the king." Emyr's voice was friendly but firm. "Please let us pass."

"He and the queen were about to retire for their

afternoon tea—"

"Perfect. We can join them after Father meets my friend." Emyr stepped forward, and the guards didn't move to stop him.

Gil followed behind nervously, grateful for the unexpected support from his half brother, though he doubted Emyr would be so willing to assist him after the truth came out.

The guards both glared at him as he passed, but Gil kept his head high. His heart thumped against his chest, two beats for every step he took. The walking stick slipped under Gil's sweaty palm, and he tightened his grip on it.

"Father! I have someone who wants to meet you." Emyr grabbed Gil's hand and pulled him forward across a soft carpet that felt good against Gil's tired feet.

All thoughts of the sudden comfort faded as Gil raised his eyes to look upon the man he'd come so far to confront.

At the end of the long green carpet sat three chairs, the largest one flanked by two smaller ones. Two were occupied, but Gil's gaze was riveted on the occupant of the center throne.

The man had graying brown hair underneath a simple crown studded with sparkling green stones. His clothes were even richer than Emyr's, and his hands lay folded in his lap. But the most surprising thing was his kind expression and the gentle smile he wore as they approached.

"You have perfect timing, Emyr. Would you and your friend like to join us for tea?"

Gil stopped and wrenched his hand from Emyr. Ignoring the prince's surprise, he glared at his father. For a moment, the words he wanted to speak clogged his throat, refusing to budge, but he drew in a sharp breath and forced them out.

"Father, I've come to confront you." No sooner had

he begun than the entire speech he'd rehearsed for years tumbled from his trembling lips. "I doubt you remember me, but let me refresh that memory for you. Eighteen years ago, you were transformed by a scheming witch into a frog."

The king's eyes narrowed, and he opened his mouth to speak, but Gil kept talking.

"Though at first you were distraught, you found peace and happiness in a small forest pond. There you met Alese, a greater spotted frog like yourself, and you fell in love. However, not long after your first clutch began to hatch, a woman came to the pond looking for you. She came every day for months, calling your name and crying. You told Alese not worry, that the woman did not interest you, but soon after that, she awoke one morning to find you conversing with the woman. Before Alese could intervene, the woman snatched you up and kissed you, breaking the enchantment you were under...and dooming my mother to die from the cold, sharp ache of heartbreak."

Gil pointed an accusatory finger at the king. "You killed my mother, King Idris." His words echoed off the polished stone walls.

The king stared at Gil for a long, long moment, not a hint of emotion touching his hard expression. In the corner of his eye, Gil could see Emyr looking between the two of them, but the prince did not matter at the moment. He'd finally done it. He'd finally confronted his father.

Why then did grief still squeeze his heart? Why then did the weight that had settled over him the day of his father's departure, the weight made more heavy with each sob his mother cried until her ultimate passing, why did that weight still lie on his shoulders?

The first to speak was not the king, or the prince, but a third occupant in the room. Her voice was frozen honey, and her words held nothing but contempt. "How dare you barge in here and speak to the king in such a disrespectful manner. Guards, escort this vagabond from the castle."

Gil's gaze darted to the woman sitting beside his father, and he flinched. Red hair, silver at the edges but still bright. Green eyes the same shade as Emyr's. Skin almost as pale as Gil's own. This must be the queen. The woman who stole his father away.

Several guards standing at the edge of the room started forward, but they stopped when the king raised his hand.

Without speaking, the king rose from his throne and walked down the carpet toward his sons. He had a slight limp, but each stride was long and purposeful. Before Gil could react, his father embraced him.

"Welcome, my son!"

Gil pushed the king away, taking a step back as confusion scattered his thoughts. *What's going on?*

The guards took another step forward, perhaps expecting an attack, but the king gestured at them again before turning back to Gil.

"I am so glad to see you. Come, we shall get you out of those dusty clothes into something more fitting for a prince."

Gil moved back, shaking his head. "What are you talking about? I didn't come here to—"

"Let it be known," the king said, raising his voice, "my son, Crown Prince Gilbert, is alive. Let this be proclaimed throughout Araliss, and let no man or woman speak against him, for he is the heir and hope of this kingdom."

A shriek came from the queen, and Emyr gasped. Gil stared at his father in shock. Questions swirled through his mind, each one more important than the last, but before he could protest, the king had two guards escort him from the room.

***

The next few hours were a blur of activity that Gil only half understood. He was escorted to a different room where his clothes were removed before he was plunged into a hot pool that smelled like wildflowers. Two men, wearing identical green outfits rather than armor, scrubbed his skin and hair with a slimy substance that smelled even more like flowers, almost overpoweringly so. Unsure what would happen if he resisted, Gil lay limp in the water and wished he were back in his nice, cool pond.

They pulled him out of the pool—bath, one of the men called it—rubbed him down with a large, soft cloth, then dressed him in much softer clothes than those he had worn before. Gil had the presence of mind to ask after his original clothes, and they promised to store them away for him, but he couldn't help wishing he still wore them. They were the last reminder he had of Eveline—besides his new body, that was—even his walking stick had vanished in the bustle. He missed her calm, supportive presence. She'd know how to get him out of this situation.

Once dressed, he was led to a chair in front of a rectangular wooden box topped with an oval, reflective surface. Gil touched it to see if the water would ripple and was startled to feel a cool, dry, stone-like material instead.

"Never seen a mirror before?" asked the man tugging something through Gil's hair.

Wincing, Gil shook his head.

The attendants didn't speak much beyond the occasional order as they finished cleaning him up. As a finishing touch, one of them pulled open part of the box and drew out a thin circle of gold with a single green gem at the front. He settled it on top of Gil's dark curls.

Gil stared at his reflection, more uneasy than ever. With the crown on his head and the fancy clothes, he looked too much like his father. Unable to meet his own gaze, he looked away, a heavy swirl of emotions twisting his stomach into knots.

He had come to the castle to confront his father, and he had done so, but he had never considered what would happen afterward. Well, perhaps he expected—hoped—that his father would beg for forgiveness. Part of him had thought his father would show no remorse. He had never been quite sure how he'd handle either of those situations, but the one he was currently entrenched in was even more difficult. Nothing could have prepared him for being welcomed with open arms—as the crown prince, no less. Gil scowled. *Whatever Father is scheming, I want no part in it.*

Emyr entered the room, disrupting Gil's thoughts with a cheerful, "There you are!" The prince skipped over to the chair Gil was sitting in and rested a hand on his shoulder. "You can go."

Finally! Gil started to rise, but the attendants bowed and headed for the door.

"Not you." Emyr leaned against the box and folded his arms. "Is everything you said...true?"

Settling back into the chair, Gil met his half brother's gaze squarely. "Yes."

The prince's expression grew more troubled, and he looked at the floor. "I can't believe Father would have done something like that. He's the kindest, most compassionate person I know. But..." His shoulders slumped. "He did call you his son. So that must mean it's true."

"Yes."

Emyr raised his head, curiosity chasing away the shadows for a moment. "But if he was a frog when you were born, how are you..." He gestured at Gil.

"A mage called Eveline transformed me into a human." Gil tugged at the collar of his shirt—it was much tighter than the one she had given him.

The prince's eyes widened. "*She* was with you? Really?"

"You know her?"

"I know of her." Emyr looked impressed. "I can't believe you met her." He slid down until he was sitting on the floor and wrapped his arms around his knees loosely. "Did it hurt, turning into a human?"

"A lot." Gil didn't want to talk about this. He needed to see his father again. Ask questions and get some answers. "What do you want, Emyr?"

The prince blinked. "I want to get to know you. You're my brother, after all." He grinned. "I always wanted a brother, but Mother couldn't have any more kids after me." His face fell again. "She's not happy you're here. I should probably warn you of that, since she's scary when she's angry. But don't worry! I'm sure she'll like you once she gets to know you."

"You don't even know me," Gil snapped.

Emyr hunched his shoulders. "But I want to!"

"I don't." Gil jumped to his feet, fidgeting under the weight of the layers of cloth he now wore. Why did humans have to wear so much clothing? He glanced down and winced a little at the crestfallen look on the young prince's face. As angry as he was at his father, as much hatred as he'd carried festering in his heart for most of his life, Gil knew he shouldn't take it out on his brother. Emyr wasn't at fault. He'd done nothing wrong, and although his existence was just one more reminder of everything his father had cast aside, Gil couldn't help but feel a twinge of pity.

"I'm sorry, Emyr." He held out his hand, and after a moment, the boy took it and pulled himself to his feet. "I will not be staying long, but I will try to answer your questions if I can."

"You're not staying?" Emyr frowned. "But you're the crown prince. Father said so!"

I don't want to be! Gil bit back that response before it leaped off his tongue. "You aren't upset at him giving away your title?"

The prince shook his head. "I never wanted to rule the kingdom. Mother lectures me all the time, and the tutors are strict, and Father insists that I sit in on all the long, boring meetings the council holds, but I don't want to do any of it." He scuffed the toe of his boot against the carpet before glancing shyly up at Gil. "I've never told anyone that before. It'll be our first secret!"

"What do you want to do instead?"

"I want to become a mage!" Emyr held out his hand and furrowed his brow in concentration. After a long moment, something bright red flickered around his fingertips. "See? Fire's easy." He held it out.

Gil eyed it cautiously, sensing the heat rising from the flames. "You can create fire with magic? Isn't that dangerous?"

Emyr shook his hand, and the flames went out in a faint puff of smoke. "Not really. And you can't tell anyone about this, either. Not even Mother knows."

"How did you learn to do it, then?"

"I love reading almost as much as I love magic." Emyr smiled. "I found some books in Mother's private study about the fundamentals of magic, so I've been studying in secret. It's a lot more interesting than history or etiquette."

Gil wondered if those books might hold a key to reversing his transformation, but that was a matter for another time. "Emyr, where can I find the king?"

The prince tilted his head, looking thoughtful. "He might be in his study. I'm not supposed to disturb him when he's there, though..."

"Could you show me where his study is? Please?"

***

Gil followed Emyr through a series of similar-looking hallways. The only distinguishing features were the random placement of doors and side hallways and the various paintings and tapestries of fancily dressed humans and strange creatures that decorated the stark white walls. Emyr's boot heels clicked against the smooth wood floorboards. Gil had chosen to go barefoot after trying on boots himself—they squeezed and rubbed his feet in a skin-crawling way. Clothes were bothersome enough.

They'd been walking for only a few minutes when a sickly sweet voice called out from behind them, "What are you doing here, Emyr? Shouldn't you be at your history lesson?"

Dread left cold tracks down Gil's spine as he and his brother turned around. The queen strode toward them, her gown swishing against the floor like the whispering wings of a hawk. "What have I told you about skipping your lessons? You'll never rule this kingdom properly if you don't apply yourself."

"But I'm not the crown prince now," Emyr protested, shrinking back a bit as his mother loomed over them. She was taller than both princes, and her glare dove off her sharp nose.

"This"—she scowled at Gil—"vagabond is no crown prince, whatever your father might say. *You* are the true heir of this kingdom, and you will conduct yourself as such. Now off with you, or there'll be no dinner for you tonight and a double session of history tomorrow."

Casting an apologetic glance at Gil, Emyr slunk off down the hall. Gil took a step back himself, not wanting to be alone with the queen, who reminded him even more of a bird of prey now. One about to sink its claws into its helpless prey. Should he try to run? He wasn't sure how far he'd get without his walking stick for support.

The queen took a step toward him, green eyes

piercing him as though she peered at his very soul. "You are no prince, little froggie. You had best hop back to your forest pond where your slimy mother raised you. This castle is no place for the likes of you."

I don't want to be here! The words sat frozen on Gil's tongue.

"I will not have you speak to my son in such a manner, Marietta." The king's voice was colder than it had been before but just as firm as when he'd proclaimed Gil's status in the throne room. He had approached from the direction Emyr had been leading Gil.

"You can't be serious about replacing Emyr with this, this fake! I've—*we*'ve worked for years to train our son to rule this kingdom. How can you expect this mongrel to do so?"

"He'll have time to learn. I don't plan on dying any time soon." King Idris rested a hand on Gil's shoulder. "Come, son. I'm sure you have questions for me."

Gil shook him off. "Yes. I do." Under different circumstances, he might have blurted them out then and there, but the queen's cold gaze chilled him to the core.

He followed his father down the hall and into a room smaller than any he'd seen so far, though still rather grand in decoration. Intricately carved shelves lined the walls, most filled with leather-bound objects. *Are those books?* Gil had gleaned some new words from the men who had bathed and dressed him, though he had no idea what the other items on the shelves might be. Some were round, others square, still others long or oddly shaped. Their colors ranged from dull black to bright blue, often patterned. *Do they have a use or are they decorative like the paintings?*

At the far side of the room, dark green drapes flanked a large stained-glass window depicting a green and brown frog wearing a golden crown. Grimacing, Gil averted his eyes to the massive desk below the window. Made of dark brown wood, its legs were carved in a similar fashion to the shelves, vines and leaves twisting up and around the edges. Two matching chairs sat on opposite sides of the desk, their seats covered in green fabric.

The desk's surface was buried beneath piles of papers and books, and the king brushed some papers aside as he sat down.

"Please, sit." He gestured toward the other chair.

Gil sat. The chair was comfortable, but this situation was anything but. "Why—"

"Do you know why I named you Gilbert?" King Idris interrupted, looking out the window at the courtyard below.

"No?" Gil ventured, his thoughts disrupted by the unexpected question.

"Your mother teased me once that I chose it because we could call you 'Gil,' an amusing name for a tadpole who does, in fact, possess gills. However, I picked that name for our firstborn for an entirely different reason. Gilbert means 'noble youth,' as in a prince. Even then, I thought that perhaps one day..." The king's voice trailed off, and he turned to face Gil, sorrow etched deep into his features. "Well, it seems that day has come, more or less, though under far different circumstances than I could have hoped. I'm glad you're here, Gilbert. This kingdom needs you."

"To be the crown prince?" Gil snorted. "I'm not interested. All I ever wanted from you was—"

"An explanation? An apology?" The king shook his head and sighed. "If I begged your forgiveness, would you leave? If I swore on your mother's soul that—"

"Leave her out of this! You don't have any right to speak of her, not after what you did."

King Idris looked down at his clasped hands resting on the desk. "I know how much hate and resentment you must hold for me, but the situation now is far greater than either of us. Your arrival here has offered me an opportunity, one that I must ask, must plead for you to accept. This kingdom is as much yours as it is mine, and if you were to leave now, it would do far more harm than good."

"Why should I care?"

The king raised his head and stared solemnly at Gil. "Because you are, like it or not, my firstborn son, and the responsibilities of crown prince rest on your shoulders. You've never been one to shirk your duty, Gil, have you?"

Gil had been the one who stayed by his mother's side while his siblings played in the shallows or chased minnows through the pond. Gil had been the one who laid her body to rest beneath her favorite flower patch. Gil had been the one who remembered how his mother died even as his siblings grew up and found mates and started their own families, their parents little more than a shadow of memory. None of the others had wanted to find their father and confront him. They thought he was crazy to try. But he'd owed it to Mother. How many times had he woken in the night to hear her crying? How many times had he heard her whispering "Why?" to her reflection? How many times had she sat at the edge of the pond, staring into the trees?

Those memories stiffened Gil's shoulders. "You abandoned us. I don't owe you anything."

"No, you don't. But don't do this for me. Do this for the thousands of people dwelling in our kingdom. They need a strong leader. A brave leader. You came this far, risked so much, to face me. I know you have the courage and compassion to care for this country and its people."

"What about Emyr?"

"Emyr is a dear boy, but he's never wanted to rule. Some say that's a good trait for a king to have, that a power-hungry man will only drive his kingdom to ruin. But a king still needs the will to work for his country even when he wishes he didn't have to, and Emyr does not have that focus. I fear that he would soon abdicate in someone else's favor."

Gil's brow furrowed. "Who?"

The king stood abruptly. "I've said all I can for now." He glanced at an object hung on the wall and frowned. "I'm late for a council meeting. You are welcome to join me if you wish?"

Gil shook his head and jumped to his feet. "I still have questions—"

"I'm sorry, Gil. They'll have to wait." King Idris strode out of the room without a backward glance.

"Argh!" Gil kicked the leg of the desk, grimacing at the sudden pain that radiated up his foot. Grumbling to himself, he stalked out of the study and then stopped short. Where should he go? He glanced up and down the hall before picking a direction at random. Eventually he'd run into someone who could give him directions. Where to, he wasn't sure.

As he trudged down the hall, his thoughts ran rampant against his will. Why was his father so adamant about him becoming the crown prince? And how could he even think that Gil would be willing to do so after what he'd done to his family?

Unbidden, a conversation he'd held with his mother long ago rose to mind.

"Father's really never coming back?" he'd asked her, only a few days after his father had vanished.

"He has responsibilities that are greater than us." Mother's voice was always soft when she spoke about Father, but grief threaded through every word. "He's the king of this land. I always knew a time would come when he had to leave, but I'd hoped..." She choked on her words and blinked away tears. "I'd hoped we could go with him."

"Why didn't he take us with him? Why'd he leave with *her?*"

"Only a princess could break the spell he was under." Mother raised one webbed foot, stared at it for a moment, then patted Gil's head. "He left us behind to protect us. I'm certain of it. A king always has enemies. If the truth got out, we could be hurt or killed. Besides, we're much happier here, aren't we?" Her voice quavered. "We have a simple, safe life here."

Safe, yes. Simple, no. Tragedy might separate a normal family of greater spotted frogs, but never had one abandoned their family before, not as far as any of those living in the pond could remember. That, coupled with the fact that his father had been a transformed human, well, the whispers of gossip from other families never really stopped, even after Mother passed away. Gil couldn't blame his siblings for wanting to put it all behind them, but he couldn't do it. Not knowing that his father was somewhere living happily with a human princess while his family fell apart.

Yet, his father hadn't seemed happy. If anything, he seemed almost melancholy, though oddly pleased about Gil's arrival. Yes, something was definitely going on, and maybe if he could find his half brother, Emyr could shed some light on the situation.

"Ah, Gilbert, is it? Or do you prefer Gil, like the froggie you are?" Venom had replaced the sweetness in the queen's voice, and Gil turned around slowly.

"What do you want?" he asked, every muscle in his body tensed. *Was she waiting to corner me again?*

"I want you to leave. You're not welcome here, and you're certainly no crown prince." She circled him, haughty gaze raking over him head to toe. "They can dress you up, but it doesn't change the truth. You're the spawn of a slimy little frog, and you have no right to come here and interfere with all that I've worked so hard for."

Gil straightened his shoulders and glared back. "All *you've* worked for?"

"Years of planning and careful execution, and you'll undo it all in an instant? Hah!" She raised her hand. "I won't give you that chance, little runt."

"I can't believe my father left Mother for you." Gil clenched his hands.

A sly smile curved her lips. "Yes, he did choose to come with me, didn't he? After all, the alternative was losing everything he loved." She waved her hand back and forth, fingers flickering. "I would have roasted that precious little pond of his along with his slimy family. Perhaps I should have, but with the wedding preparations, and then all the responsibilities of queenhood, and then my pregnancy, well, what did I care if a couple frogs were still hopping around in the woods? I never imagined one of his spawn would come looking for him." A glow began to form along her fingers, growing brighter with every second. "No matter. Once I've disposed of you, everything will be back on schedule. In a few years, this kingdom will be mine, and I will make it the greatest country in the world."

Gil turned and ran. Two strides down the hall, he stumbled but caught his balance and kept going. *I have to escape.* His heart pounded in his chest as he tripped again and almost fell. *I have to escape.* If he had any breath to spare, he would have called for help, but his aching lungs seemed empty despite his heavy breathing. *I have to—*

The queen's laughter bounced off the walls behind him, and then something slammed into his back. Searing pain enveloped him, and he crumpled to the floor, crying out.

The last thing he saw before blacking out was Marietta looking down at him, her wicked smile widening in triumph.

***

Gil's eyes opened slowly, even the sliver of light making him wince at first. Blinking, he tried to raise his head, but everything ached.

His surroundings came into focus, first as blurs and then as sharper shapes that at first didn't make sense. What he mistook for trees were too straight and smooth, made of the same cold gray material that he lay upon. They appeared to form a circle around him, that much he could see with some slight movement of his eyes.

"Where—" The rest of his question died in his throat, drowned by the quiet croak that vibrated through his body.

Surprise outweighed pain for a moment, and he struggled to his feet. The odd sensation of swaying made his stomach flip, but he gulped air into his lungs and looked down.

Webbed toes, smooth green skin with brown spots—he was a frog again. Shock made his skin twitch, and he took an experimental hop. Everything felt natural and unnatural at the same time, familiar movements now unfamiliar after his stint as a human. If it weren't for his strange surroundings, he might have thought it had all been a dream, but the metal under his toes said otherwise.

"Where am I?" He wobbled as his prison swayed and finally looked beyond the metal bars.

The cage he was trapped in hung from a metal chain attached to the ceiling. Similar cages dangled nearby, all of them empty. Soft yellow light from wall sconces lit the small room, which was lined with crammed bookshelves. The only furniture was two tables, one covered in papers and the other with strange objects, and a chair tucked into the wall opposite the door.

There was only one other occupant in the room, and Gil shrank back when his eyes landed on her.

Queen Marietta smirked as she looked up at the

swaying cage. "Ah, finally awake, are you? I thought of tossing you out for the dogs to play with, but greater spotted frogs are prized by some potionmakers."

Gil flinched. That didn't sound good, whatever potionmakers were. "Please, let me go. I never wanted to be crown prince—"

"Stop that horrid croaking. Without a translation spell, no one can understand you. You're just a pitiful little frog, stuck in that cage until I find a use for you or you wither away." The queen pursed her lips. "Either way, you've got nothing to do but sit there and wish you hadn't come on some foolish mission to avenge your mother, or whatever it was you wanted to do."

She set aside some papers she had been flipping through and walked toward the door. Pausing with her hand on the doorknob, she glanced back. "If it's any comfort, your father won't be a thorn in either of our sides for much longer. He had no right to take Emyr's birthright away from him."

The door slammed shut behind her, and in unison, the sconces' light flickered out, leaving Gil in the darkness of the room and his own troubled thoughts.

Could his father really have left to protect his family? If that were true, why had King Idris remained married to the queen for all these years? Was she the reason Gil's father had wanted him to stay and be the crown prince? But what could he do against a mage that powerful? She'd reversed Eveline's spell with ease.

Gil paced back and forth in the cage as it continued to sway. There wasn't anything he could do. He was just a frog. But a small part of him regretted that.

Would Father have stayed if the mage had never come for him?

That question, and many others, simmered on the surface of his growing anger—anger at his father for allowing this to happen, anger at himself for failing to do anything, and most of all anger at the mage who had destroyed his family.

A soft creak drew his attention to the door, and he took a step back, pressing himself against the cold metal bars.

As the sconces' flames leapt up, Emyr peered into the room. Gil blinked. *What is he doing here?* The prince crept in, easing the door shut behind him. He had a book tucked under one arm, and he made a beeline for the bookshelf on the far wall.

"Emyr!" Gil couldn't be sure his half brother wasn't in on the plot, but he didn't have any choice. The prince might be his only chance for escape. "Emyr!" He hopped up and down, making the cage swing back and forth. If he could only get the boy's attention, maybe there was still a chance he could help their father. Somehow. "Emyr!"

The prince froze and looked over his shoulder, face pale. He relaxed a little upon seeing the swinging cage and edged over to peer through the bars. "Oh, you poor thing. Did Mother lock you up?" After setting the book on the nearest table, Emyr flicked open the latch on the cage's door and slipped his hand in. "Come on, I won't hurt you."

Gil leapt into his half brother's hand. "I know you won't." The deep croak of his normal voice sounded odd to his ears. "I'm glad you're here."

"I guess the cage was scary, wasn't it?" Emyr patted Gil gently on the head. "I wish I could understand you. Maybe you could tell me why Mother was in such a foul mood."

"Father is in danger!" Gil hopped up and down, pleading with his eyes since his words fell on deaf ears.

"You do seem rather agitated. I better take you home... But where's home for you?" The prince snapped his fingers and gently slid Gil onto the table. "Wait there a moment, I know just the thing!" He bustled around the room, skimming the spines of books with his fingertips. "Aha!" Snatching a large tome from the shelf, he darted back to the table and opened it. "See? I saw this spell a few months ago, but I haven't tried it yet."

All Gil could see was black markings on the white pages—it reminded him a little of bird tracks. But it seemed to make sense to the prince, for Emyr mumbled to himself as he ran a finger across a few lines.

"Got it." Emyr turned to Gil and made a few quick gestures with his hands. A faint silver glow drifted from his fingertips toward Gil, who held still, recognizing the same communication spell Eveline had used. "I hope it worked... Can you understand me now?"

"I could understand you before." Gil hopped to the edge of the table. "We don't have a lot of time, Emyr. We need to find Father."

The prince's jaw dropped. "*Gil?* You're a frog again? But... How..."

"I'll explain on the way." Gil hopped up and down impatiently. "We don't have time to waste. You're a mage, right?"

"Well, I know a few spells..."

"Do you know any that can prevent someone from using magic?"

Emyr shook his head. "I don't—"

"We have to stop the queen." Gil paced along the edge of the table, heading for the door. "We'll figure something out on the way." *If only Eveline were here...*

"What's going on, Gil?"

"Did you know your mother is a mage?" He gestured with a foot at the room. Every fiber of his being wanted to flee, but without Emyr's help, he couldn't even make it out the door.

"I thought she must be, but whenever I ask her

about magic, she tells me not to worry about such things." Emyr folded his arms. "Is she in trouble? Did something happen?"

"Your mother happened. She threatened to destroy my family; that's why our father married her."

"What?" Emyr's brow furrowed in confusion. "That makes no sense."

"She's angry that Father tried to make me the crown prince. I think she's planning to do something to him, and we have to stop her. Do you know a spell that would help us?"

Emyr shook his head. "Mother can be scary when she doesn't get her way, but I can't imagine she'd kill Father..."

Gil released a frustrated sound, a deep croak that made the prince jump. "If I'm wrong, you can have me thrown out of the castle yourself. But if I'm right..."

Turning in a circle, Emyr's eyes swept over the shelves of books. "I might be able to find a spell that would work, but I've never tried casting something like that before. Blocking someone else's magic would be a very advanced spell."

Every time he'd seen a mage cast a spell, it had involved hand movements. "What about a spell that could freeze someone in place for a few minutes? Would that work?"

"Yes!" Emyr rushed to a bookshelf and grabbed a slim tome from it. "I think this is the book..." He flipped through the pages as he rushed back to the table. "Here." The prince slammed the book onto the table and jabbed a finger at a particular set of bird-track markings. "These spells were originally meant for animal training"—he grimaced—"or what the awful author thought animal training should be like. I considered burning it, but Mother might have noticed."

"Focus, Emyr, we don't have much time."

The prince mumbled to himself as he traced a few lines with his fingertip. At last, he looked up. "I think I've got it." He held out his hand. "Come on, let's go."

Gil stepped onto his half brother's sweaty palm. The salty damp made his skin itch, but of more concern was the trembling that traveled up his limbs. He gave Emyr a gentle pat with his foot, remembering how Eveline had done something similar to comfort him. "You can do this."

"I hope so." Holding his hand close to his chest, the prince pushed open the heavy door. Almost too quiet for Gil to hear, he murmured, "I hope you're wrong."

I wish I was. Gil huddled in the gentle cradle of Emyr's fingers as his half brother raced through the halls. *I just hope we're not too late.*

***

The king's study was empty, and so were his bedchambers. Gil's chest ached in sympathy as he listened to his half brother's labored breaths. Every mad dash they made left the prince more winded, and the trembling from before had become a deeper shaking.

"The castle's always quiet at night, but I haven't even seen any of the guards." Emyr gulped down air.

"The guards won't do any good against her magic."

"Neither will I, if we can't find Father." Emyr drew another shaky breath. "Let's try the throne room."

Something warm and wet dripped onto Gil's back as the prince took off again. He looked up to see tears streaking Emyr's face. There were no words of comfort he could offer, though. Not until they knew for sure the king had not yet been harmed.

The guards who had stood outside the throne room that afternoon were conspicuously absent. Emyr muttered a curse and flung open the doors.

"Father?" the prince called.

Gil squinted, trying to make out the room in the dim light of a few wall sconces. After the surprising sharpness of human eyesight, his own seemed woefully inadequate. But at the far end, near the thrones, he could see two figures standing, both bathed in shadows.

As the humans turned toward Emyr, light revealed two very different countenances—one, his father's, drawn in fear, and the other, the queen's, twisted into a mixture of triumph and shock.

"What are you doing here, Emyr?" Queen Marietta demanded. "You should be in bed."

"Is it true?" Emyr's voice wavered, as did his hand beneath Gil's feet. "Are you really trying to kill Father?"

The queen's voice turned soft and sweet. "Your father and I are in the middle of a discussion, dear. Be a good son and go to your chambers."

"Go, son," the king said, his own voice stern but strained, like a pondweed pulled almost to the point of snapping. That tone, more than anything, chilled Gil to his bones. It told him the king did not expect to make it out of the throne room alive but hoped the prince would.

Emyr took a few more steps forward, until barely a pace separated him from his parents. "Not until you tell me what's going on."

"Enough!" Queen Marietta raised her hand, a soft orange glow already flickering to life around her fingers.

Without magic of his own, there was only one way Gil could help.

Leg muscles flexing, he gathered himself up and leaped from Emyr's hand. It wasn't a far distance, all told, even with his legs wobbly with fear. But it seemed like a deep void lay beneath him as he launched through the air.

For a brief moment, all seemed suspended around

him. Even Emyr's gasp and the king's cry hung frozen in the air.

Then Gil slammed into the queen's face, his feet flailing as his toes sought something to hold onto.

Her shriek made his eardrums ache, and sharp nails dug into his sides as she grabbed him. He let out a weak croak of pain before the queen hurled him aside. The world began to spin. Gil tensed, expecting any moment to impact the hard stone floor.

Instead, soft flesh cradled him.

Somewhere in the distance, Emyr's voice rang out. Gil hoped that meant his half brother had cast the spell. *Did he stop the queen?* Gil wished he could turn to see, but his body ached and his head ached and everything seemed to be going dark...

"Gilbert!" His father's voice was the last thing he heard before he blacked out.

***

Gil slowly stirred. The cool mud he was burrowed in soothed his scratched skin. Had he been attacked by a crow? Sometimes those scavengers lurked around the pond, waiting for a leaping meal. But he didn't remember a crow passing by the day before, only a human with hair the color of sunshine—the mage!

Everything came rushing back, and Gil raised his head from the soft embrace of the mud. His eyelids slid open.

"Gil! You're all right!"

Emyr's cry made Gil wince and shrink back into the mud. "Not so loud."

"Sorry," his half brother whispered.

"Good, you're awake." A familiar face came into view, wearing a relieved smile.

"Eveline?" Gil exclaimed. "What are you doing here?"

She chuckled. "King Idris sent messengers after me, begging me to come back and help. Apparently your brother praised my spellcraft a little too well. I told him I wasn't a healer, but, well, here I am. Thankfully, it looks like you just needed some rest."

"How long have I been asleep?"

"Almost a week." Emyr held up a jar full of fat, buzzing houseflies. "I caught some flies in case you were hungry when you woke up. Father said that you'd like them."

Gil's stomach certainly did ache, but his curiosity was an even stronger hunger. "What happened...?"

The prince set down the jar and looked away, his shoulders slumping. "You were right. Mother really was trying to kill Father."

"Did your spell work?"

Emyr nodded. "I kept casting it until Father could fetch a sleeping draught from a healer. They're keeping her sedated, and she's awaiting trial now." The prince fidgeted. "Thank you, Gilbert. If you hadn't distracted her, I wouldn't have had time to cast the spell."

"Is Father all right?"

"Yes. He's in a meeting right now, but he'll be back as soon as he's done."

"He's been spending every spare moment at your side," Eveline added, tucking a curl behind her ear. "Though I am glad he's not here now."

Gil blinked. "Why?"

"You have a very difficult decision to make, the details of which I have yet to share with him."

"What do you mean?"

"Queen Marietta made a right mess when she transformed you back into a frog. She wasn't powerful enough to reverse my spell, so she simply added another on top of it. Your body has healed, but your spirit is being torn in two by the opposing spells and your own unique self—a boy born of frog and man."

Gil looked down at himself, realizing she had spoken true—the scratch marks were gone. But the ache was still there, lurking just under his skin. "What's going to happen to me?"

"With the help of your talented brother"—her compliment drew a blush to Emyr's cheeks—"I may be able to reverse one of the spells, but not both. Before, you had the choice to be man or frog, and you chose to risk a lifetime as a man. This time, the decision will be permanent. Which would you prefer?"

Gil glanced from her calm blue eyes to Emyr's pleading green ones. No wonder she hadn't said anything to his father. He knew Father would want what was best for the kingdom. Emyr wanted a brother and a chance to become a mage as powerful as Eveline.

But what did Gil want?

In the confusion following his father's announcement that he would be crown prince, Gil would have given anything to return to his peaceful life in the forest pond. But now that he knew the truth behind the king's abandonment all those years ago, he was torn.

Part of him wanted to stay, to get to know his father better, and his brother. To learn more about the kingdom beyond the small glade where he'd grown up. To see the world he'd just barely glimpsed.

Part of him wanted to go home. Home, where there was no magical threat, only the everyday danger of animals who hunted frogs. Home, where his sisters and brothers still raised their offspring, never dreaming of how small their corner of the world was. Home, where he had buried Mother.

Had Mother known the truth? Had she guessed it?

Had her broken heart been, not because of Idris's abandonment, but because she had thought him dead for trying to protect their family?

Gil had no way of knowing and no way of reassuring her now. All he could do was try to honor her memory. She would want him to stay in the castle, wouldn't she?

Her voice echoed in his mind. *We're much happier here, aren't we? We have a simple, safe life here.*

Safe was relative. There were always enemies. Simple...well, the answer was never simple, as he was swiftly learning. At the pond, it had been simple to dream of confronting his father. And yet the answer, the truth, had been anything but. Just like the choice he had before him now.

It was his father's turn to whisper in his memory. *I know you have the courage and compassion to care for this country and its people.*

Perhaps he had started this journey as a simple frog who wanted nothing but a simple answer, but he had become more than that. He was a prince—the crown prince.

Gil opened his eyes—although he didn't remember closing them—and looked from Emyr to Eveline. "I wish to stay."

On the Wrong Foot

Allie May

"And they lived happily ever after." The prince fingered the last words on the page before closing the thick volume of fairy tales and looking up at his friend. "Don't you see my dilemma?"

Daniel's dark hair hung over his face as he slouched in the plush red chair.

The prince cleared his throat.

Daniel's eyes widened as he snapped to attention and straightened his gray jerkin. "I'm not sure I do, Charlemagne."

The prince's eyes narrowed. "I told you to call me Charming. I can't have my story immortalized with subpar qualities attached to my character."

Daniel sighed, a smile playing at the corners of his mouth. "I'm sorry, Prince Charming. But I still don't see the problem."

Charming discarded the book onto the table with a heavy thunk. "These stories are all so perfect."

"Well, they are fiction." Daniel shifted in his chair, leaning forward to adjust the ties on his boots.

"But my story isn't! How can I ensure my story lives up to these? My story needs to be told throughout Donia until its end, and beyond! How else will I be remembered?"

"A peaceful reign? Hard work? Good deeds that win

over the love of your citizens?" Daniel pushed the book to the side, hoping Charming would forget about it.

"Oh, be serious, Daniel. These are the kinds of stories that withstand the test of time. Stories of drama, heartache, loss, good defeating evil, love overcoming all." He thumped his fist against his chest to add emphasis. "That's what people want to hear. Not some ordinary ruler who did ordinary things."

"So why am I here, again?"

"Because my parents have finally granted their permission for me to marry!" Charming rubbed his hands together, his brown eyes shining with glee.

"I'm at a loss for words." Daniel rolled his eyes.

The prince stood and paced, tramping down a trail in the thick blue carpeting. "I need your help planning my ball. Please, Daniel. It has to be perfect. It has to be remembered."

Daniel grabbed Charming's arm, halting his pacing.

Charming exhaled and slumped back into his chair.

Daniel propped his feet up on the table. "Of course I'll help you, and it will be perfect. I just don't understand why you're so set on this whole perfect romance thing."

Charming frowned. "That's easy for you to say. You already have a girl. And it's the perfect story, too! You grew up next door to each other and spent every day of your childhood getting to know her. I'm not a child anymore, so it's too late for that to happen to me. I need something as perfect as your story."

Daniel's feet thunked against the floor as his face flushed with heat. He waved his hands in protest. "Whoa, Emma and I haven't even seen each other in five years. We grew up together, and we had a thing before I left to work here, but that doesn't mean that she still—"

"Of course she does. That's how it always works."

Daniel's tongue fumbled in his mouth. "In books,

yes, but this is—"

"You invite this girl to the ball, and I'll show you how a little of this," Charming tapped on the thick leather that bound the storybook in front of him, "can create magic for you and…whatever her name is."

"Emma."

"Sure. Now, we must start planning. I insisted to Mother that the ball be this weekend. We only have three days to get everything in order."

Daniel sighed. "Then let's get to work."

The prince's eyes glinted as he clapped his hands together. "That's the spirit!"

***

Charming considered the preparations a huge success. Three days was plenty of time to throw a ball for every maiden in the kingdom. Only half the servants had been up all night sewing the silver and gold drapery that now decorated every inch of the ceiling and walls. Clearly there wasn't enough work to do.

He stood at the top of the grand staircase, directing the placement of the last few ice sculptures of himself, while servants carried in decadent sweets from the kitchen to fill the eighteen banquet tables. Clustered in the corner, a handful of maids wiped down the tile floors, polished doorknobs, checked for spots on the windows, anything the prince might want them to clean for a fourth time.

"You're sure this isn't a bit…extravagant?" Daniel stood a step below the prince so that Charming appeared taller. He scrutinized the glittering ballroom, hardly recognizing it through the perfumed haze. A band struggled to fit their eighteen-piece orchestra between an ice sculpture of Charming and a polished suit of armor.

"Extravagance is what the kingdom expects!

Extravagance adds detail to the story of my life. Did you get that, scribe?" Charming turned back to the royal scribe he had documenting his tale. "Make sure to note exactly how many platters of food the servants are laying out. And you need to count the maidens as they enter so that it can be noted how I knew my future bride from all the others the second she walked into this room."

"Of course, Your Highness." The scribe, Morley, scribbled more notes on his roll of parchment. He pushed his glasses back up, smearing ink across his thin nose, then scurried down the steps to count the trays.

"And don't forget to note each different dessert I am serving!" Charming called after him.

Morley turned while still descending the staircase, causing him to slip and tumble down the rest of the stairs. He stood, straightened his jerkin, and hurried off toward the refreshments with his head down.

"Oh, it's impossible to find good help these days." Charming sighed. "There better not be any ink on that staircase."

Before Charming finished speaking, a maid grabbed a rag and started dabbing at the nonexistent stain.

"Don't be too hard on him. This is a lot for one scribe to note." Daniel gestured up to the jewels dangling off the chandeliers that reflected glittering lights across the whole room. "I mean, you used eight different kinds of diamond, not to mention the rubies, sapphires, emeralds, and whatever else you convinced the royal jewelers to give you."

"Isn't it perfect?" Charming leaned on the railing and grinned at his friend.

"I guess that depends on your definition of perfect," Daniel carefully answered.

Charming frowned. "I'll see if the ice master can carve another statue of me."

Daniel waved his hands to stop the prince. "What I meant was you can tell which guests are right for you by the way she reacts to your decor. If she doesn't think it's perfect the way you do, then she's not the one."

Charming's smile perked back up. "Precisely, my good friend!"

"So, how exactly do you plan on finding the right girl if you're inviting every single girl from the entire kingdom? I mean, you're going to waste your entire night being introduced to them. How are you going to get to know anyone?"

"Nonsense. I don't need to get to know her." Charming gestured for the servants to shift one of his statues to the right.

"If you don't get to know her, how will you know she is the one for you?"

"Really, Daniel, you need to read more often." He shook his head and motioned for the statue to be moved back to the left.

Daniel sighed, unsurprised. "I'm not sure that clarifies it for me."

"The most fitting way to meet my love is to find the maiden who makes the grandest entrance, one who turns the eye of everyone. So I'll be judging every maiden on her ability to enter a room. The one with the best entrance is surely meant for me. After all, this is my ball. Or maybe the one who can find the most serendipitous way to meet me. I believe they call it a meet-cute."

"That's practical." Daniel nodded, careful to bite back his sarcasm.

"I thought so." Charming smiled at his friend before sighing and stomping down the stairs toward the servants. "No, no. This is all wrong. Switch it with that one over there." He pointed to another ice sculpture, this one across the room, sending servants scurrying to switch the two.

Daniel followed behind, taking the steps two at a time. He put an arm on his friend's shoulder. "It looks perfect, Charming. You've done a great job. Let the servants have a break, and we'll go get ready. Your guests will be arriving within the hour."

Charming clapped a hand to his forehead. "Of course! How can I impress my future bride unless I am as extravagant as this ball itself?"

"Not exactly what I said, but I'll let it slide because I know you already had outfits designed for us." Daniel scratched his side in anticipation of the stiff and hot fabric he'd be stuck wearing for the next few hours.

"But are they enough? We match the decor. How are we going to stand out?" Charming's brow tensed as he examined the room.

"You don't want to overshadow your decorations, Your Highness."

"As always, Daniel, I knew I could count on you. Now, to find my bride!" Charming turned on his heel and strutted out of the hall.

Daniel waved the servants away. "You all deserve a break before the ball starts. Thank you for your help."

"Thank you, my lord," they murmured as they breathed a unanimous sigh of relief.

***

Charming yawned as another maiden approached him on the dais and curtsied.

Daniel nudged the prince, ruffling the poofed-out sleeves of Charming's golden jacket.

"Thank you for coming." The prince waved a hand to dismiss the girl then shifted his shoulders. The golden fibers dug into his back, and he was confident there'd be a rash for the next week, but it would all be worth it once he found his future bride.

"How are you doing?" Daniel tugged at his own silver collar.

Charming sighed, his shoulder puffs drooping. "Who are all these girls? And why are all of them so…ordinary?"

"What do you mean?"

"So far, not a single one of them has done anything to grab my attention! All they've done is smile, curtsy, and bat their eyelashes at me from behind a fan." Charming felt like he was reliving his fifth birthday when some lord gifted him a horse that was the wrong color. Nothing was going right. All his grand plans were collapsing around him, and he would be left alone and humiliated, forgotten as time passed—no! This was not acceptable!

"It's almost as if they've been told that there's a proper way to greet royalty, and anything else wouldn't be acceptable." Daniel motioned to Charming's parents on the opposite side of the room, stiff and formal as various nobles curtsied and bowed. No conversation between them.

Charming frowned. That may be how his parents wanted people to act, but it was not what he wanted. "And the impression these girls want to make is that they are exactly like everyone else?"

Daniel cleared his throat as another young woman approached the dais.

The prince slapped a generic smile on his face as he tipped his head toward the girl, her parents beaming behind her.

"Your Highness, thank you so much for this wonderful opportunity to—"

"Yes, yes. Of course." Charming waved her away. "Doesn't this kingdom have anyone with a flair for something original, unconventional, nonconforming?"

"Obviously these girls didn't grow up with the thesauruses that you did." Daniel smirked.

"What am I to do? None of these girls live up to my expectations. How did you get so lucky to meet your one true love while I waste away alone in this palace?" Charming's hands twitched in his spotless white gloves. "By the way, Daniel, I forgot to ask. Did you invite what's-her-name to the ball?"

"I sent an invitation to her house, but I didn't get to speak to her as I was too busy, you know, trying to keep you from baking diamonds into the pastries."

"I still think that would have been a dazzling surprise." He pouted. "Well, let me know if she appears. I'd love to meet the girl who sent you to work in my stables. Without her, I wouldn't have my best friend."

The corners of Daniel's mouth quirked upward. "You remember that?"

"Of course! I'm shocked that you think I would forget."

"Well, seeing as you can't remember her name is Emma…"

Another young woman approached, fanning herself so fast it looked as though she might take flight. "Your Highness!" She squealed then slapped a hand over her mouth and dipped into a curtsy so fast she wobbled.

Charming held out a hand to help her stand. "Thank you for attending. Please, help yourself to some treats and enjoy the dancing."

The maiden's head bobbed up and down. "I will, Your Highness." She stared into his eyes with such sudden ferocity, the prince backed away in fear.

Daniel coughed to cover a snort and motioned for the girl to leave.

Charming exchanged a glance with Daniel. "This is not going well. And I'm starving. What fun is this ball if I can't even enjoy my own delicious refreshments?"

"I will sneak you something. Never fear." Daniel

chuckled and stepped off the dais, disappearing into the swarm of women waiting to meet the prince. Daniel had scarcely been gone a minute when Charming spotted something unusual out of the corner of his eye.

A young woman in a glittering purple gown burst into the room through one of the side doors. The doors slammed closed behind her, shaking the crystals on the chandeliers and sending lights dancing across the wall. The thud interrupted the musicians and startled the guests, who all turned to stare at her. With wide eyes, the maiden put a hand to her mouth and profusely apologized to the guests closest to her. The room filled with murmurs, presumably about her rude interruption of the festivities.

A huge grin broke out on Charming's face. This maiden certainly knew how to make an entrance. He pushed through the crowd of smiling girls, his gaze locked on the one in purple. He could only hope Morley was following behind, noting every detail about this moment for posterity. Pausing briefly to take a deep breath, he stopped in front of the maiden with his hand extended. "May I please have this dance?"

The maiden's eyebrows rose as she glanced around the room of frowning guests before her eyes locked onto the crown sitting on Charming's head. "Your Highness." She dropped into a deep curtsy.

"There's no need for formalities between us. You may call me Charming."

The corner of her mouth lifted into an adorable half-smile, but she covered it with a hand. "Of course, Charming."

The maiden never accepted his hand, so he reached out and took hers. He smiled at her before turning to the crowd. "Maestro?"

In the corner, the musicians raised their instruments and started a soft, slow refrain.

Without missing a beat, Charming spun the maiden toward him and began leading her in a minuet. "Isn't this nice?"

"Yes, Your—" She cleared her throat. "I mean, Charming."

His palms grew clammy as he gripped her hand. This could be his future bride. Now he had to discern the most important things about her to plan a perfect proposal. But also because Daniel said it was important, and he wanted to prove that he could listen. "Do you like it here in the palace?"

"Oh, uh, yes. It's a little overwhelming at first. I got separated from my family because I was looking for—"

"So you do like it?" he interrupted. "The decor, I mean. But also the rest of my home, too."

She blinked. "Yes. There's so much color and history here. I got distracted by all the tapestries and paintings everywhere. Your family tree is astounding and full of stories, I'm sure. I'd love to take a peek inside the library."

His heart fluttered, sending a tingling sensation down to his fingers and toes. "The library's my favorite part of the whole palace!" This was it. This was the feeling he had been reading about his entire life. This was love.

"Charming, I hate to be a bother, but I was looking for someone when I got separated from—"

"Never mind them." His cheeks hurt from grinning at her. "Do you feel that?"

"Feel what?" She glanced around the room.

He pulled her so she was looking at him again. "This warmth between us. It's like magic."

She stuttered as her eyes widened.

"It's okay, fair maiden. I feel it too. It's undeniable."

"What is?" Her voice quivered, and her eyebrows tightened.

"This connection we have. It's what I've been

reading about my entire life. It's love at first sight."

She shook her head. "I'm very sorry, Your Highness, but I don't know what you're talking about."

He locked eyes with her, and he couldn't help but smile at his own reflection in them. He looked kingly. "You don't have to play coy with me. Although, even when the men say that, the women in the stories still do. So if you want to continue…" He chuckled and stepped closer.

She pulled away. "I think you may have the wrong impression, Your Highness. I should go."

Charming gasped. "You're right! How could I forget the basis of every love story in existence!"

"I'm sorry?"

He released her hand. "The story doesn't revolve around the first meeting. Every romance involves some sort of separation to add to their longing and love before they are to wed! You are a genius! Please, this way." He put a hand on her arm and began leading her back to the door.

"To wed? I don't think— Where are we going?" She pulled away, looking around the room again. "I'm still trying to find my friend—"

"Shh…" He put a finger to her lips then squeezed her hand. "It's better this way. I promise. We will go down in history." A giggle escaped his lips as excitement burst through him.

"Your Highness, please. Can I at least find my sisters? They'll be looking for me." She fought against his grip, but he continued to steer her to the door.

A servant opened the door for him at the snap of his fingers. "Fair maiden, until we meet again." Charming pushed her out the door.

The girl stumbled, losing one of her shoes in the process. She frowned and reached for it.

He snatched it up. Gold. The same shade as his outfit. "This couldn't go more perfect if I had written it myself." He squealed then cleared his throat so a more manly pitch would come out when he spoke. "This is my only clue."

Her eyebrows pinched together, and she held out her hand. "May I please have my shoe back?"

He hugged the shoe to his chest, grinning. "I promise I will find you again!"

"How? You don't even know my name."

"Your shoe, of course!" He chuckled, waving the shoe in the air. "It will fit on your foot, and your foot only."

She stepped toward him, but a guard held her back. "I don't think that's— It's not even my—" She huffed, making one last grab for her shoe. "Why don't you just use my name instead? It's—"

He turned away, his hands over his ears, and the guard closed the door in her face.

Daniel hurried to the prince's side, treats piled in one hand. "What just happened?"

Charming grinned from ear to ear, bouncing on the balls of his feet. "I found her! I found the one!" He waved the shoe in the air.

"And then you shoved her out with only one shoe to make it home?" Daniel ran a hand through his hair.

Charming chewed on his lip. "I now see how that might be a problem."

"Yes." Daniel reached for the shoe, trying not to drop the refreshments in his other hand.

"Well, it'll add to the drama of the story!" The prince shrugged and accepted a chocolate. "I'm sure it'll be fine. Say, did you ever find what's-her-name?"

Daniel's face turned a shade darker. "I did, but she had to leave unexpectedly."

Charming clapped his shoulder. "It's a shame I didn't get to meet her. Hey! Maybe she can come to my wedding!" Charming smiled and walked away, cradling the gold shoe.

***

"Emma!" Daniel rounded the front of an extravagant blue carriage, bumping into a coachman.

"Excuse me!" The coachman huffed.

"I'm so sorry, sir." Daniel smoothed the ruffled silver fabric of his shirt and peered inside the next carriage, this one with pink roses painted on the side.

Empty again.

He glanced down the long line of carriages parked out front of the palace and sighed. He would never find her at this rate. "Emma? Are you out here?"

A grumpy face framed by brunette curls poked out of a window three carriages in front of him. "Daniel?"

"Emma!" He bit back a grin as he ran to her carriage and opened the door.

Emma sat there in a gorgeous purple gown, her legs crossed with her bare foot sticking out toward him. "Fancy meeting you here."

His hands froze as his breath caught in his chest. He wanted to hug her, run his fingers through her hair, stare into her blue eyes forever. But that might be awkward for her. He still wasn't sure where their relationship stood, and it had been five years since he had last laid eyes on her. So he settled for a simple, "Hi."

"Hi." She raised an eyebrow, the same side of her mouth twitching with a smile. "I like your suit. Is this how you dress now, Lord of Administration and Royal Oversight?"

"I don't—I mean—It's not—" His face warmed.

"I see your vocabulary has improved over the past five years. Must be all the time you spend with the prince." Her smile thinned as her mouth soured. "Is your friend always that charming?"

"Oh, Emma. I am so sorry that happened. And to

you. I have one job—to keep the prince from causing trouble. I stepped away to get him something to eat, and everything went wrong. I never imagined things could go that horribly."

"It was truly spectacular." A grin broke out on her face.

He smiled back. Her smile had always been contagious. "How are you?"

"Well, my foot's a little cold since the prince stole my shoe." She wiggled her toes at him.

"Aww, would your toes like my jacket?" He hopped up into the carriage to sit across from her.

She rolled her eyes. "Is he really going to use the shoe to find me?"

"Apparently so. Should be interesting, right?"

"I knew the prince was…odd, at least from how you described him in your letters, but I never thought he could be quite that…" She held up a hand and grimaced.

Daniel snorted. "I know what you mean. There's a reason why I have a job."

"Good thing you were working in the royal stables to stop the prince from testing whether or not he could stop his stampeding horse by calling to it with his mind."

"And speaking of that, I should probably get back before something even worse happens." Daniel stood and stepped out of the carriage.

"Daniel?" She put a hand on his arm.

He stopped and turned back to her. "Yes?"

She pulled away and looked down at her lap. "I don't want to marry the prince."

He watched her fingers pick at the beading on her skirt, and he refrained from squeezing her hands to relax them. "I'll figure something out, Emma."

***

"She had green eyes…" Charming tapped his chin as he paced in front of the scribes. "No, actually they were blue. Definitely blue. I think. And blond hair."

"Are you sure?" Daniel raised an eyebrow. He couldn't exactly sabotage the prince's search, not when so many others would recognize Emma from the ball.

Charming looked at Morley for reassurance. "She was blond…"

Morley shook his head.

"I mean brunette. She was a brunette."

The scribe nodded.

"I knew it." Charming puffed out his chest before turning back to face the shoe, placed on a silver-cushioned pedestal in the center of the room. "The shoe will fit her foot. That's how we'll know it's her. Make sure you note that I intend to marry the maiden whose foot fits the shoe. It needs to go in the decree."

"Are you sure this is practical? Think of all the houses you'll have to visit. What if she's not home when you show up? Or what if the shoe fits the wrong girl?" Daniel stepped between Charming and the shoe. "This isn't what your parents meant when they told you to find a bride."

"I will find her, Daniel. For the sake of our story, I have to." Charming faced the scribes, his façade firm to hide his anticipation. "Send word to every household in Donia. I expect everyone who attended the ball to be waiting for me in their homes when I arrive. We leave immediately."

The scribes tucked away their parchments and left the room to send off every available page.

"Daniel, I want you by my side when I find her. I plan to marry her as soon as possible, and I need you to help her and her family transition to palace life."

"Of course, Your Highness, but I'm still not sure that this is the best idea. You don't even know her. Your parents never met her at the ball. Even I didn't get the chance to meet her." Daniel still hadn't told Charming that the shoe belonged to Emma. He wasn't sure how to break the news, and the longer he took to figure it out, the worse he felt for lying to the prince, his best friend.

"I don't exactly need your approval for marriage." Charming frowned.

"That's not what I mean. But what if she isn't fit for the life of a princess? What if she can't leave her family? What if she doesn't want to marry you?"

"Nonsense! She would be lucky to marry me!" Charming marched to the front door of the palace, where servants would already be waiting with horses for their journey.

Daniel sighed. "What if she's betrothed to someone else? Or what if she's already married? You didn't give her much of a chance to introduce herself."

Charming paused, biting his lip. "I guess you do have a point. We'll cross that bridge if we come to it." He smiled, though his eyes contained worry. Setting his shoulders back, he opened the front doors and waved to the crowd of guards gathered in the courtyard.

Daniel trudged down the front steps behind the prince. It was his fault they were in love with the same girl. He thought that if she used the side door, she could avoid Charming long enough for him to fall in love with some other girl so he could safely introduce them.

As Daniel mounted his horse, he leaned over to Charming. "Whatever happens with this mysterious girl, remember that I want you to be happy."

Charming smiled and sat straighter in his saddle. "Thank you." He glanced over the crowd of soldiers that were to accompany them before snapping his reins and sending his horse into a gallop.

Daniel nudged his horse forward, and the rest of the party followed behind. Past the castle wall, the copse of trees that surrounded the gate, and down the hill to the main town.

They rode in silence until they arrived at the first house. It was nice enough. Stone walls with a thatched roof, a flourishing garden out front fenced with dark wood, and a handful of animals around the side.

A young page waited at the front door, standing up so straight, Daniel thought he had to be on tiptoes to seem taller for the prince. When Charming dismounted, he passed the reins to one of the guards. Daniel followed suit. Another guard accompanied them up to the house, followed by Morley with his quill and parchment.

The page opened the door, announcing the arrival of the prince.

Charming stepped inside, Daniel on his heels, to find a gaggle of girls curtsying and whispering as they smiled at him. A man and a woman, probably the girls' parents, stood in the back corner with their hands clasped tightly together.

"Please, take a seat." Daniel motioned for the girls to sit on the large sofa behind them.

The girls clambered to take their seats, plastering smiles on their faces.

Charming glanced over the girls. "The page told you why we are here?"

The girls nodded, giggling like schoolchildren.

Daniel held out a hand to the guard who produced the single shoe and passed it over. "This shoe was left at the ball by a girl. Do any of you recognize it?"

"My shoe!" Their cries tumbled over each other, and the girls all grabbed for the shoe. As they claimed the shoe, they stared daggers at their sisters, shoving each other out of the way.

Daniel rolled his eyes as he backed the shoe away from them, while Charming grinned and puffed out his chest again. He passed the shoe over to the prince. "Well, if you can't decide whose shoe it is, then you will all have to try it on."

Charming knelt in front of the first girl while she unbuckled the shoe she was already wearing. He slipped it over her toes, but it was too large. "Thank you, but it does not fit."

The girl pouted and slumped back in her seat.

The prince turned to the next girl, who had already taken off her shoe. Once again, the shoe slipped over her toes but didn't quite fit over her heel.

"Thank you, but it does not fit," Charming repeated.

Morley scratched notes onto his parchment as Charming tried the shoe on each maiden's foot.

The next maiden slipped her foot easily into the shoe. "It fits!" She jumped to her feet.

Confused, Charming stepped back.

"It's me, Your Highness." She stepped toward him, but the shoe slipped off her foot and the maiden fell.

"Thank you, but it does not fit." Charming breathed a sigh of relief before turning to the last girl. "May I?"

She nodded and stuck out her foot. The shoe fit over her toes and onto her heel. Surprised, she glanced down to double-check that the shoe fit.

"It fits?" Daniel's breath hitched in his chest. Maybe Charming would believe this was the girl, and he and Emma would be off the hook. Charming didn't remember what Emma looked like. He just wanted his story to be romantic. Morley could weave a wondrous tale of how fate led them to the prince's bride first. That was romantic enough for the prince, right?

Charming frowned and stepped back. "We have to make sure it fits."

"Of course." The maiden walked in a large circle around the room. The shoe stayed on her foot the whole way.

Charming turned toward Daniel and Morley. "This isn't the girl. What do I do?"

"Are you sure?" Praying for Charming's memory to work in his favor, Daniel held his breath.

"Of course I'm sure." Charming huffed.

Daniel's elation deflated back to worry. "You have to do something, Your Highness. She expects to marry you now."

Charming tapped his chin before turning back to the maiden and motioning for her to sit back down. He dropped to one knee.

The girl clasped her hands to her chest as she stared down at the prince in wonder.

"Thank you, but it does not fit." Charming pulled the shoe off her foot, avoiding her bewildered gaze, and gave Morley a pointed look.

The scribe crossed out the notes he took on the last girl before packing up his scroll and quill.

The parents stared before stuttering and talking over each other.

Charming stood, cutting off their pleas, and headed for the door as he passed the shoe back to the guard.

Daniel tipped his head toward the girls. "Thank you for your time. We are sorry to have bothered you." He hurried out the door after the prince, avoiding the confused calls from the girls and their parents behind him.

The page shut the door, staring up at Daniel.

"Continue on to the next house." Daniel nudged his shoulder, and the page scurried off. He took the reins to his horse back from the other guard and mounted.

Charming still stood next to his horse.

"What's wrong?"

"I don't understand. She wasn't the girl. Why did the shoe fit?" He looked up at Daniel and chewed on his lip.

Daniel shrugged. "I fear she may not be the only

maiden whose foot fits that shoe. You have to be careful so as not to anger any others."

Charming took a deep breath and mounted his horse. "My parents are not going to be happy about this, are they?"

Daniel shook his head. "I'll deal with them later. Let's continue. This is going to take all day, maybe tomorrow." With any luck, Charming would tire of his endeavor before they reached Emma's house.

The prince snapped his reins, and the convoy hurried to the next house.

***

"That shoe fit my daughter! Come back here!"

Guards held back an angry man waving a frying pan as Charming and Daniel fled to their horses. The shoe had fit a foot in almost every house so far.

"This is so much harder than I thought." Charming's face and neck flushed as he mounted his horse. "How can one shoe fit on so many feet?"

"I warned you this might happen." Daniel struggled to swallow with his dry throat. The next house was Emma's. He was out of time.

"Daniel, didn't you live around here?" Charming glanced around.

Daniel nodded. "My parents live up the road a ways. They would be honored to meet and host you, Your Highness." He pointed to the sun, now lowering toward the horizon. "We should stop for a meal. You could regale them with your many adventurous tales of bravery. Would you like to head there straightaway?" Maybe he could distract the prince long enough to forget about Emma's house and move on to the next one.

"No, let's head to the next house. And we'll see how

I'm doing after that." Charming spurred his horse forward.

Daniel's chest tightened as he followed the prince up the road.

The copse of trees opened around a turn, and the gray stone walls of Emma's home came into view. Emma was by no means wealthy, but her family's house still stood much taller than Daniel's across the lane, visible in the distance.

"Your Highness, my parents live right there if you want to stop. I'm sure the soldiers would appreciate a break for some food."

"It's fine, Daniel." Charming waved a hand as he slowed his horse. "I can handle one more family."

Daniel closed his eyes and took a deep breath. "Then let's get this over with." He dismounted and passed the reins over to a guard.

"That's the spirit." Charming sighed and brushed off his suit before heading for the door.

"Oh, don't tell me you're suddenly regretting this." Daniel shook his head.

"No. For the sake of my legacy, I have to keep going. I will find her. But…" Charming trailed off and ran a hand through his hair.

"We could stop right here. Morley will gladly scratch all of this from the record. The guards will round up the pages before they reach any more houses—"

"No. Absolutely not. I have to finish this." Charming's fists clenched.

Daniel nudged his elbow and grinned. "Why? You never finish anything else."

"That's why." Charming looked at his feet.

Caught off guard, Daniel stepped back. He hadn't meant to offend the prince.

"You don't think I know what my parents say about me when they think I'm not around? About how my head is up in the clouds and how they pay you to stay by my side every day because they don't trust me. They want to give the royal council control over every decision I make when I'm king. They're afraid I can't follow things through."

Daniel's heart sank. He knew that the King and Queen were worried about Charlemagne's future, but he hadn't known how much.

"I have to do this to show them that I can do hard work. I can go to every house and talk to every person. My subjects will know my face as well as my name. And they will see that I am determined and I can follow through. It doesn't matter how tired I am. Because I have to do this."

Daniel stuttered, unsure what to say.

"But beside that, I honestly believe that this hard work will make me appreciate her more. I need to work for it. My parents are right. Not everything can be handed to me. And I want her to know that I will do anything in my power to keep my future bride happy."

"Wow. That's actually romantic."

The prince raised an eyebrow. "You sound surprised." He turned back to the door and knocked.

"Wait, there's something I need to—"

The door opened, and Daniel found himself face-to-face with Anne, Emma's younger sister.

She looked identical to Emma, except her eyes were green instead of blue. Her eyes opened wide when she saw Daniel, then she turned her head and saw the prince. "Your Highness." She curtsied and opened the door wider.

Daniel followed Charming inside, shaking his head once at Anne. He would find a way to explain everything later. A guard and Morley followed behind him.

She led the way through the large entry hall. "If you are hungry, I could bring up some tea and biscuits."

"What kind of tea?" Charming asked as he glanced around the hall.

"We have all kinds, Your Highness. Jasmine, chamomile, or perhaps you're more interested in mint?" She smiled warmly at him.

"Mmm… I'm not sure I could choose just one." He clapped his hands together. "I know! What if I tried them all?"

Anne tilted her head to the side. "You want me to make you six different cups of tea?"

"Of course not. Just mix them all together!"

Anne stifled a chuckle with her hand. "Are you sure you will enjoy the taste? Maybe you should try mixing two flavors to start with."

Daniel raised his eyebrows. Anne's response was better than the one he had planned.

"What an excellent idea, miss." Charming raised his eyebrows and glanced toward Daniel, smiling.

"Are you planning on staying long?" She paused.

"No." Daniel coughed and motioned for her to keep moving.

"Of course." She broke eye contact with the prince and kept walking, past the grand spiral staircase and into the sitting room on the right, where Emma and her older sister Daphne waited with their mother, Vera. All three curtsied when the prince entered. Only Emma's eyes didn't widen when Daniel entered the room.

Charming motioned for them to take a seat on the couch.

Daniel knew the house well. The portrait of Emma's father still hung on the wall above the couch. Out of the corner of his eye, he spied a faded stain on a green chair. A stain from his own spilled tea.

"Your Highness, it's a pleasure to host you this afternoon." Vera dipped her head toward the prince.

"You know why we are here?" Daniel held out the shoe. "This was left behind at the prince's ball. It belongs to one of the maidens in Donia. Do any of you recognize it?"

Vera glanced between Daniel and the prince. "That shoe is actually mine, Your Highness."

Charming's jaw dropped, and he backed away from the women.

Daniel choked back a laugh.

"I didn't wear it to the ball, Your Highness. Don't worry. My daughter borrowed it along with one of my gowns. I was surprised when she returned home without it, but I was more surprised when she shared her story from your ball." Vera motioned to Emma.

Charming gasped when he noticed Emma standing in the back, then turned to Daniel. He put a hand on his friend's shoulder and turned away from the women. "That's her! I remember now!"

Daniel swallowed. "Well, what are you going to do?"

"Well, this isn't a thrilling enough climax for my story. It needs some extra…drama." He smiled warmly before turning toward the women. "You have lovely daughters, my lady, both of them."

Morley's quill scratched against the parchment. "You mean all three?" he whispered to the prince.

Charming cleared his throat. "Both of them." He gave Morley a pointed look.

The scribe groaned as he scribbled out his notes and started over.

Emma's sisters exchanged confused glances, while Emma folded her arms and leaned against the wall. "Just pretend I'm not here." She raised her voice louder than necessary and raised an eyebrow at Daniel.

He shrugged just enough for Emma to see.

Charming took the shoe from Daniel then knelt in front of Daphne. "May I?"

"Of course, Your Highness." She unclasped her shoe and placed it on the ground next to her.

The prince slipped the shoe over her toes, but it stopped just shy of her heel. "Thank you, but it does not fit."

Daphne replaced her own shoe without a word.

Charming turned to Anne. "May I?"

Anne smiled. "Of course, Your Highness."

He placed the shoe on her foot. It fit over her heel nicely. He quickly pulled it off. "Thank you, but it does not fit."

"I am sorry, Your Highness." She continued to smile at him, and he grinned back.

Daniel cleared his throat. "What now, Your Highness?"

"Hmm?" Charming broke eye contact with Anne. "Oh, yes." He frowned and stood, fingering the heel of the shoe as he stared at Anne's foot.

"Your Highness?" Daniel repeated.

Charming glanced back up at Emma then toward Vera. "My lady, are there no other maidens in this household?"

"Umm." Vera turned back toward Emma then looked to Daniel for advice.

He shrugged.

She sighed. "I guess not, Your Highness."

"Very well, then. We will be on our way." Charming gripped the shoe and turned to the door. "Come, Daniel."

Daniel followed Charming, completely lost as to what he was getting at. "What about…"

"Goodbye!" Emma called, waving a hand.

"What is that I hear?" Charming cupped a hand to his ear.

Emma groaned.

"I hear another maiden calling." He turned back to face Emma. "Alas! Another lady of the house." He took her hand in his and guided her to a seat. "Where have you been hiding?"

"Hiding?" She guffawed.

"I fear your family has hidden you from me out of jealousy! No… Your step-family!" He snapped toward Morley. "Write that down."

Morley glared at Daniel.

"No, this is my regular family. No steps involved." Emma raised an eyebrow at the prince.

"You're in denial about your family. I see. They must force you to do all their chores for them because they don't care for you. Have they hidden you up in the dusty attic with the rats?"

"Actually, Anne and I share a bedroom."

"Well, there's not enough space for three daughters in this tiny farmhouse." Charming gave Morley another pointed look.

"Farmhouse!" Vera stood, her hand to her heart and her anger turning her face a shade of red.

Daniel stepped forward to calm her.

Charming waved a hand. "It's just for theatrics, my lady. No need to get upset. Everyone loves a rags-to-riches story. They appeal to a wider audience."

"What are you talking about?" Emma tried to stand from the chair, but Charming held her down.

"Please, maiden. Try on this shoe. If it fits, I will rescue you from this awful life."

"But I actually like—"

"Shh." He put a finger to her lips. "Try on the shoe."

She scowled but held out her foot.

Of course, Charming slipped on the shoe and it fit, just like it had fit at least twenty-five other girls that day.

At least, the shoe mostly fit. The heel slipped off, leaving the gold shoe dangling off her toes.

Charming's brow scrunched up, then he forced the shoe back over her heel. He feigned surprise. "It fits! You are the one I have been looking for!"

"Hooray?" She kicked off the shoe and tucked her foot back under her skirt.

Charming stood and pulled Emma to her feet. "Please. You must come with me to my palace where we shall be married! You must meet my parents." He turned away from her and locked eyes with Anne again. "Your whole family must join you at the palace."

"I thought they hated me?" Emma folded her arms.

Charming scowled at her. "Just go with it. You want to come to the palace with me, I assume?"

Before she had a chance to respond, Charming giggled and clasped his hands together. "Of course you do!"

"Umm…" Emma held up a finger.

In his excitement, Charming either missed or ignored her. He cheered and spun in a circle. "I did it! I actually did it!" He turned to Daniel, beaming with glee. "I will head back to the palace immediately to tell my parents. You and the guards will escort these ladies and prepare them to be introduced." He turned back to Emma. "My parents will love to meet you…" He chewed his lip as he studied her face. "What is your name?"

"Emma."

"Great. Nice to meet you, Ella." He tossed the shoe back to the guard and hurried to the door.

"It's Emma, not Ella."

"Yes, of course." He swallowed, glanced briefly at Anne once more, and disappeared out the door with Morley close on his heel.

"Daniel, what just happened?" Vera put a hand to her mouth.

Daniel ran a hand through his hair. "It's a long story, and I promise I will be back to explain, but first…" He turned and chased after the prince.

Charming paced outside, mumbling to himself and shaking his finger enough to make the horses prance nervously.

"Charming? May I speak to you alone?"

The prince jumped. "Of course, Daniel."

He led his friend out of earshot of the guards. "What is going on? You finally found her. Why did you run out of there?"

Carefully, Charming inhaled before answering. "What if… What if I go through all this and don't end up happily ever after? She hardly seems like my type. Her sister was a lot more friendly and welcoming. Why couldn't she have been the one who lost her shoe?"

Daniel wanted to remind Charming that he was the one who kicked Emma out of the ball and stole her shoe, but he held his tongue. "Well, how do we proceed?"

"I can't back down now. My parents will never let me hear the end of it." He shook his head and groaned. "We proceed as planned. I'll figure out a way to make it work. I need to go home and think." He turned and shuffled back to his horse.

"Of course, Your Highness." Daniel bowed his head then muttered, "And by that, you mean *I'll* figure out a way to make it work."

***

"I think it's quite sweet." Anne sat on a chair in Emma's temporary bedroom inside the palace. It was about the size of their sitting room back home, only the center was filled with an enormous bed draped with lush pillows and comforters in every color imaginable.

"Of course you do. Because it's not happening to you." Emma threw her head back as she collapsed onto the bed with a muffled thud.

Daniel paced, treading in a circle. "There has to be some way to get you out of this."

"Why do you want to get me out of this so badly?" Emma turned onto her side and grinned at Daniel.

His face warmed, and he turned away from her.

"Stop tormenting him, Emma." Anne's eyes narrowed, and her smile turned into a smirk. "Before he decides he's no longer in love with you and lets the prince marry you."

Emma's face darkened to the same shade of pink as the bedspread. "Do *you* want to marry the prince?" She threw the pillow at her sister.

Anne deftly caught the pillow and shrugged. "Why not? He seems nice enough. If maybe a bit extravagant." She fingered the tassels on the pillow as she stared up at the ceiling.

"More like crazy." Emma's legs dangled over the edge of the bed, her feet swinging back and forth.

"It's romantic!" Anne threw the pillow back at Emma. "He really does care about you."

"Does he? He doesn't even care to know my name."

"He was close." Anne's foot also bounced, unable to stay still.

"He called me Ella! And then ignored me when I corrected him."

Anne huffed. "He's trying. Give him a chance."

Emma huffed back, her arms folded across her chest. "I really don't want to."

"I wish someone cared for me enough to search through the entire kingdom to find me." Anne slouched in her chair.

"It would've been much easier for him if he hadn't shoved me out of the ball in the first place." Emma sat back up and tossed the pillow at Daniel. "Can't you sneak me out of here or something? Put some other girl in my place. I'm sure there are thousands who are dying to marry the prince and wouldn't mind being called Ella for the rest of their lives."

Daniel glanced between Emma and Anne. Except for their eyes, they looked almost identical. Especially with their raised eyebrows and slight pouts. "You know, that gives me an idea."

***

Anne wrung her hands, pacing out in the hall. "Are you sure this will work?"

Daniel shrugged. "I'm never sure when it comes to the prince. Are you sure you're okay with this?"

Anne peered through the doorway and saw Charming sitting with his parents on their thrones. A smile crept onto her lips. "Yes. I'd like to get to know him better."

"Then this is the best idea we're going to have. He'll realize you aren't the girl from the ball, and he'll have to slow down. But if you both like each other in the way I think you do, then you'll have time to get to know each other before rushing into anything." He put a hand on Anne's arm before peeking through the doorway himself. "They're almost ready for you."

A sizable crowd had gathered in the throne room. Up on the dais, the king stood from his tall purple throne and addressed the people gathered there. He motioned to the prince then at the shoe, resting on a pedestal next to Charming.

Daniel nodded at Anne, and she entered the room. She walked up the aisle and stopped at the bottom of the dais.

After taking a shaky breath, Daniel slipped into the room and waited at the back of the crowd.

Emma appeared next to him. "Do you think this will work?"

Daniel chewed on a nail. "Why not? He couldn't

remember your eye color anyway. It was easy enough to bribe Morley to change it in his notes."

Charming took Anne's hand and led her up the steps onto the dais by the shoe. His brow furrowed a bit as he studied her face.

She smiled at him, and his face brightened. He seemed to recognize her, though his brow remained furrowed. He glanced around the crowd until he spotted Daniel and Emma and raised an eyebrow.

Daniel shrank in the back row, clenching his fists. Charming knew.

Emma leaned over and took one of his hands in hers.

He sighed, relaxing toward her.

Charming knelt down in front of Anne, with the shoe in hand. He slipped it onto her foot in front of the crowd, and it fit perfectly over her heel. He blinked up at her then breathed in relief as a smile spread over his lips. "It fits!" He stood, taking Anne's hand in his and holding it up for everyone to see.

The crowd burst into applause.

"So that's it? They're engaged now?" Emma squeezed his hand.

"I guess so. But I still have a lot of explaining to do. I can't hide you from him, and I'd prefer he hears the truth from me. But for the sake of his story, this works. Morley will make it work."

Charming put an arm around Anne, whispering something in her ear. She smiled then covered her mouth with a hand.

"And what a story it will be." Emma leaned against Daniel, her head resting on his shoulder. "The strangest love story ever written."

Daniel casually draped his arm over her shoulders, pulling her in a little closer, and couldn't help but smile at the prince and his new fiancée. "They'll live happily ever after. I'm sure of it."

"And what about us?"

Daniel's face warmed as his heart thumped in his chest. "What about us?"

She bit back a smile. "We'll see."

Beauty in the Beast

Martia Benson

Daria stumbled through the dark forest. She'd lost track of the path she'd been on, she was sure of it. What if she was entering the territory of the Beast that was rumored to live in these woods?

The air trembled with a roll of thunder. And now a storm was coming. She could catch her death of cold or even get hit by lightning!

Maybe she shouldn't have left her town behind. But she'd had no choice. Gustav wouldn't take no for an answer—even after she finally worked up the nerve to try to tell him so. It wasn't a woman's place to make such objections.

Lightning flashed. A tall figure barred her way, an axe on his shoulder. Daria stopped short with a gasp, stepping back.

"What are you doing on my land?" the man growled.

"I…didn't know it was yours," Daria stuttered in a small voice. "I just…got lost, and now it's dark and cold…" Thunder rumbled again in the distance.

He stared at her for another expressionless moment. "Come with me." He turned away.

Released from his intense gaze, Daria let out a breath. At least he wasn't dragging her off. But she couldn't bring herself to move. *What if he's the Beast?* Did she dare to go with him? Did she dare not to and risk incurring his wrath? She didn't want to be left behind either, not when it meant being caught in the rain. She hastened to follow him before he went out of sight.

As they passed into the even deeper blackness beneath the trees, the man stooped to gather up a bundle of chopped logs under one arm. Daria felt some measure of relief. Of course. That was why he was out here in the forest with an axe. But that didn't mean he couldn't still use it for other purposes.

The man continued leading the way through the evergreens. Soon they emerged onto a narrow dirt path, which wound halfway up the slope before them to a large building that loomed there. Another lightning bolt revealed it to be a decrepit residence with grayed plank walls and a steep shingle roof that harbored a single turret. It looked just like the cursed manse of lore. Where the Beast took his victims.

With every step up the incline, Daria felt a greater tightness banding her chest. Why was she doing this? She could be walking right into a death trap!

But she forced herself to calm down. She knew better than to put too much stock in hearsay. There could be any number of men living out here in remote cabins. Besides, if the man meant her harm, why hadn't he acted on it already? He hadn't even looked over his shoulder to see if she was following.

They went up a few steps onto a roofed porch, lined with square wooden columns, to enter through a weathered side door.

The interior was just as bare and lifeless. Gray sheets were draped over a few high piles of irregular shape.

The man sent the door swinging closed behind Daria. He crossed to a dormant hearth on the other side of the room and deposited the logs onto the floor beside it, leaning his axe against the wall. He squatted before the fireplace and set some wood inside.

He eyed her over his shoulder then took something out of his inside coat pocket. He touched the object to the logs, and they caught alight immediately. Surprised, Daria craned her neck to try to see it better. How had he done that? There had been no strike of flint on steel. But he tucked the thing away again and rose, taking his axe with him as he went through a left-hand archway ahead.

The sky lit up one more time, and then the patter of rain started on the windowpanes, growing louder until it was a constant drumming. Daria was briefly grateful she hadn't been caught out in it after all, but the feeling soon withered under her apprehension of being inside this forbidding residence.

She waited, but when the man didn't return, her eyes drifted to the light of the hearth. The warmth of the blaze drew her closer, and she came to a stop a few feet before it, holding her hands out to the heat.

The looming shadow of the man reentered, and Daria took an involuntary step back, withdrawing her hands.

He pointed at the high-backed armchair facing the fireplace. "Sit."

Watching him, she hesitantly backed into it, hands on the armrests as she lowered herself onto the seat.

He came to stand beside the mantelpiece and folded one arm atop it. He fixed Daria with his stern gaze. "What brings you into the middle of the woods, at night, alone?"

With a discomfited twinge, she dropped her eyes, fingering the stitching on her skirt. "I…left Nordham. This morning. There's nothing for me there." She sighed. "I guess I didn't give much thought to where I was going, as long as it was away."

The man watched her in silence. Then he looked out the rain-streaked window, the ragged ends of his lank black hair brushing his shoulders. "There's no settlement for miles." He returned his gaze to the mantel. "The other rooms aren't any more accommodating than this one, so you'll have no need to enter them."

Daria studied him. The ruddy glow from the fire cast his long angular face in stark shadow. Before she accepted any hospitality, however grudgingly alluded to, she had to know who he was. "Are you…the one they call…the Beast?"

He looked over at her with a dark, silent glance.

She went on hastily, "It's just…you don't look the part, and…this doesn't seem like very beastly behavior."

His expression seemed a bit placated. "They call me that, yes," he admitted levelly. "But it is undeserved."

Daria's mind brimmed with curiosity. "They say you're as wild as the wolves and that you…prey on whoever crosses your path."

He pressed his mouth into a thin line. "I don't perpetrate violence," he said quietly.

"Then…all those rumors…?"

His eye glinted. "Purely folktales."

Daria knew that every fable had a kernel of truth, though. "What made them invent such things about you?"

"Anything mysterious or unexplained is fodder for superstition. They don't understand why I live in a run-down shack in the middle of the woods."

"Why do you?"

He regarded her for a moment. "It was once my family's estate. It was abandoned many years ago and has since fallen into disrepair. I have returned to attempt to restore it."

Daria found herself relaxing a little. The nearby flames had warmed this nook of the chilly house, enough to start thawing her to the bone. "And nobody's ever come up here to greet you?"

He shook his head. "Never bothered. They don't seem to realize I have a name."

"Then what might it be?" she asked gently.

He eyed her sidelong before responding. "Geordon."

Nothing monstrous about that. She gave a small smile. "Mine's Daria."

He looked away before long and straightened off the mantel, shifting one foot. "It's late," he said, changing the subject. "Do you need to eat?"

"No. But thank you," she murmured. "I brought some rations with me." She'd had enough forethought for that, at least. She still had some provisions in the pouch at her hip, but only enough for another small meal.

Geordon nodded. "Settle in. I'll be upstairs." He turned and went back out through the archway.

Daria looked over her shoulder at the door. Now that he was gone, it might be her one chance to get away. But the downpour was still pelting out there. And besides, he had provided ample cause to believe he wasn't the Beast, or any such thing. She tucked her feet up under her on the seat and leaned one elbow on the armrest. *He's just a man, as normal as any other.*

Even after a considerable time had passed, she wasn't sure she could get any rest in this unfamiliar place.

But eventually, the beat of the rain on the walls began to lull her, along with the warmth of the fire. Under the drowsy weight of the late hour, she lowered her head onto her folded arm, watching the mesmerizing flames until her eyes slowly slid closed.

***

Daria stirred, lifting her head—and started when the first thing she saw was Geordon. He was watching her from beside the right-hand archway, leaning against the wall with his arms folded. Daria levered herself upright in the armchair, rather self-conscious. How long had he been there?

The morning sky out the window was white with clouds, and the rain was long gone. The fire had also dwindled to embers.

"Get enough sleep?" Geordon prompted.

"Uh…I suppose so." She briefly sank her fingers in her brown hair.

He headed to the other side of the room, and Daria watched him around the corner of the backrest then got up from her seat.

"Urdstrom is five hours southeast of here."

Daria drifted after Geordon, at a bit of a loss as to what he was talking about.

"A path at the bottom of the hill leads there." He turned back to her and opened the door.

She gazed at the view beyond. "You mean…you're letting me leave?" She lifted her eyes to his. "Even after you told me all your secrets?"

Geordon smiled faintly. "The truth is no worse than rumor." He gestured with one hand. "You're free to go."

Slowly, Daria stepped outside but paused just past the threshold, eyes on the porch. "I…" She turned to look back at him. "I don't know anyone there," she murmured. "I don't have enough money for room and board, let alone a new place to live." Her gaze drifted down again in despondence as she realized the extent of the predicament she was in. She hadn't fully considered how much it would take to start over.

Geordon glanced to the side. "You can stay here," he said, and Daria met his eyes, feeling some surprised hope. "At least until you decide what to do."

Even so, she was still hesitant. Taking shelter from a storm for a single night was one thing, but taking up longer residence with a strange man she barely knew…

Geordon's mouth quirked. "It's not much of a place, but at least you're welcome to it."

Daria's heart was touched with gratitude. Despite his curt manner, he kept offering to help her at every turn. Definitely not the actions of a Beast. He was more of a gentleman than many men she knew, in his own rugged way. "That's very generous."

Geordon simply gave a grunt and spread an arm back toward the inside of the house.

After they reentered, Geordon prepared a meal of porridge and bread in the kitchen, though he left Daria to eat hers alone in the armchair before the dark hearth. Afterwards, Geordon gave her a flint and steel to light the fire with, but that didn't take much time. He even found her a leatherbound book to settle down with by the fireside, but she couldn't concentrate on it for long.

Throughout the day, he always seemed to be lurking around, as if to make sure she didn't get up to anything. He showed up especially whenever she wandered near one of the archways to the front room, blocking her way, often ready with some new remark or suggestion of a pastime for her. Daria squinted past him, but there was nothing noteworthy about the dim parlor beyond. What was he trying to hide?

Finally, when dusk fell, Geordon told her that she could stay in a room upstairs.

He led the way into the dark parlor with its ceiling twenty feet above. Around the three far walls ran a ledge lined with sculpted wooden columns and railings on all but the side closest to the front double doors. Atop stood several items and small pieces of furniture, which looked quite out of place and precarious up there. There were also more heaps of objects on the floor, but some of them peeked out from underneath the sheets. Daria tried to get a look at them in passing.

Geordon eyed her sidelong. "Don't touch anything," he warned.

They went up a few steps onto the raised stage covering the far half of the room then climbed the grand staircase to the colonnade. At the end of the hall, Geordon opened a worn door. The room beyond was wide and furnished with a few more large shapes covered by gray sheets. Three long windows, framed by diaphanous curtains that stirred in the indoor drafts, were spaced out across the wall ahead, looking south. A low, rickety cot stood in the rough middle of the floor, with several layers of dusty blankets serving for a mattress.

"This is the best there is," Geordon said.

Daria wondered if she wouldn't rather sleep on the armchair again anyway. But she couldn't very well turn down the chance to have a room to herself. "It's enough," she replied instead.

"There's firewood beside the hearth," he said. When she nodded, Geordon turned away and pulled the door closed on his way out.

A second later, a click came from it. Frowning, Daria crossed to it and tried the knob. The door wouldn't budge. She rattled the knob, tugging on the door in desperation. He'd locked her in! Maybe this had all been a ruse to keep her captive here after all. Just when she started thinking she could trust him, he did something like this!

Finally, she gave up the effort and tried to reassure herself. It didn't mean he had ominous intentions for her. Maybe he was just paranoid and didn't want her wandering around his house in the night. Daria turned back to the room, but there were no other ways out. The windows were too high up to climb out of, and they didn't even open.

Her eyes fell on the blanket-draped heaps. She was still immensely curious as to what was really underneath them. And if she was going to be sequestered in here anyway, she might as well have a look. If Geordon didn't want her to, he shouldn't have put her in the same room with them. She went over to one and lifted a corner of the dark gray sheet to peek behind it. All she saw were some old chairs and end tables piled up together. She checked all the other ones, but it was nothing but more furniture. She sat on the edge of the cot in disappointment. Of course he'd only put her in a room that had no secrets to uncover.

***

The next morning, Daria stood rubbing the small of her stiff back with one hand when the doorknob jiggled. She looked at it then drifted closer. A minute later, a key turned in the lock, and Geordon opened the door.

He met her eyes. "Sorry, this faulty old door locks sometimes when it's closed."

Glad understanding swept through Daria. A grain of doubt remained, though, as to whether he was just contriving that story. But why else would he have tried to open the door before going to get the key?

Her final piece of certainty was restored when he handed her the key. "In case it happens again."

Daria looked down at it in her palm. She should really stop thinking the worst of him, when time and again it turned out to be nothing but a misunderstanding.

Geordon half-turned back to the doorway. "Want to go for a walk?" She glanced up at him in surprise. "For some fresh air."

It *would* be good to stretch her legs, after being cooped up in this room all night. Daria tucked the key into her belt pouch and nodded.

They headed downstairs and went out the same side door. They proceeded down the porch steps and onto the pale dirt of the path. Everything had dried up after the rainstorm of two nights ago, but the low overcast remained. The sparse grass that covered the ground was dead and matted, a dull yellow-brown that matched the rest of the drab landscape.

Geordon gestured to the eastward lane. "That leads to the farther town of Rodendard." He walked the other way, and Daria accompanied him. He looked down the sloping path on their left, which looped around to become the one they had first taken up to the house. At the foot of the hill it split, veering southeast. "That way's Urdstrom."

Daria looked at him, wondering if he was listing her options.

As they kept onward, they neared a crossroad, beyond which the course they were on continued west. "And that's back to Nordham."

She drifted to a stop. "I'd rather not be heading closer to that place."

Geordon glanced at her. Then he tilted his head toward the trail that crossed in front of the manor to rise north up the hillside. "That one goes to the dam. If you don't mind a bit of an uphill climb."

The bushes nearby rustled, and a timber wolf emerged, followed by a whole pack that trotted up to them. Daria gasped, shying back.

"Don't fear," Geordon reassured her, setting a hand on one wolf's fur. The others circled around them, more like curious dogs than predators. "They won't hurt you, not if you're with me."

She watched them with wide eyes. "So you really can speak to the animals."

Geordon lifted the corner of his mouth wryly. "Not in so many words. We just understand each other."

A wolf nosed at Daria's skirt. With her arms tucked up before her, she kept her hands to herself and resisted the urge to pull away.

"You can give them a pat, if you like," Geordon told her.

Daria considered extending a tentative hand onto the wolf's head—but then decided that was too close to its jaws, and it would be all too easy for it to bite her hand off. The wolf lowered its snout to the ground and turned partly away, but still stood close to her. Daria reached down and lightly sank her fingers into the brownish-gray fur on the wolf's back. It was coarse, but thick and warm. The wolf's shoulder shifted, and Daria whisked her hand back.

The wolf wandered over to the others, and they started tussling and playing together. Without the element of danger, Daria began to feel a sort of appreciative wonder. She'd never seen a wolf up close. She hadn't thought she wanted to, before.

Geordon started up the northward path, and Daria hastened to keep pace. Some of the wolves swung about to jog along with them, tongues lolling. They frequently loped off into the woods, only to rejoin them later. Daria eyed them uneasily, finding it stressful to try to keep track of where they all were.

"Would you prefer if they didn't accompany us?" Geordon prompted her. Evidently, the expression on her face was answer enough. He turned to the wolves. "All right, gang, as you were." They all regrouped and lolloped off into the forest.

Daria stared after them. "Do they always do what you tell them?"

"They'll do as I ask, because they decide to," he qualified. "I don't control them."

That was a bit of a comfort. The only people she'd heard of—in stories, anyway—who were capable of commanding animals were evil witches or necromancers.

The two of them continued up the incline. The still air was crisp, but the exercise kept her warm enough.

"You can come out here whenever you want," Geordon told her. "You're not obliged to stay inside."

Daria looked over at him. The way he said it made her wonder if he'd prefer her to be out of the house, so he wouldn't have to keep an eye on her, like he had yesterday.

She returned her gaze to the ground. It might be nice to have the freedom to roam the grounds at leisure—but then again, she wasn't sure she'd want to be out here on her own when there were wolves roving about. Geordon had only said they wouldn't harm her *if* she was in his company.

A dark shape moved in the woods ahead, and Daria looked up. A big black bear had risen onto its hind legs and was watching them.

Her breath caught, and her step faltered. She glanced at Geordon, but he didn't seem the least bit concerned, so she kept walking, keeping her eyes on the bear. At least she had Geordon between her and it.

The bear dropped to all fours again and started ambling over to them.

"He a friend of yours too?" Daria prompted Geordon, in a voice that was a bit too tenuous to be casual.

He smiled faintly. The bear joined his side, and Geordon briefly ruffled a fond hand on its head. "They all are."

Daria studied Geordon with a trace of impressed admiration. If he could tame the wild beasts with just his presence, there must be something about him that was gentler than the average man.

***

That evening, the two of them sat before the fireplace in the side room. Geordon had pulled up a chair, obtained from one of the blanketed piles.

"You really don't want to return to Nordham?" he asked Daria gently. "What made you leave?"

Her eyes were downcast. "I have no family to stay

for. The people there are so…uncaring, so spiteful. They make the place even more bleak than it already is. And there's this one man, Gustav, who fancied himself my suitor. He was determined to make me his wife, and I'd have little say in the matter. With no father or brothers to speak on my behalf, none of the villagers would interfere. But I could never marry a man like that, who would only see me as the token of another successful hunt."

Geordon studied the floorboards, as if trying to find the words. "You shouldn't have had to face that."

Daria looked up at him, poignantly moved by his compassion. No other man had been on her side about it. He was so different from Gustav. He expected nothing, demanded nothing. He just let her be who she was. She appreciated it more than she could say.

***

On the fourth morning, Daria came down to find Geordon loading more logs into the fireplace. As he headed away, she stood with her hand on the back of the armchair, gazing at the hearth. She remembered how he'd inexplicably kindled it before, without seeming to first strike a spark.

"Geordon…" she said, and he paused to look back at her. It was the first time she'd spoken his name. "Can I ask you something?"

His expression became a bit droll. "You've done so before."

She turned her eyes to him. "That thing you used to light the fire the first night…what was it?"

Geordon considered her for a long moment. "Well, you already know everything else about me." He turned and went through the archway into the front room. When he came back, he held in his hands an object that looked like a brass oil lamp but more compact. "It's a lamp of dragonfire.

Its ever-flaming liquid will set fire to anything it's poured on."

Daria drew in a breath of awe. No wonder the logs had ignited so spontaneously.

"I collect magical artifacts like it, from all across the land. I brought them all back here, so they would have a safe and secluded place to stay. My family had several of their own, passed down as heirlooms. They're what first inspired me to become a collector."

She never imagined she'd encounter magic in her own lifetime! "There are other artifacts?"

"Want to see them?" Geordon's gaze turned earnest and intent. "I trust you won't tell anyone else about this."

"Not a soul!" Who would she tell, anyway?

He studied her for another moment, then smiled and nodded. He went back into the parlor, and this time she followed. He flapped back the dark gray sheet on one heap and carefully set the dragonfire lamp inside a stone chest behind. Of course; that must have been what he'd wanted to keep her from finding under the blanketed piles. Artifacts. Then he beckoned her over to a stack of crates beneath the ledge and climbed them, pausing and turning back each step of the way to help her up.

Sitting catacorner on the ledge was a narrow cupboard that came up to her shoulder height. It was painted powder blue but was so scuffed and battered that nearly as much of it was white beneath the peeled and flaking coat as not.

"This is a teleportation cupboard," Geordon announced. "If you get in one and close the door, it transports you to the other one."

"This? But it looks so…ordinary."

"Most artifacts do. That's what makes them so hard to track down." Geordon set a hand on top of the cupboard. "Its twin stands in the turret on the third floor. The door to the turret was bricked over long ago, so this is the only way to get in and out of it." He regarded her sidelong. "Need a demonstration?"

"Well, that would help convince me," she admitted. "It would be my first time seeing magic."

"Feel free to take a look inside it after I go—but make sure you close the door again, or I won't be able to get back here."

Daria looked at him questioningly.

"One door can only open if the other's closed," he explained. "That way, there can't be two people trying to teleport at the same time and ending up occupying the same space."

She grimaced. She could imagine why they'd want to avoid that.

Opening the cupboard, Geordon crouched a little to step in and pulled the door closed. A flash of blue light beamed through the cracks on either side. Daria snatched the door open again, but the interior was empty. She stared then looked all around the inside. There was no false bottom, not when it stood on a ledge over the sitting room. She sidestepped to peek behind the cupboard, but there was no back door either. She came back in front and closed the door. A second later, it opened again, and Geordon stepped out, just as if he had been inside all along.

"Incredible," Daria murmured.

Geordon showed a small, teasing grin. "You want to try it?"

"Oh…I don't know…" she began dubiously. "I've never teleported before."

"You barely feel a thing. Other than a little disorientation when you get out," he added. "I'll go first, so I'll be waiting in the room when you get there." He climbed back in, and once he'd gone through, Daria took her turn at it.

She got into the cupboard and, after a hesitation, made herself close the door. She stood there in the cramped dimness for a few moments, but nothing seemed to happen. Did it only work for Geordon? She opened the door and stepped out, but found herself in a small hexagonal room. Her mind swept a little.

Geordon stood before her, half-holding out a hand as if to steady her, a trace of a smile on his lips. "Weather your first trip all right?" he prompted.

Daria also felt a touch of vertigo, her body realizing she was a story higher than she just had been. "I…think so." She studied the room until she got her bearings back. There were a lot of artifacts here too, but they were arrayed neatly on shelves around the walls and carefully polished so they gleamed in the veiled midmorning sunlight from a small window. "What do the rest of these do?" she asked, heading over to them.

Geordon came up beside her, following her gaze to a round brass bauble, as big as a fist and carved with interlocking patterns. "That one's a returning sphere. It comes right back to your hand after it hits what you throw it at. Handy in a fight." He went on to introduce the rest of them to her, from an inexhaustible cornucopia that provided Geordon with all the provisions he needed without ever having to go to town, where he might not be welcome—to a coil of grappling rope, which would wrap itself securely around anything it was tossed at—to an orb of levitation, a sphere of clouded crystal sized to fill the palm of the hand, which would let the holder float down safely from any height instead of falling—among dozens more.

Daria studied him. All this talk of artifacts brought out a vibrant aspect in him that made him seem five years younger—more like her age. Though she might be considered past her prime at twenty-five. It was quite in contrast to how grim he'd been at first. He clearly had a passion for what he did.

Daria found herself tempted to venture a playful comment. "Out of all these things, don't you have some sort of…magic hammer that restores buildings instantaneously?"

Geordon's mouth quirked. "Unfortunately, no. I've yet to find an artifact that convenient." His expression turned thoughtful. "I do have one that's quite the coincidence, though." He reached into his shirt and drew out a thin leather cord he wore around his neck, from which hung a silver medallion in the shape of a wolf's face. "This amplifies my connection to the animals across distances. Without it, we'd only be able to communicate if they were in my immediate presence. I was fortunate to find it. To anyone without the inherent bond, it would serve as nothing more than a trinket."

It filled Daria with wonder to imagine there might be more people like Geordon who could run with the wolves. "Are there others with abilities like yours? I mean, there must have been at some point, or there wouldn't be a medallion for it."

"It did give me validation that there have been other instances of it. But it's rare. I haven't found many accounts of it in history—but then again, it's not something that most would admit to being capable of." He tucked the medallion away.

Daria turned back to the objects on display. "Do you ever use the rest of these?"

"Only when I have occasion to."

"Could it be that the possession of all these magical artifacts contributed to your reputation?"

Geordon cocked an eyebrow at her. "Yes, I'm sure it did. If anyone passing by saw them in action, that would add further to the unnerving mystique of the unexplained that others ascribe to me. It was a reason I refrained from mentioning before, since the existence of such priceless treasures is not something you share with a stranger."

Daria twisted her mouth wryly. She started strolling back along the shelves, looking over all the artifacts. "Can anyone use them?"

"Yes. Most of them are simply activated by the touch of living skin, and then they do as they're made to, upon the wielder's will and direction." Geordon gave her a no-nonsense look. "But I don't advise that you toy with them on your own. You don't know how to wield all of them, and one misstep with something like the dragonfire lamp could burn the whole house down."

She made a face, both daunted and dissatisfied. "Point taken." She ran her fingers along the shelf and tapped them in front of the cornucopia. "Shouldn't this be in the kitchen?" she wondered.

"It used to be," he admitted. "I moved it up here, along with a few other things that were lying about, after you arrived." Daria eyed him sidelong. "Didn't want you catching on to what they could do by accident."

When they teleported back into the parlor, Geordon took some of the artifacts with him and returned them to their proper places. They had no secrets from each other anymore.

Daria did a lot of thinking the rest of that day, trying to figure out her next steps. She wouldn't want to overstay her welcome. But neither of her current options—return to her old town or take her chances in a new one—was appealing. And, despite how run-down this place was, it was starting to grow on her. Most of Nordham wasn't in much better shape, and the company was worse. It seemed Geordon wasn't as gruff as he'd first let on, and she felt herself growing a certain esteem for him and his unique abilities. And where else would there be so many magical artifacts! It was to her own surprise that she found she didn't really want to leave, despite how eager she once might have been.

The following afternoon, Daria found Geordon outside, checking on a rain barrel off the side porch.

"Geordon," she began hesitantly, stepping up to him. "You said I could stay until I decided where to go, but…" She looked up at him. "My prospects aren't any better now than they were before. There's no guarantee I'd be able to start over in any other town—and I'm *not* going back to Nordham." Her gaze drifted down to the side then across the manor grounds. "I think…I want to stay here." She met Geordon's eyes. "This place feels more like home to me than anywhere I've been in a long time."

He looked upon her for a moment. "You're the only one I've trusted with all this." His voice was soft, too. "You've made this house much less lonely."

A tentative hope began to rise in Daria. Had he come to feel as much fondness for her as she did for him? She thought he'd simply tolerated her before, like an inconvenient interloper that was too nosy. But there was no mistaking the tenderness in his gaze now.

Geordon set a gentle hand on the side of her neck and slowly stroked down it, running his palm around the front to rest on the skin below her collarbone. She could feel her heartbeat thumping against his hand. Then he withdrew it, still meeting her eyes.

As the days went on, Daria began lending a hand with the restoration efforts around the house, starting with uncovering some of the furniture, dusting it off, and moving it into the rooms where it belonged. She also carried planks and supplies to where they were needed for actual repairs, such as a leaky part of the roof in the attic, and held them in place while Geordon hammered. She managed to rustle up an old lumpy mattress that wasn't too musty to use on her cot instead, and in an antique wardrobe, she even found some decent dresses that she could launder and repurpose for herself.

But after a while, a worry began to nag at her. She hadn't told anyone in Nordham she was leaving. She was sure none of them cared—but it was only a matter of time before Gustav would notice she was gone. It might not have been right away, since he didn't come to court her every day. After all the time he'd spent on her, he wasn't likely to give up what he considered his rightful property. He might even think it the perfect opportunity to finally win her over, by "rescuing" her from her captor in a blaze of heroic glory. And if he *was* on his way, Geordon had a right to know.

Daria brought it up the next time she saw him. "The man I told you about, Gustav—once he hears I went missing in your territory, he will come looking for me."

Geordon's brow creased with concern.

"He'll probably think I was captured by the Beast."

"And if he does?"

"I don't know what he'll do. He was already possessive and relentless in his pursuit of me. He might stop at nothing to get me back, even in the face of a Beast."

"Then I'll explain to him that you want to stay."

"He's not one to listen to reason. And he won't believe you, not when he still thinks you're the Beast." Daria was silent for a moment. "He could be dangerous."

"Do you think he would bring any villagers with him?"

She considered it and twisted the corner of her mouth wryly. "No. They're too apathetic to be recruited to a cause just to get me back."

Geordon's expression became a little complacent. "If he comes alone, I can handle him."

Daria wondered if he was just putting on a show of confidence to reassure her. She knew he wouldn't actually fight Gustav if it came to that, since Geordon wasn't a proponent of violence. But she doubted Gustav had any such qualms. That's what worried her.

The day after, Daria was wiping dust off a dresser in the side room. When Geordon came back in with the firewood, his face held a troubled look. He met her eyes and put his load down by the door. "The bear saw someone lurking in the area this morning. A pale-haired man with a sword."

Daria got a sinking feeling. It was as she'd feared. "Gustav," she breathed.

"I don't want you going out there," Geordon went on. "I'll send the wolves out to make sure he's not still around."

A few hours later, the pack reported they hadn't come across Gustav. Geordon still had the animals stay on the lookout and keep him apprised.

Daria was pacing in her room the next afternoon, lost in unsettled thought. She drifted over to the west window. She thought she glimpsed a figure at the treeline below, and her heart jumped. But when she looked again, no one was there. It hadn't been Geordon; he was still in the house. The fleeting sight had resembled Gustav. Maybe it was just her anxiety playing tricks on her.

She went straight downstairs and told Geordon.

His expression darkened. "How dare he come that close," he growled. "I'm going out there." He started for the front door.

"What about you?" she protested. "He has a sword."

"I have an axe," Geordon countered grimly. "And wolves, and artifacts, and a reputation. Even Gustav would think twice about coming at me when he's outnumbered." He took up his axe from where it leaned against the wall and brought the returning sphere out of his pocket. "Bar the doors behind me."

Once she'd obliged, and he'd called the wolves to him, Daria watched him from an upper window. He stood on the path in front of the house, scanning the woods with a sharp eye. With the axe propped on his shoulder and the pack of wolves around him, he made quite a formidable figure. He patrolled for hours, sometimes sending a few wolves out scouting further. But after no more sightings of Gustav, Daria began to wonder if the intimidating display had successfully deterred him.

When Geordon came back in, he even checked the magic mirror that stood in his room. It indeed showed Gustav passing through the forest—but there was no way to pinpoint where exactly he was, just from the trees visible in the background. Even if Geordon and the wolves went after him, by the time they came across the right location, Gustav would be long gone. In any case, Geordon could tell, based on which side of the trunks was lit by the glow of the setting sun, that Gustav was heading west, back to Nordham. Geordon didn't trust that he wasn't up to anything, but he couldn't watch the mirror every second. He still consulted it each day, though all it displayed was Gustav walking around in town. Maybe he wasn't coming back after all.

***

Geordon sat in a chair by the kitchen wall, sanding a piece of wood to be a new leg for the couch. He looked up when he heard Daria come in.

"All this waiting is making me restless." She sighed. "I feel like taking a walk."

He frowned in concern. "Gustav could still be out there."

"There's been no sign of him in days. And I haven't been out of the house for a week."

Geordon was still reluctant. "All right. But let me have the wolves keep a wide perimeter around you, to make sure he doesn't get anywhere near." He saw her to the front door and stayed in the threshold, looking out at the forest as he contacted the distant pack. His medallion momentarily glowed a faint silver. When he was done, he looked at Daria again, touching a brief hand to her elbow. "Don't be out too long. It'll be dark soon."

She gave him a slight smile. "Promise."

Geordon watched her walk up the path to the dam until she was out of sight. Then he slowly turned back inside and closed the door. The wolves would alert him if they caught any trace of Gustav, and they'd close ranks around Daria to protect her until Geordon could get there.

As the minutes passed, a thicker cloud cover rolled in, bringing night early. Geordon couldn't focus on his work; a grain of worry was still gnawing at him. *I'll check the mirror, just to be sure.*

He went up to his bedchamber and crossed to the cheval glass. He set his hands on either side of the dark wood frame, activating its magic with the contact, and looked intently into it. "Show me Gustav."

The glass clouded over into a dull gray then cleared to show a scene in the benighted woods. Gustav stood on a hill above the trees, speaking soundless commands to the man beside him, who was setting up a catapult. With a smirk of grim satisfaction, Gustav turned and pointed out where to aim it. The view shifted to reveal their target in the distance. The great wooden wall of the dam.

Geordon's stomach dropped. If the dam burst, the floodwaters would wash straight for the manor. And Daria was out there. It'd reach her first.

Releasing the mirror, Geordon raced out to find her.

As he charged up the path that led to the dam, Geordon cursed himself. He should've sent a vanguard of wolves with Daria too. He should've checked the mirror first before letting her leave. If anything happened to her…

A wolf stepped out from the trees ahead, yellow eyes

glowing faintly in the dark, to see why Geordon was in such a rush and if he needed any assistance.

"No! Stay away!" Geordon called without stopping, waving a hand for it to go back. "There's a flood coming!"

The wolf turned tail and lolloped back into the woods to warn the rest of the pack—and hopefully some of the other animals, too. One by one, howls rose into the night from all corners of the forest, near and far.

Geordon could have had one of them run ahead to find Daria, and they might have gotten there sooner than he, but he didn't want to send them into the path of danger. She might not have understood them, anyway, and none of them had been closer to her than he already was.

He got an impression from one of the wolves' minds; he'd last seen Daria not long ago, halfway up the hill. Geordon made his legs pump even faster.

A distant boom rumbled through the air. Then another. But it wasn't thunder. Gustav had started bombarding the dam.

Geordon caught sight of Daria ahead. She stood looking around with a slight frown, probably made wary by all the howls. She turned to him as he came running up.

"Gustav's coming tonight," Geordon told her. He caught her hand and started pulling her along with him as he hastened back down the trail. "We must get out of here. He sabotaged the dam."

"What?"

"His plan must be to come for you after he flushes me out with the flood."

"But…that's mad!" she breathed. "It'll fill the whole valley."

Geordon clenched his jaw. "I doubt he cares about that."

A few cold droplets landed on his skin, and soon a light rain began to fall from above.

Daria stared at the ground as they ran. "I'm so sorry," she whispered.

He glanced over at her. "This wasn't your doing."

"But he's doing this because of me," she insisted. "If I hadn't stayed here, I wouldn't have brought this on you."

After a moment, Geordon tightened his hold on her hand. "I wouldn't have had it any other way." Someone like her deserved to have refuge when she needed it. And at least he'd gotten the chance to know her, even for just a short time.

Far behind them, there was a ponderous, groaning *crack* that shook the very earth, followed by a thunderous rushing rumble. Geordon glanced over his shoulder to see a massive torrent of muddy water surging toward them. There was no way they could outrun it now.

He dashed for the side of the path with Daria in tow. He reached for a branch of the nearest tree, intending to climb out of harm's way or at least hold onto it as a lifeline.

But his hand was still an inch away when the tide rammed into them from the side, bearing them under its freezing waters as it charged downhill. The shock of the impact nearly robbed Geordon of his consciousness. Awash in the churning darkness, he didn't know which way was up—but he still held on tight to Daria's hand and rowed with his other arm, until his chest burned with the desire to breathe. He fought his way to the surface, pulling Daria up with him, and they each gasped lungfuls of air.

The raging current tossed them about and cascaded over their heads again. Spluttering and struggling to stay afloat, Geordon laboriously drew Daria nearer, cinching his arms around her—though they were starting to go numb from the cold—and holding her close to him. The coursing waves dashed them against tree trunks, but Geordon tried to take the brunt of the impacts with his back so as to spare Daria. Low branches and driftwood scratched them as they whipped past. Trees were pushed over and even uprooted, and the flood spread out wide through the forest, being added to from above as the rain turned into a downpour.

Finally, the manor came into sight ahead. Beyond it, the rampant river split, one course continuing onward down the steeper slope, the other running past the far side of the house.

As they rapidly neared it, he pushed Daria out from him so she would be caught up in the flow that headed toward the manor. "Get to the house!" he called to her.

"Geordon!" she cried out in anguish as she was swept away from him.

He continued on downhill, far, far along, until the torrent lessened enough that he could try to get his footing on the ground again. He washed up at the lowermost curve of the path and staggered to his feet. Turning, he made his way around the bend to start climbing up the slope of slick mud. His body ached all over from bruises and scrapes gained during the buffeting, and he walked with a slight limp. He plowed on through the heavy downpour, which plastered his bedraggled hair over his forehead and continued soaking him to the skin. He frequently slipped in the muck and even fell onto it a few times, sliding several yards back downhill— but he always got back up, eyes fixed on the hilltop ahead, putting one foot in front of the other with dogged perseverance. He would get back to her before Gustav did. Of that, he was determined.

At last, Geordon made it to the crest and was relieved to see Daria standing on the side porch, an arm around one of the wooden pillars. She must have been able to grab onto it as she coasted by. She was watching anxiously for him and now discerned his form amidst the darkness.

"Geordon!" she breathed and rushed down the steps to meet him in the rain. She set a hand on his chest, accompanying him the rest of the way. "Are you all right?"

"If you are." He touched her chin tenderly. There was a nasty abrasion on her cheek, but he hoped he'd been able to shield the rest of her from the worst of it.

Facing forward, he put an arm around her shoulders, but it served more for her to support him than for him to protect her.

They went up the stairs and into the house. A film of water coated the room's floorboards and was slowly draining through the gaps between them into the cellar. It must have washed in through the cracks under the doors. Geordon set his jaw. This would set back his restoration efforts by months.

The two of them shuffled over to the fireplace and dropped onto the hearthstone before it. Thankfully, the fire was still burning. Slumped with an elbow on his knee, Geordon sank his fingers in his hair and waited for the heat to dry his clothes. Daria shivered and huddled closer to the flames. The silence was singularly miserable, with only the drip of droplets from their sopping hair landing on the floor.

After a while, the mud on Geordon's clothes began turning to caked dust that he could brush off. The rain outside seemed to be dwindling off.

"He'll be here any minute," he said dully. He lurched to his feet and helped pull Daria up. They stumbled into the front room, and he went to heft up the thick wooden beam, barring the front double doors with it. It was only a cursory precaution, since it would make little difference if Gustav thought to look for another way in.

But no sooner had they set foot on the stage than there came a pounding on the door. Geordon turned back to it.

"Take to the cupboard," he told Daria quietly.

She looked at him with alarm. "Geordon..." she murmured.

A man's bellow came through from outside. "I'm

here to reclaim what is *mine*, Beast!" The door rattled on its hinges as Gustav started ramming his shoulder against it.

"Leave the door open on your end, so he won't be able to follow you there," Geordon went on to Daria.

"But…" That meant Geordon wouldn't be able to escape to the turret either.

The old beam began to buckle.

"Go," he said again. "I'll hold him off."

Daria climbed up the stack of crates to the cupboard, then got in and teleported in a flash of blue.

The wood bar splintered as the doors burst open.

"Daria!" Gustav called out, storming into the foyer, sword out. "Where have you hidden her, you foul brute?" He cast about, craning his neck to look through the curtained archways into the other dark rooms. "Release her to me!"

Geordon glared at him. "No."

Gustav paused in his tracks and slowly turned to look back at him with a dark gaze. "No?"

"She does not wish to return with you," Geordon told him. "She has decided to stay here, of her own free will."

"You lie!" Gustav cried. "She would never choose to remain with a creature like you!" He whirled on Geordon, blade at the ready.

"You clearly don't care much for her," Geordon said coldly. "That stunt of yours with the dam could have gravely injured her."

Gustav's face showed a moment of surprise, as if he really hadn't thought of that, but he quickly covered it with indignation.

"You just assumed she would be locked up inside, and I would be the one out hunting, did you?" Geordon clenched his fists. "Not only that, but you caused the destruction of miles of land," he growled. "Did you even stop to think of the ramifications your actions would have on the forest you flooded and all the creatures that live there?"

Gustav's face hardened. "The fate of the common beasts is none of my concern," he spat. "Typical of you to side with your wild brethren over humankind. There's nothing I wouldn't do for my Daria."

"That's where we differ," Geordon said quietly, a steely glint in his eye. "Daria is not *yours*, nor does she belong to anyone else. And only a weak man would so easily forsake his conscience."

Gustav let out a roar, brandishing his sword. "Enough of this talk! Tell me where she is!" Gustav charged at him, but Geordon leapt nimbly up the stack of crates onto the ledge. "Where is she?" Gustav yelled again.

Geordon stopped beside the leather sword case that leaned upright against the wall. "Somewhere you'll never find her," he said grimly. He opened the latch, stepping back. "Excalibur, go!" he called out, and the sword burst out to sail through the air, pointing straight for Gustav, loyally dedicated to protect its master.

Gustav parried it, but it kept coming at him, swinging and slicing as if wielded by an invisible hand. "What sorcery is this?" he demanded amidst the clangs of steel. "Come out and fight me like a man, you cowardly beast!"

Geordon backed up to the teleportation cupboard and used an arm tucked behind his back to try the door. He tugged on the knob a few times, but it didn't budge. Good. Daria had done as he'd advised.

Geordon crouched down to rummage in a small pile, looking for the returning sphere. It wasn't there. He gritted his teeth. He must have left it on the other side of the gallery. He stood up again.

"Excalibur, you traitor! How could you fight for the

Beast?" Gustav knocked the sword aside with such force that this time it went flashing across the room to stab into the door of the cupboard right in front of Geordon's face, quivering there for a moment of helpless defeat.

Geordon turned back to Gustav in frustration. "What will it take for you to realize?" he demanded. "I want no part in violence!" He started heading around the side of the colonnade. "I'm not the Beast everyone thinks me to be. I am just a man who wants to be left alone. Your own superstition and fear has built me up into something I'm not." He was about halfway around now, almost to the artifact…

The teleportation cupboard flashed, and out stepped Daria, holding the orb of levitation and looking around for Geordon.

"No!" Geordon cried out to her. "Get back to safety!"

Gustav barked a derisive laugh. "You hid her in a cupboard?" His tone was saturated with ridicule. "Daria! Fear not! I shall have you rescued from this craven beast in a moment." He faced back to Geordon with a casual flourish of his sword.

But Daria turned to Gustav, squaring her shoulders and setting her expression sternly. "I don't need to be rescued." Gustav looked at her in surprise. "I don't *want* to be rescued. I am under no duress or coercion. Geordon is a good man who took me in when I needed it. I came here, of my own accord, to get away from *you*."

Gustav recoiled as if slapped.

Geordon looked at Daria with profound admiration.

"He must have bewitched you!" Gustav spluttered.

"He did no such thing." The orb in Daria's palm began to glow an eerie green. She stepped off the ledge and floated down serenely until her feet touched the floor. Gustav stared at her with wide eyes. "It is entirely my decision to stay here. I won't be returning with you, and I certainly won't be marrying you."

Geordon tossed a grappling rope at one of the columns, then vaulted over the railing and slid down to reach ground level.

Daria started advancing on Gustav, the orb shedding unnatural light on her face. "Now I suggest you leave us in peace."

Geordon moved to keep pace behind Daria, backing her up with his tall presence. He had to fight to keep a properly forbidding face. She was just so impressive.

"If you persist in antagonizing us, we'll be forced to dissuade you by less pleasant means. You don't want to see what else our artifacts can do."

"You've gone mad," Gustav breathed, backing away from her. "You've joined forces with *him*!" Then his face twisted into a mask of scorn. "You never were that much of a catch, anyway. Now I'll have my pick of all the finest women, the ones that are *worthy* of being mine." Whirling, he fled out into the night.

Letting the glow of her orb fade, Daria drifted to a stop and watched him run down the path to town, while Geordon came up beside her.

A howl went up nearby, and Gustav shot a glance over his shoulder as the pack of wolves crested the hill. They charged after him with a series of yips, nipping at his heels.

Daria couldn't help a grin of victory. She turned to Geordon and wrapped her arms about his neck in a hug. He held her close too, one hand on the back of her hair.

"I'm so proud of you," he murmured by her ear.

She backed up to give him a savvy look. "So you admit I'm not the type that needs to be hidden away in an ivory tower?"

Geordon smiled wryly. "No. You're definitely better as a partner in action."

Daria stroked the orb in her hands, harboring suppressed satisfaction on her face. "So, what's our next step for the restoration efforts?" she prompted.

Geordon quirked the corner of his mouth. "I believe I have an enchanted sponge that should make short work of the flooding in the cellar…"

Together they turned away, sending the door slowly swinging closed behind them. Above the manor, the clouds parted to reveal the white glow of the crescent moon, and in the distance, one of the wolves howled one more time.

This Little Piggie

Alexander Thomas

They say no plan survives first contact with the enemy. That goes double when you're trying to murder your idiot brothers. You really need to be adaptable to pull off a successful fratricide, but I'm getting ahead of myself. My name is P.G. Everest, and I should probably start at the beginning.

This time six months ago, I was waiting down at the veterinarian's office for the final word. I can still hear those damn fluorescent lights humming over the constant beeping of my mama's heart rate monitor. The problem was whoever replaced the bulbs didn't do them all at the same time, so they were out of sync. One had been running a lot longer than the other two and was going to snap again real soon. It was enough to make me grind my hooves.

I swore under my breath as I tried to spoon more applesauce into my mama's mouth. "Come on, Mama, eat for me. We need to keep that strength up."

"Ain't no point, P.G. I'm dying today, and the last thing I eat on this earth will not be store-bought applesauce. No, sir." Mama struggled to push my hand away. "Now, where are your brothers?"

"They're not here." I placed the sauce cup on her bedside tray and bit my lip.

Mama smiled and laid her head back on her pillow.

"Those rascals, they get that aversion to punctuality from your father."

"It's been a week, Mama. Ain't no excuse for it."

"Now, now, they're good boys, P.G. Not as good as you, but they mean well." Mama cradled my face against her hoof. "They're gonna need you when I'm gone."

A tear slid over my round cheek. "I don't know if I can do it without you."

"They're your family, they need you." Mama closed her eyes and sighed. "I want you to make them partners in your firm."

"Absolutely not. Those chuckleheads wouldn't know a hard day's work if it jumped in their arms and called them Papa. They'll ruin me."

Mama coughed, causing her whole juicy body to spasm. "I know they have some growing up to do. But you can help them along. Give them something to care about, a stake, and they will mature right before your eyes."

"But…"

"No buts, boy. What do I always say?" Mama's beady blue eyes scanned into the blueprint of my soul.

"Sometimes all a plant needs is a better place to grow." I bowed my head and wiped my eyes. "I'll give them a chance, for your sake, Mama. I'll try."

"You're a good boy, P.G. I love you."

She fell asleep after that, never to wake again.

Now, O.G. and Q.G. didn't turn up until Mama's wake. Their whooping and hollering announced their presence long before their perfidious odor. Mourners across the parlor turned to me, shame and pity clear on their faces. I nodded and shuffled out to meet the chuckleheads.

My brothers crawled out of their lowrider as I stepped onto the veranda. They were clearly intoxicated, stumbling over themselves, and carrying on. O.G. fell flat on his face, rolled over onto his back, and laughed up a storm.

His ears had new piercings, those holes idiot kids stuff in their heads so their brains have somewhere to leak out. RIP MAMA was tattooed across his neck.

Q.G. wore a long-sleeved plaid shirt to cover up his track marks. A beanie covered his bald head. His toes was covered in orange cheese dust. Thick, red veins crossed his dilated eyes. He'd left the motor running.

I exhaled a ragged breath and joined them in the yard. "You boys are late, again."

O.G. sat up, belly still heaving from his giggle fit. "We're sorry, bro, we was down gettin' my new ink fixed up. Whatchu think?" He gestured to the script below his chin.

"I think that's the Cowrean word for 'Don't hire me.'" I spat on the ground beside him.

"Aw, lay off him, P.G." Q.G. patted me on the back. "He's just trying to honor Mama."

I wheeled on my other brother. "He coulda done that by coming to see her in the hospital."

"We was goin' to, but something came up." Q.G. inhaled, trying to hide the smell on his breath.

"Are you really high on truffles at your own mama's wake?" I swallowed my anger, trying not to blow a fuse in front of Mama's company.

"It's just to take the edge off, man."

"You ain't got an edge to take off, you soft sack of rotten tomatoes. How dare you?"

O.G. stood and got between us. "Look, P.G. we know you're hurting. We're hurting too. Let's not fight."

I scowled and turned away. "Fine. Just be on your best behavior. We got some respectable animals here today."

"That's mighty brotherly of you, P.G." O.G. smiled and pushed Q.G. along. "Oh, before we go in, I just need to know: what did Mama leave the two of us in the will?"

I balled my hoof in front of my mouth. Anger wormed from the crown molding in my mind all the way to the foundation of my shoes. "What did you say?"

Q.G. chimed in. "Yeah, how much did Ma give us? My ride needs mods, and O.G. needs to pay off his ink."

"Mama didn't leave you a red cent." I turned to face my brothers, my voice low. "She left you a job. Wanted me to make you partners at Everest Construction."

"Nice." Q.G. and O.G. high-fived.

"Finally, a job we ain't gotta pass a drug test to get." Q.G. danced in place.

O.G. rubbed his hooves together. "We're going to make so much bank, bro. You will not regret this."

This should come as no surprise to you, but I did in fact regret it.

Sure, it would have been fine had we all been equals. We certainly was paid like equals, but my brothers, O.G. Everest and Q.G. Everest, were the laziest, most deplorable little pigs I have ever had the displeasure of knowing. You see, I believe in taking my time. Dependable materials and quality craftsmanship create lasting prosperity for our customers, but that attention to detail must not be genetic.

Now you might be asking what was it that set me over the edge? What was it that prompted me to murder these idiots, rather than just fire them? Well, six months into their tenure at Everest Construction, they did something so boneheaded, so lazy, that it threatened not only the lives of my customers but the honor and integrity of my company's name. Honor's all we got in this world, I know that for sure. Stains on your good name, especially in this connected age, will sink your entire life. The Internet don't forget, not never.

So on that fateful day, I headed down to answer a complaint at one of the properties my brothers were tasked with constructing. I received a phone call from the Williamses, a family of tree frogs for whom I'd designed a house. Frogs are a persnickety people by nature, so it wasn't uncommon to make some friendly accommodations for them. However, this complaint was not nitpicking. Apparently, there were some…deviations from my sound blueprint.

Naturally, I drove down there in my trusty pickup truck. I could see the problem right away. The entire lot was flooded with wet straw and broken sticks. Mr. Williams, a neon green frog, was surveying the site. His two tadpoles sputtered about in a kiddie pool nearby. He puffed up his air sac as I got out of the truck.

"Is this a joke, Everest?" Mr. Williams's voice resonated in my chest. "I thought we agreed on a brick house with an inground pool."

"We did." I fumbled in my briefcase. "I've got the plans here somewhere."

"Clearly, whoever you hired didn't follow those instructions." Mr. Williams reached down and held up a few strands of wet hay. "I thought you knew what you were doing, but my kids can't use a straw swimming pool."

"I know, Mr. Williams…"

"My precious little poles could have died. Who's going to pay for this?"

I swallowed hard. Anger seeped out of the pores on my chinny chin chin. "I assure you, we will be giving you a full refund, and I will draft up a new design, absolutely free of charge. I'll oversee the construction personally."

"Just give me my money back." Mr. Williams ribbeted as he shook his head. "You really think I give second chances to the swine who tried to kill my babies? Those beavers at Dam Good Construction know what they're doing."

"Of course, Mr. Williams. I'll write you a check."

Mr. Williams folded his arms. "It's a pity, P.G. Everest used to be reputable company. You bet your bacon I'm telling everybody to give you a wide berth."

I held onto my rage the entire drive to my brothers' bachelor pad. I had known deep down that this was never going to work. Why had Mama hoisted these fools into my care? She should have sold them as bacon when we were kids. She had to have known what fools they were. Anger carried me from the parking lot to the front door in a red mist.

"Why the hell did you make a swimming pool out of straw?" I used the slamming door for punctuation.

O.G. was sitting in the living room. A bubbling bong sat in his lap. GAME OVER was written on the TV screen. Q.G. was snout deep in a greasy bucket of fried chicken. He poked his up, breading still stuck on his fat face.

"I saw a chance to save some money." O.G. put his lighter down and turned on the couch to face me.

"You almost killed Mr. Williams's babies. I specifically wrote that he needed an inground pool attached to his brick house." I stamped my hoof, cracking their cheap wooden floor.

Q.G. nodded and tore into a drumstick, chewing as he spoke. "Yeah, we saw that. We thought it was a good chance to improvise. Prove our know-how to you."

I clapped my hands together. "Improvisation has no place in construction. Not in the name of laziness or convenience. When I give you a blueprint, it is less flexible than the Scripture."

O.G. turned back to his hookah. "You never give us a chance to just be us." He took a deep drag and coughed. "Sometimes the moment calls for something more personal. You just feel it, man."

"I had to refund them, and the Williamses are taking their business to those damn beavers." I walked over to the window and rested my arm on the wall, seeking strength from somewhere. "Do you have any idea how much you just cost us? This company can't afford screwups like this."

"Whatever, P.G., you got the money. Screw those no good salamanders." O.G. closed his eyes and leaned his head back on the couch.

"They're frogs, not salamanders."

"It's all amphibians to me, bro. Slimy is slimy, am I right?" O.G. looked to Q.G. for validation.

Q.G. licked his lips. "Especially the girls. Holler." My brothers high-fived.

"It's not about the money. It's about prestige, you junkie waste of space."

"Whatever, man. I feel good about it."

"Just. Just." I screamed and punched a hole in the drywall. "Don't do it again. I'll see you tomorrow. Heaven help you if you're late."

I stormed out of the room. I gripped the steering wheel of my truck and shouted at the sky. Their smug faces flashed across my mind. No sense of shame or remorse in their beady eyes. *I deserved better than this, Mama.* Those morons were never going to shape up. They would drag me down into the mud with them like some…pig.

Warm drops hit my lap. Blood spilled from above my hoof. I must have scratched myself punching the wall. I pulled my handkerchief from my pocket and held it to the wound. It's funny how such a little accident could cause so much pain. It was too bad my brothers couldn't have an accident. Wasn't it?

It was in that moment I knew they had to die. I knew I needed to hire a hitman.

You might be calling me a monster right now. You should know that I do not consider myself to be a monster. I had a moral obligation to rid myself of those morons. Not only were they hampering my professional advancement, they were disrespecting the memory of our beloved mama, God rest her juicy ham hocks. She'd do the same thing if she knew her boys were down here making a mockery of themselves. So my conscience was clear.

Finding a hitman wasn't hard. The Internet sells all kinds of wild things. I was perusing Stagslist late one night and came across a fella by the username Big_B@D_W0lf23. His ad said that he was the expert in ferrying folks to the other side.

So I logged in and sent him a message:

"Dear Mr. (or Miss I suppose) Big_B@D_W0lf23,

I saw your ad on Stagslist, and I feel like you are offering just the services I need. You see, I have two employees who are single-handedly sabotaging my business. I need them to disappear. What would be your fee for this kind of job? I can provide you with their work schedule, habits, personal information, addresses, and anything else you think would be important for dispatching them quickly and quietly.

Signed,

Mr. Pig."

I thought it seemed candid and professional enough. My mama always taught me not to beat around the bush with folks you was hiring.

The response came a few minutes later:

"Mr. Pig,

Thank you for reaching out. The less you know about me, the safer it is for both of us. Needless to say, I am very capable of handling the aggressive unemploying of certain individuals. I charge $20,000 for a hit, but I happen to be running a buy one get one half off special this week. So $30,000 for these two. If that price is acceptable, send me their names, addresses, schedule, known allergies, medical history, and when you need the job completed by.

Regards,

Big_B@D_W0lf23"

$30,000. That sum stared at me from the computer screen. That, plus the cost of Mr. Williams's contract, would be well over six figures from Everest's coffers in one day. Could I really afford to drop that kind of money on making my idiot brothers go away? It's not like I couldn't just off them myself. I was a proud gun owner, after all. But could I get away with it?

I'd watched dozens of cop shows in my life. Criminals who got caught were just stupid. I wasn't stupid, was I? Maybe those were just the cases they showed on tv so they wouldn't let the smart criminals know all the smart ways cops could catch you. No. I had to hire an expert, as much as it chafed my chops.

I emailed Big_B@D_W0lf23 again:

"W0lf,

$30,000 is perfectly reasonable. Send over the account information, and I'll make the transfer right away. Their names are O.G. and Q.G. Everest. They live together at 57 Glenwood Ave, Porkersburg, AL. They will both be working two construction jobs this week at 65 High Perch Parkway and 1991 Old McDonald Way this week. The only thing they're allergic to is hard work, but they are avid truffle abusers. I want them gone ASAP.

Mr. Pig."

The wolf messaged me back right away and said that they could "handle a couple of stoner pigs."

That was false advertising if ever I heard it.

I sent the money off to the account of my lupine assassin. They told me to consider it done, but something didn't sit right with me. How did I know I was going to get my money's worth? Sure, this hitman claimed to be able to get the job done, but when would I know? Besides, a part of me really wanted to see my brothers get it.

O.G. was working on a barn out in the countryside. I decided to head down and see if I couldn't get a view of the murdering. I'm a hands-on kinda swine like that. I threw my pistol in the glove compartment, drove down to the lot, parked on the dirt road, and settled in for a good ol'-fashioned stakeout.

A couple of hours passed. The cabin of my truck began sweltering like the inside of an oven, so I snuck and crawled into the hedge. Got a better view that way too. I watched that no-good bastard roll some straw into a box shape, clap his hooves together like it was a job well done, and pull a flask out of his truck. Why was I cursed with a brother like this? Straw is for eating not building. It's like constructing a candy house for humans.

I spied the wolf as O.G. knocked back his second flaskful. He certainly lived up to the name. Easily eight feet tall at the shoulder, wearing a threadbare vest and scarlet pants. The stomping of his paws made the ground shake. Globs of drool dripped off his sparkling teeth. My brother spotted him right away, on account of the thunderous steps he was taking. The straw hat shot off O.G.'s chubby head as he hightailed it for the straw house.

I slapped my knee and laughed. It served him right for sticking with that straw. That fool was about to be bacon. I snuck closer for a better view.

Big_B@D_W0lf23 paused outside the barn and cleared his throat. "Little pig, little pig, let me in."

"Screw you, pal." O.G.'s voice shook like a jackhammer on concrete.

"Then I'll huff, and I'll puff, and I'll blow your house in."

"Go ahead, ain't my—"

The wolf inflated like a hot air balloon and rained hell on my brother's shoddy little shack. The clouds in the sky scattered from the wind, thunder exploded in the little clearing, and my car alarm started ringing to High Heaven. The straw flew away, leaving O.G. standing in the foundation I'd laid.

His eyes was saucers staring up at that wolf. It was

time for him to go meet Mama, so she could tan his behind across Kingdom Come.

Or, at least, it should have been.

Turns out survival is a stronger motivator than money for my brothers.

O.G. squealed like a pig, but not just any old pig. He was like a teacup pig who got left in some starlet's purse in the cargo hold of an airplane. Frantic and desperate for anyone to come bail his spoiled self out. He disappeared in a cloud of dust. Poof. Gone. I had no idea that porker could run so fast. The wolf loped after him, and I ran for the truck. Mud kicked up from that old dirt road as I peeled out and made tracks for Q.G.'s jobsite.

It made sense to me that O.G. would turn to the middle Q.G. for help instead of me. They was always closer with one another than with myself. It ain't my fault Mama turned to me to help raise those little hellions after Daddy left. It also ain't my fault that they was so much like our deadbeat father. Mama always said he was lazy too and thought he wasn't strong enough to handle a real woman like her anyhow. That's besides the point though. What matters is that my little brothers grew up together, and they was gonna die together.

I pulled up at Q.G.'s excuse for an apartment building just as our youngest brother ran inside. This building was supposed to be home to a large number of different animals. My blueprint clearly said that it needed to be brick to support the various habitats we needed to install.

He had taken the liberty of fashioning a dreadful tenement out of some bundles of sticks lashed together with straw. You could damn near see through the outer walls. Wind whistled through the gaps. More subpar workmanship tainting my good name. Where in the hell did it say Everest Slumlords on the sign? They had to go.

O.G. sprinted to the front door and threw himself

inside. I could just make out Q.G.'s form in the window. He raised his little hooves in panic and ran deeper into the building. I chuckled from the safety of my truck.

Thunder announced the wolf's arrival, but the afternoon sun gave me my first good look at him. He was not the proud creature I assumed I'd hired. He leaned against the "Everest Construction" sign and panted, catching his breath. Jagged ribs peered through the holes in his vest. Big_B@D_W0lf23 reached into his pocket and grabbed an inhaler.

I done hired me a defective hitman.

The wolf choked down a few extra gulps of air. "Little pigs, little pigs, let me in."

Q.G. answered him, "Ain't no pigs in here, just a couple of barbers."

"You sound like pigs."

O.G. this time. "What are you trying to say? Pigs can be barbers. You have any idea how many chin hairs we have to deal with?"

Heh. Moron.

"Got ya." The wolf reared back on its hind legs. "I'll huff, and I'll puff, and I'll blow your house down."

I don't rightly know where he got the strength to knock down that apartment, but he sure did. The maelstrom uprooted trees behind the building, knocked a crater in the ground, and shattered the sticks into splinters.

Q.G. and O.G. took off once more. I swore to myself. More and more, this plan was not going my way. The wolf dropped back to all fours and crawled after them. I raced back to the truck to cut them off. They were probably heading to my house, and I'd only have one more chance to nail those idiots.

A man's home is his castle, and mine, I'm proud to say, is a marvel of porcine architecture. I lovingly crafted it from brick, with walls reinforced by rebar. There ain't a storm on God's Green Earth that can level my baby. Ain't an army that can storm my keep. That wolf wasn't going to be able to blow down my doors, but maybe I didn't need him to.

I took a shortcut and beat my brothers home. I grabbed the pistol from the glovebox. I held its weight in my hoof for a moment. That hitman had failed twice now to deal with my brothers. I'd paid good money for him to bump off a couple of idiots, and he couldn't even get that right. I'd have to do this job myself. Unfortunately, there were no refunds for assassins. I was going to have to kill him too if I didn't want him to just run around with my thirty grand.

A devious idea settled in my mind.

I racked the chamber on my pistol and tucked it into my waistband, then headed into the house. It was nice to return to some semblance of order after the day I'd had. Everything was placed exactly where it needed to be. I set a massive pot in the fireplace, got a fire burning, and waited. Sure enough, Q.G. and O.G. came running down and slammed on my door.

"Let us in. Let us in," they cried together.

I opened the door and leaned against the doorjamb. "Now why are you boys running around raising hell? Did you get those jobs done today?"

They pushed past me, pulled me in, and slammed the door. O.G. clambered into the living room. He grabbed my favorite wingback chair and tried to shove it against the door. "The…the…there's a wolf after us."

"He won't stop." Q.G. joined in the fortification efforts.

"A wolf?" I stoked the fire beneath the cauldron. "He say what he wanted?"

O.G. stopped, his mouth open and his brow furrowed. "He's a wolf, moron. He wants to eat us."

"Don't you think you're overreacting?" I beamed at them. "That feels like profilin', son. Maybe he's just lookin' for directions."

Q.G. stood at the window. "Shut up, you two. He's here."

Big_B@D_W0lf23 had seen better days. He dragged himself along the ground, claws burrowing into the dirt. White foam leaked out of his snout. His chest rose and fell like a thumping rabbit's foot. He sucked on his inhaler and broke into a coughing fit.

"Little pigs." Wheeze. "Little pigs." Wheeze. "Let me in."

I grabbed a paper and pen from my end table, which was now stacked on my couch against the door.

O.G. raised an eyebrow. "What do you think you're doin' there, P.G.?"

"I've half a mind to bargain with him. Unlike you swine, I've got some money saved up." I moved to the window and placed the pad against the sill.

Q.G. and O.G. high-fived. "That's a pretty good idea, P.G. Mama always said you was the smartest."

Oh sure, now they listened to Mama.

I wrote, "Come down through the chimney, you'll surprise them." on the piece of paper and plastered the note right in front of the beast.

The wolf nodded and staggered to his feet. I waited for him to start climbing and turned to my brothers. "He didn't buy it, he's climbing up to the roof. Quick, get that fire going."

Q.G. and O.G. lunged for the fireplace to stoke the flames. The water in the pot boiled. My brothers stepped back and clung to each other. The wolf's thundering steps carried down the chimney as he climbed inside. The smoke got him hacking. His cough rattled the house as he fell into the pot. It was now or never.

My brothers leapt for joy. O.G. danced a jig. "We did it. God thank you for a brother like P.G."

"Good job, fellas, get over here for a family hug."

When they turned around, I reached into my jacket pocket, pulled out my pistol, and shot O.G. through his stupid neck tattoo. He gasped and clutched his throat before falling to his knees. The look of shock was a reward all its own.

Q.G. charged forward but caught a bullet in the brain for his effort. His head snapped back, and he fell to ground, bleeding. Hopefully, Mama was waiting to smack some sense into them in that big smokehouse in the sky.

Big_B@D_W0lf23 screamed as best he could, but his asthma kept him from carrying on like that for too long.

"Mr. Wolf. I hired you for a very particular job. Do I look like the kind of pig who needs to be engaging in fratricide?"

"Let me out." Wheeze. "I'll give you your money back."

"This isn't about the money. It's about the prestige." I put the gun back in my pants. "You see, I'm going to need to build a lot of shelters and orphanages to cleanse my soul of the evil you made me inflict today."

"You were going to kill them anyway." Big_B@D_W0lf23 grabbed the pot, feebly trying to tip himself over.

I shook my head. "No, you were going to kill them so that my hooves would be clean. You must be punished for pushing me into this."

The wolf's voice was caught by another coughing fit before he passed out. Once he was nice and cooked, I knocked the pot over and let him spill out on the floor. Then, I took a massive paw in my hooves and raked his claws all over my brothers' bodies. The worst part was scratching myself. I tore open part of my belly and placed the gun in the wolf's hand.

Of course, I called the police to let them know somethin' right horrible had happened. The papers called me a hero. Said I was clever for cookin' the wolf like I'd done, but it was too bad about my brothers. These days, I'm raking in a fortune at Everest Construction, my family's name is saved, and somewhere my mama is proud of me. Of course, I got to live happily ever after; I told y'all I'm adaptable.

Out of the Tower

Kristy Perkins

Jehoram didn't want to intervene in the verbal battle between Rapunzel and the elf selling the apples, but he was pretty sure if he didn't do something there would be a repeat of the tower battle.

"But there's not a second L in apple." Rapunzel had a fixed smile on her face that was becoming more rigid by the second.

The elf behind the stall smiled right back. "Then you fix it."

Jehoram's memories of his fiancée were spotty, but he knew she was capable of handling herself. She'd tossed the evil witch Feliveg out a window, for goodness sakes. Hard to tell what she might do next. She was making this little wrinkle with her nose, and that made Jehoram nervous.

He made up his mind when Rapunzel's braid stirred without a breeze to move it. Jehoram grabbed Rapunzel's arm and steered her away from the apple cart, with a pointed look back at the elf. They were in a small market in a small town, so there weren't a lot of other places to go, but at least they were out of spitting range.

"That man was so…peculiar," Rapunzel said, the innocent tones of her voice ringing like bells. She wrapped her arm around his.

"Well, he is an elf. As long as they're not on a killing spree, we try to put up with the weirdness."

"Oh!" She smiled widely and kissed him on the cheek. "That makes sense."

Moments like that, Jehoram understood how he could have asked her to marry him. "Are you done with the market, or is there something left you wanted to look at?" he asked, wrapping an arm around her waist.

Rapunzel sighed. "I found a few things I'd like to buy, but I don't want to pay very much money for them. How does that work?"

"I can help. Just give me one minute to check the heft—"

"Oh, never mind." She cut him off with a pat on his shoulder. "I'll be fine, Jehoram. I can figure out a few things for myself."

Rapunzel skipped away, her long blond braid flowing behind her. That was weird. She almost sounded sarcastic. Jehoram decided he was imagining it.

Part of him wanted to follow her and make sure that Rapunzel didn't end up anywhere strange. Another part desperately needed the space to think about her and their apparent relationship.

He didn't know a lot about her, but he knew that she was charming and sweet. She was tough, too, taking down Feliveg all by herself after he'd been blinded and tossed out of a six-story tower, and then she'd healed his injuries. After all that, it was his turn to protect her, to help her adjust to the world outside the tower. He could put up with a few mood swings.

Right?

The sound of laughter broke him out of his reverie. Jehoram looked around. The familiar face snickering by the bounties board waved. Zachonicon was his best friend and the first person he'd thought to contact after the Feliveg incident. Jehoram had butted heads with him on more than one occasion—not literally because Zach was huge and it would have ended in a concussion—but there were few people he'd rather have watching his back.

"You made it!" Jehoram grinned.

Zach bounded over and clapped him on the back. "Of course I did. You're engaged! Apparently. Are you sure about this whole marriage thing? She could just be in it for your crown."

"Maybe. I don't know what she thinks of royalty." Jehoram scratched his neck and avoided eye contact.

"Dude, you're a prince. How has that not come up?" Zach raised an eyebrow.

Jehoram flinched and wished Zach could shut up for once. "I don't know."

That got him a befuddled look.

Jehoram huffed. "Getting thrown out of the tower made everything fuzzy. I don't remember most of what happened before that. I'm relying on what little I do know and the things Rapunzel mentions."

"Oh." Zach looked around at the marketplace. "So that's why you're hanging around this dinky little place. You're stalling until you can work out what's up."

"Yeah." Jehoram sighed. What he really needed was a quest so that he'd have an excuse to spend time with Rapunzel. He just needed the time to figure her out.

"Portraitists everywhere will rejoice, what with your brooding dark-haired hero look and her being all blond and flowery." Of course Zach wasn't done poking fun. "You're sure you're engaged?"

"Yes!" Jehoram groaned and swatted at his friend. "We're getting married. I just need the chance to get to know her better, before any big decisions come up." Something he kept telling himself over and over, to the point he actually sounded confident when he said it out loud. "And I can do that as soon as I can get her to the palace and figure out how to explain to my parents that I destroyed a local witch to save a girl."

"Didn't your letter say she was the one who destroyed the witch?"

"Yeah, but my parents are going to see it as me showboating no matter what I tell them."

Zach winced and clapped a hand on his friend's shoulder. "They're still not happy about the whole hero gig, huh?"

Jehoram glared imperiously at his friend. It was the full royal-blooded I-can-kill-you-for-your-insolence staredown. Zach was almost completely immune, but blessedly, he still backed down.

"Man, you need a quest. You're getting way too wound up," Zach muttered. "There's got to be something to do around here."

"I don't know." Jehoram looked around at the marketplace, which bustled with cheerful energy. Simple peasants trotted around, dressed in their charming smocks, bidding their welcomes to all in sight. There was a spell in the air creating a subtle golden glow around everything. "I think Feliveg and her tower was the biggest thing around." He waved at Rapunzel, who was presently looking through a meager shelf of books like it was a chest of dragon gold. She was pretty great, even if he wasn't sure about their getting married.

Zach shrugged broadly. "Who knows? Maybe she left something nasty behind."

An out-of-place thump put Jehoram's senses on high alert. With his hero training, he smelled them long before he saw them. Like everywhere else, there needed to be villains around to keep things chaotic. In this case, the appropriate evil was a band of thugs, who overturned apple carts and pushed the weak and elderly to the ground with a sneer. They had masks and empty bags, so they were definitely on their way to rob someone.

His natural sense of justice kicked in, and Jehoram leaped out of the alleyway shadows with a righteous roar. Zach followed at a leisurely pace, grabbing a fence post as he went. The ruffians stared. Some gaped openly.

Jehoram drew his sword and fell into the clash with ferocious joy. The bandits weren't quite up to his usual grade of villain, but aside from Feliveg, he hadn't had any kind of opponent in ages. He kicked one man through a fruit stand and threw a handful of flour in the face of another. Ignoring a peddler's squawking, Jehoram catapulted across a cart. He jumped over fences, dodged through laundry lines, and hacked and slashed the robbers' gear until it disintegrated. He also sliced through a few display racks, but he could probably pay for replacements later.

The thugs ran, crying and yelling rude things about Jehoram's magnificent bladework. At the other end of the street, Zach whacked them over the head with the fence post, leaving a tidy pile of unconscious bodies.

Jehoram wiped his blade clean of fruit pulp and sheathed it, satisfied. "Rapunzel, did you see that?" He looked around. No sign of her.

He wheeled around twice more, taking in the wrecked marketplace. She was nowhere to be seen. Panic started to set in until he caught sight of her gleaming hair near the village chapel. "Rapunzel!"

She turned, her unbraided hair flying in a halo around her head. She looked wonderful, almost exactly how he'd seen her after she healed his sight, short hair and all.

But Rapunzel wasn't alone. She was pulling along another woman, who was armed with a cudgel. The woman was wearing something like a gray uniform with a serpent embroidered on the sleeve, so she was still clearly something sinister.

"Rapunzel, stay back! This woman is a villain." Jehoram dashed over, drawing his sword as he went.

"Yes, I know."

Jehoram blinked.

Rapunzel beamed at him. "She offered to give me a haircut, but then she and some others tried to kidnap me for ransom." Rapunzel's nose wrinkled. "It was a nuisance, but all's well that ends well."

Jehoram had a brief moment of self-pity at having missed either the chance to rescue his fiancee or see her in action. Then his brain caught up. "Kidnapped?! Rapunzel, are you okay? Did they hurt you?"

Zach cleared his throat. Before he could say anything, Jehoram held up a finger in warning.

Rapunzel didn't appear to have noticed. "Oh, no. I should have stretched beforehand, but otherwise I'm fine. It wasn't a terribly complicated fight, and I was able to use my hair for most of it."

"So why are you taking this woman with you?" Jehoram tried to step in and get the woman away from Rapunzel, but she turned and kept hold of her captive.

"I turned her friends over to the authorities, but this woman fell ill as we were fighting, so now I'm taking her to the doctor." She frowned. "That's what you do when someone is sick, right?"

"Generally." Jehoram eyed Rapunzel's companion with new distrust. How much of this was an act, designed to get the woman out of jail time? Her skin did look kind of blue, come to think of it. He stepped in closer.

She vomited a stream of glowing blue liquid on his boots.

Jehoram grimaced then took up a place at the woman's other side and helped Rapunzel drag her along.

The village didn't have a doctor, but it did have a midwife and an apothecary who set up shop together. They pulled the would-be kidnapper through the doorway. Jehoram tried to just drop her, but Rapunzel had a good grip and kept the woman from falling. With a reproachful look, she placed their prisoner on an empty pallet.

Not that there were many of those. The shop was filled with beds, and those beds were filled with people whose skins were varying tints of blue. There were so many that even a few tables had people on them.

The apothecary charged over. "Not another one."

Jehoram frowned. "Another what?"

"Plague victim." The woman crouched down next to Rapunzel and took the victim's pulse. "I'm Genevieve. Usually I'm just an assistant, but as you can see, we're a bit short-staffed."

Genevieve leaned back against the wall wearily then pushed to her feet again and checked on the next patient. Jehoram followed, stepping carefully around the people lying on the floor.

The patient coughed, and Genevieve sighed. "We've no idea what is causing it. People get sick, turn blue, and then fade into a cloud of blue smoke, which means we're reasonably certain it's magical in origin. So far we're handling it, but it's left other places decimated."

Rapunzel was still kneeling beside the young woman they brought in, murmuring comforting words. When the patient was settled, Rapunzel moved on to the next person and the next. Genevieve took full advantage of having three extra sets of hands. Zach grumbled about helping, but he took the chance to show off by carrying two people at a time.

Jehoram took a second to admire his fiancée before he started shifting patients to places where Genevieve could get to them. Poor woman was frazzled enough without having to climb over sick people. It was a relief to see Rapunzel throwing herself into the work. Her having a good heroic instinct was probably one of the reasons he fell in love with her.

The plague was a nasty one, and it was an hour's work before Jehoram was able to take a breath. He caught Rapunzel before he lost her to the maze of patients and took her aside. "I think I saw a messenger raven stall in the market. I'll send off a few messages, get the band together, and we'll figure out a way to stop this."

"Why is it up to us to stop it?" Rapunzel carried on preparing a tincture, deftly mixing in the ingredients without even measuring. "I thought diseases were for doctors to heal, not heroes."

"Yes, but this is a magical plague, so there's got to be someone causing it, and we can fix that." He grinned at her.

What a relief. The chance to quest with Rapunzel, to get to know her in a way that didn't involve heartfelt conversations and possibly rehashing things he'd already told her. He just didn't want to hurt her.

Jehoram knew by her pursed lips that she wasn't convinced. "Come on. It'll be an adventure. We can explore the world and help people while we're at it."

She gave him a dubious look, but then she sighed and kissed him lightly on the cheek. "All right. I suppose traveling a little wouldn't hurt. And I wouldn't mind being farther from the tower. Feliveg was brewing something nasty before she died, and it'll probably leave a horrible miasma for weeks even if she's not around to sustain it."

Jehoram could hear someone complaining about fool heroes in the background, which stung his pride and strengthened his resolve. He really hadn't meant to make such a mess of the courtyard. "So we're agreed. We'll go and investigate the source of this magical plague."

"And find my parents, like you said before."

Jehoram blinked, willing the panic and confusion out of his face. He knew bluffing like that was going to come back to bite him, but he didn't want to risk hurting Rapunzel. She deserved someone who could remember all the details, and he was determined to make up the gap in his memories and get back to where they were, even if it was a little awkward.

"Right!" He scratched the back of his neck. "We'll work on that, too. But we should probably investigate the plague first, just in case they end up being infected or something. So we can cure them. Just in case."

"You've said that twice now," Rapunzel said placidly. "Are you feeling all right? Oh, you probably should have stretched before your fight too. You must be feeling terrible. I'll ask the apothecary for some ointment."

All the alarm bells went off at that. "Oh, no," Jehoram babbled. "Heroes don't use ointment. They use potions, elixirs, shirts for bandages, crude poultices, even salves in a pinch. But not ointment. Ointment is…" He looked to Zach, who had come up while they were talking. His friend's evil grin was no help at all. "Ointment is just bad."

Maybe Jehoram's aversion was a bit strange, but he had his reasons for the mild phobia. Besides, there were lots of other ways to treat wounds that didn't involve flashbacks to the time he was held prisoner by that lunatic physician.

"Oh. I see."

Rapunzel walked away slowly. She looked back twice, and each time, the wrinkles on her forehead were more pronounced. Jehoram groaned. Sometimes he could get away with ridiculous explanations of things he didn't want to talk about, but more and more, Rapunzel was catching on. He had no idea what to do about her.

"Dude, you are clueless when it comes to that girl."

"Zach, you have no idea."

***

By the time Jehoram got Rapunzel out of the village,

it was sunset. It wouldn't have been a problem, except that some of Jehoram's guildmates weren't permitted within five miles of that particular village, so it was a long trek to the clearing they'd set as a meeting place. Rapunzel chattered the whole walk about the wonderfully ordinary things she'd discovered that day.

When Jehoram and company arrived, the others were already there. Jehoram cleared his throat, cueing the stares. "Guys, this is Rapunzel, my fiancée. She's joining us on this quest." She elbowed him with surprising vehemence. "And we're also looking for her parents."

He pointed to the woman in dark leather who was throwing knives at squirrels, barely visible in the twilight. "That's Kimna. She's technically a thief, so if a guard asks, you definitely have not seen her."

Next, he gestured to the dwarf stirring a pot of blackened stew. "That's Thezzag. He's pretty traditional, so no bad-mouthing his grandma, even as a joke, and don't touch the axe."

Finally, he pointed to the man in the starry robes, who had taken advantage of being the last one introduced and had posed. "This is Uvdalf the Uncorruptible. He's our wizard."

Rapunzel blinked. "I'm sorry, did you say 'uncorruptible'? As if it was spelled with a 'u'?"

"He did." Uvdalf smiled slyly. "That way, it's an alliteration. Easier to remember." He winked.

"But it's supposed to be 'incorruptible.' With an 'i.'" Rapunzel smiled back, showing a lot of her teeth.

As Zach had pointed out, Jehoram was pretty clueless when it came to his fiancée's mood, but he was pretty sure it was a good idea to get her thoughts away from Uvdalf and his chosen descriptor. He cleared his throat. "Anyway, I've gathered you all because there's a crisis. Someone's cast a plague on the countryside that makes people sick and then turns them into blue smoke. Uvdalf, can you cast some light on what might cause something like that?"

Uvdalf blinked and broke pose. "Um." He stood there, calculating on his fingers for way too long. "No."

That figured. Jehoram refused to roll his eyes. It wasn't like he'd expected much from the eccentric wizard.

"We should check underground, make sure there's not something seeping up from the depths." Thezzag tapped the rock he was sitting on with his axe. "I can dig us a tunnel in less than a week."

"But they're turning into air." Rapunzel had so thoroughly entangled her fingers in Jehoram's that it hurt. "It's unlikely to have anything to do with earth magic. Air magic is more likely."

Jehoram looked back and forth between the brewing scowl on Thezzag's face and the curl of Rapunzel's lip. "So we check both. The mountains are only a few days away, and that should let us check air and earth magic at the same time." He breathed a sigh of relief when Rapunzel's death grip relaxed.

The others didn't object, so they settled in to camp for the night. Thezzag served his stew, and he and Zach set to arguing about who had killed more monsters since they'd last met. Uvdalf contributed occasionally, adding snide comments about how much more practical spells were as weapons. Rapunzel drew closer to the campfire, the light reflecting in her eyes like the sun.

"How did you get that woman to fall in love with you?" Kimna whispered harshly. She'd climbed a tree and was dangling over Jehoram's head.

Jehoram sighed. Scattered memories of quiet conversations, a desperate battle in the tower, and that was all he had. He remembered her saving him, at least, and something about the color blue. He knew he loved her, but he wished he could remember why.

"I'm trying to figure that out," he whispered back.

***

Once again, he found himself in a marketplace, watching over Rapunzel from a distance. He took Kimna with him, supposedly for her sharp eyes but really because he'd known her since childhood and needed the chance to talk to her. The other three he ordered to investigate any magical sources in the area, which they did, grumbling the whole time.

Jehoram was a hero, so even if his personal life was a mess, he had to help people, and that meant investigating the plague, even if his friends didn't make it easy. Kimna wanted to enchant her new sword in the Pyres of Amorgan, Zach dared Thezzag to hunt a chimera, Uvdalf offended a local lord, and they had to do a delivery for his mother-in-law. Fortunately, Rapunzel was a great person to have on a quest, when she wasn't wandering off to help random strangers.

Jehoram probably could have kept all of them a little more focused if he wasn't so confused by his future wife and by how he felt about her. He could probably spend years unraveling Rapunzel's personality and its contradictions. The more he got to know her, the more he wanted to fall in love with her. Hence stalking her while she shopped.

"I don't see why you're suddenly so worried about us not hunting down some crazy curse," Kimna mumbled as she slipped a silk scarf under her jacket. "It's not like the situation's getting any better or worse. Someone's bound to find the solution sooner or later. We might as well do our own thing."

"And what if someone else doesn't come along?" Jehoram dodged out from under a filmy green length of fabric and scowled. "We said we would take care of it. What if the villagers we've talked to tell other heroes not to bother helping them, and so no one ends up stopping this plague because they think we're doing it? This place is our last lead, and so far, we haven't even seen anyone with symptoms."

Rapunzel was in the process of haggling for a new dress. She was surprisingly shrewd at that, Jehoram had noticed. She was so nice that no one noticed the bargaining part.

"Villagers never turn down help. Besides, this should be giving you plenty of time to talk to Rapunzel." Kimna held up an orange scarf to her hair and looked in a mirror with a critical eye. "Don't blame me because you're looking for excuses not to talk to your own girlfriend."

"Fiancée."

Kimna huffed. "I was making a point. You're acting like this is someone you're about to dump, and you both deserve better than that."

Jehoram blanched. Before he could find an appropriate comeback, Kimna sauntered off and jumped on a ledge by a baker's cart. She snatched up two coin purses and a pastry before she vanished onto the rooftops.

"I'm not going to dump her!" he finally squawked, but the only thing around to hear him was the scarf seller's cat.

A gong clashed and boomed from across town. Jehoram took off, yelling for assistance, but didn't care to see if anyone actually listened. Finally, something to do that wasn't just thinking. There was a lot of screaming in that general direction, so at least it was easy to navigate.

He was so ecstatic to be on the move that he didn't look where he was going and crashed into a troll. The beast looked shocked to see him, since everyone else had been running away. Jehoram fell back and drew his sword, shouting his defiance to the sky.

Fighting a creature the size of a troll was not

something Jehoram excelled at. He liked banter, leaping about, and smashing. The dodging required to get through a troll's defenses required a lot of focus, and before long, he was smashing through windows and colliding with walls, and it was just very unpleasant. Hitting the heavy door of the bank was too much, and he blacked out for a split second. Where was his sword, anyway? He tried sitting up and failed miserably.

The troll hefted its club and held it high over its head, prepared to squash Jehoram into tiny bits of hero.

"I bought lunch!" Rapunzel darted out from a bakery and waved her arms wildly. She gave Jehoram a desperate look.

The troll paused mid-swing and stared back at her, a dumbfounded look on its already not-too-bright face. The expression turned to a flabbergasted smile.

Rapunzel was as lovely as ever, of course, but the thing that held the troll's fascination was her hair. It had grown out again, to the point where it swept the ground even when she kept it braided. The troll eyed that hair greedily, which was odd behavior even for a troll, but Jehoram wasn't going to protest the lack of attention as he scrambled around on his hands and knees looking for his sword.

The troll made a clumsy grab at Rapunzel, and rather than dodge, she let it grab her, pull her in close. Jehoram would have screamed for help, except that he could see the keen look in her eyes and wasn't sure what to make of the situation, so he kept crawling around for his sword.

The troll chomped down on her braid. Rapunzel screamed, a wordless cry of absolute feminine fury, and in that moment, Jehoram struck.

His sword shattered into a thousand pieces when it hit the troll. That was a bummer.

Rapunzel's hair glowed a delicate blue. The troll

yelped and stumbled back, spitting out the hair frantically. It staggered about, knocking over everything in its path, until it finally stumbled to a halt and turned to dust.

Rapunzel immediately went to Jehoram and started fussing over his injuries, which were numerous but not serious. She kept trying to use ointment on them, though, until he managed to toss it in the bushes while she wasn't looking. She complained about the loss as she bandaged him up.

"How are you doing?" He checked her over for injuries.

"Fine, I suppose." She sighed. "The world is a very big place. It might just be a little too big for me. So many things go wrong." Rapunzel looked almost sad.

Jehoram had no idea what to say to that, so he found the first topic he could and skipped right on past his own awkwardness. "Thanks for saving me. I didn't know your hair could do that." Jehoram avoided looking her in the eyes as he trimmed up the nastier bits of hair with a shard of his sword. He half expected the stray locks to start sparking or the clipped bits of hair to spontaneously catch on fire.

"Oh yes, darling, I found that out a week ago. When you were fighting the forest renegades? A wolf tried to eat me, but all he got was my hair, and then it glowed, and he was gone within minutes."

Jehoram could feel his eyes bugging out and was saved from trying to figure out what that could possibly mean when the rest of the group arrived. Uvdalf in particular became very interested in what had just happened, particularly what he saw as the flaws in the tale.

"But why would a troll try to eat hair, anyway? They're terrific eaters, but they're not that stupid." Uvdalf held court by a smashed florist's shop. Somehow, the townspeople thought that he knew what he was talking about and listened to the argument avidly.

"Trolls are attracted to magic, and my hair is probably one of the largest concentrations of magical energy in town." Rapunzel tugged at the ragged ends.

"Why would you say that?" Uvdalf scoffed.

"Because it grows at least an inch a day. I think that's more than enough proof," Rapunzel said, smiling sweetly.

Jehoram stayed out of it and wrapped an arm around Rapunzel. He was a little more concerned about the fact that she hadn't told him about being attacked by wolves. She did that a lot, actually. Wandered off and then reappeared having escaped something dreadful, smiling the whole while, and not explaining unless he noticed she was gone.

In any case, he wasn't rescuing Uvdalf. The man wouldn't get away with playing the wise wizard for much longer, especially since Jehoram had seen the whole thing, along with several confused villagers and a herd of goats.

The conversation got technical, but even if Rapunzel's arguments were superior—and a lot more accurate—the argument was ended not by a verbal victory but by the fact that Zach turned blue and collapsed. Rapunzel was the only one with the presence of mind to try and catch him.

The villagers and Jehoram all panicked. Luckily for all of them, when Jehoram panicked, he got very organized, as if his fight-or-flight instincts had once belonged to a sheepdog. Before Rapunzel was able to rouse Zach, Jehoram had summoned the local healers, organized a squad to find anyone else with symptoms, and persuaded the bystanders to build a stretcher.

The whole time, Rapunzel stayed with Zach. Just like with the bandit she'd taken for treatment, she didn't flinch from the disease. She did whatever the healers directed her to do. The cowards were too afraid to get close to Zach.

"We need to find that cure. Fast." Jehoram cursed at himself for getting distracted by his personal problems.

People were turning to vapor, and he'd let the group do whatever they wanted. Now his friend was sick.

Zach came around and insisted he was fine, but the blue tinge to his skin and the blue mucus he coughed up stated otherwise. The group crowded around him, badgering him with questions when it was clear he wasn't going to just pass out again.

Jehoram was the one to notice Rapunzel edging away. He caught her hand, because it seemed to be the thing a good future husband would do. She left it in his grasp limply, not holding on but not pulling away, either. He wasn't sure what to do. Rapunzel usually took the lead in those kinds of situations.

She had such bewilderment in her eyes. "Is it always like this? The world, I mean. Can dreadful things happen to just anyone? There's not a single apothecary we've talked to who might know how to end the plague." She had one arm wrapped around herself. "Feliveg had a supplier named Bruce in a town called Standelbart. He might know more about what's going on. I'll get us food for the trip while you check the map."

Before he could answer, she had bounded away. "We'll leave as soon as you get back!" he shouted. He wanted to go after her, but Zach was still sick even if the fainting spell did seem to be a temporary lapse. They needed to get Zach back on his feet and back to the quest before he died. Hopefully Rapunzel wouldn't end up in the middle of a bank robbery or something like that.

As soon as she was out of sight, his friends all turned back to him. "Are you sure you can handle her?" Uvdalf asked. "She's so featherbrained."

Jehoram didn't have to tell Uvdalf to be quiet. Zach used the last of his strength and punched him.

***

Apparently, Standelbart had a larger-than-average collection of villains. They had a gang, some highway robbers, the usual variety of bandits and thugs, and even a few petty vandals and deposed despots. They inspired Jehoram's creative streak, and he and his friends entered into a pitched battle in the town's central square. A few more cows got involved than would be preferred, but such was life.

By the fifteen minute mark, there was a crowd of villagers, and by twenty minutes, they were taking bets. Zach won sixty gold because he could predict what Jehoram was going to do next. It was nice to see him up to his usual tricks and not getting bogged down in the despondency that had gripped them all. Jehoram looked around for Rapunzel, but she had vanished within the first few minutes of their arriving, presumably looking for Bruce.

"What is the point of showing off for your lady love if she's not going to stick around to appreciate it?" Jehoram said, accompanied by an exaggerated huff. Of course, Rapunzel was doing something way more useful, but everyone knew that heroes were supposed to be vain, and the reference made his friends grin. Jehoram grinned back and returned to the fight with a renewed spirit.

By the end of the hour, Jehoram could freely admit that he was stalling. There were only so many times one could do the Reinhold Sweep before it got boring, and he wasn't really focusing on the fight.

One of the more stubborn despots got his hands on a flame spell. By the time that was all taken care of, the fight was pretty well over. Once things start catching on fire, there's not much of a chance for grand leaps and other fight extenders.

Jehoram handed things over to the town guard with a flourish and a twirl of the cape he'd snatched from a bystander. He got so caught up in the adoration that he almost accepted a favor token from a lovely young lady, until Kimna swatted him. In his surge of spirits, he'd forgotten his engagement. That wasn't a good sign.

When he finally slipped away, Jehoram wasn't sure if it was to find Rapunzel or not. When he'd regained his sight after the tower battle, he'd been useless. Rapunzel had been the one to dispose of Feliveg's body, and she'd healed his wounds. She could do just fine on her own. The real question was, would she want his company? It was hard to read how she felt about him sometimes.

He knew he liked her, at least. He thought she was kind, funny, and curious, and she made a fantastic traveling companion. Did that mean that he loved her? Or, just as important, did those little smiles and cheek kisses mean that she loved him?

He spotted her down the street, gliding along. Her hair flounced around her shoulders in lovely golden waves, already losing the signs of the troll attack. His heart skipped a beat. She waved at him cheerfully, and that was enough to make up his mind about whether or not he wanted her company at the moment.

"You missed the show!" He grinned at her. "And I missed you."

"You didn't. I was gone for maybe an hour." Rapunzel's half-laughing tone as she let him take her hand was almost enough to make him forget how to speak. "You probably didn't even notice I was gone."

"I always notice." He cleared his throat, a little embarrassed at the admission.

"Really?" Rapunzel blushed and glanced off to the side for a split second. Then she smiled and leaned in like she was going to kiss him, but at the last second, she pulled back, her eyes going bright. "I found Bruce. He says we're looking for a witch."

Jehoram winced. "Well, yeah. We knew that."

She nodded slowly, and if he didn't know better, he might say that she was on the verge of rolling her eyes. "I mean, he thought a particular witch might be responsible. Her name is Nasturium, and I recognize the name as a prominent figure in the Witch Guild."

"The what?"

"Witch Guild." Her expression was entirely serious.

Jehoram blinked and somehow found himself sitting down, stunned and bewildered. "Witches don't organize. They're random agents of chaos and evil. If they were organized, they might kill us all. It's not possible."

Rapunzel handed him a glass of water—retrieved out of nowhere, apparently—and a reproachful look. "Jehoram. You have your guild, and witches have theirs. Most of the world is a sea of ridiculousness to me, but in this topic, I know a little more about it than you. Feliveg's assignment was the tower she held me in and the surrounding area. Nasturium is responsible for this whole region, so Feliveg reported to her. She's definitely powerful enough to do something like this. According to Bruce, her cottage is less than an hour away. We can deal with her and cure this whole plague."

Jehoram remained stuck to the ground, still processing the terrifying thought that witches were just as organized as everyone else. What else did he have wrong?

"Are you okay?" Rapunzel wrapped her arm around his. "Because I can ask Bruce for some other solution. He's probably got some kind of ointment we could use to cure everyone."

That snapped Jehoram out of it, and he shook his head no. "Nasturium's fine. We'll go get her, and that'll fix everything. No ointment." And then he actually looked at her face and saw the mischievous gleam. "You were joking."

Rapunzel sighed, which only partly abated her grin. "One of these days, you'll have to explain that weird aversion of yours." She let go of him. "I'll go find Zach and Kimna and Thezzag, and we can get going." She swirled away down the street and looked back at him twice.

Jehoram thought about yelling to make sure she got Uvdalf, too, but hopefully one of the others would grab him. The warm feeling in his chest was utterly distracting. She knew him well enough to know how to make him focus, how to make him laugh. Somehow, that little joke meant more than all the cheek kisses and pet names that came before.

Thezzag stomped up to him, probably having heard the whole conversation. "If you marry that girl, you're going to turn into a complete sap," he said solemnly.

Jehoram wasn't entirely sure that was a bad thing.

***

"That is definitely a witch's cottage," Zach muttered from his position halfway up the tree, where he was dangling from a rope trap. The splatter of his cerulean vomit was vibrant against the dark forest floor.

"Shut up!" Kimna hissed from her spot in the spiderweb. "She'll hear us, and then we're in trouble."

Thezzag bellowed from the mud pit he was sinking into. "Both of you be qu—!"

Uvdalf slammed his staff into the ground. All three became frozen in a shimmering purple field of energy, still trapped but not giving away their position and not getting more stuck. Uvdalf sagged against a thorny bush, then yelped and jumped away. The field flickered, and he raised a hand to sustain it. With his free hand, he waved Jehoram and Rapunzel through, in the direction of the witch's cottage. They proceeded with caution.

Zach was right. It was a quintessential witch's cottage. It was downright classy, featuring skulls so polished they gleamed and a roof dark as midnight. A subtle blue fog swirled around their feet as they approached.

"Excuse me? Can I help you?" A feeble voice rang through the clearing from all around them. Jehoram spun around. The fog ghosts were eerie but not dangerous.

Rapunzel gently turned him to face the door, where a woman somewhere between elderly and middle-aged stood. She held a knobby staff, and she tapped it on the floor of the little cottage porch impatiently.

"Witch Nasturium, we demand that you cease this foul curse you've laid upon the land." Jehoram drew his sword. It made a satisfying ring. Too bad he'd have to give it back to Kimna when this was all finished.

The witch's face fell. "Oh, you're heroes." She huffed. "Here I was hoping the herbalist was finally doing deliveries like a reasonable businesswoman." She raised her staff.

Rapunzel's hair shimmered. Her long locks shot out, stretching and grabbing the staff. Not yanking it free, just holding it still. "He's the prince, too," Rapunzel added.

Jehoram twitched. Even if it was a relief that she knew he was royalty, he wanted to yell at her for giving away a crucial part of his identity to a malevolent witch. Before he could, the witch tossed her staff to the ground and swore. At least, Jehoram was pretty sure she did. The vehemence she spoke with was a pretty good clue, and the fact the skull in her line of vision disintegrated.

Nasturium disappeared into her cottage for a few minutes, and Jehoram and Rapunzel waited outside, exchanging looks of befuddlement. They could hear banging and scraping inside. Nasturium barged back outside with a pair of hedge clippers, a ladle, and a human leg bone.

"Come on, then, Your Highness. I'll get your friends out of the traps. Didn't realize our good royals would deign to let their precious children do anything as gauche as hero work." Nasturium stalked toward the trees where Jehoram's friends were hidden.

"Are you going to stop the curse, too?" Jehoram asked, as politely as he could.

"What curse?" Nasturium reached Kimna and began clipping away industriously.

Rapunzel helped unwrap Kimna from the frayed bits of webbing.

Jehoram wanted to help, but he didn't want to let go of his sword, so he stuck with his interrogation. "The plague that's spreading across the land, making everyone sick and turning them into blue smoke."

Nasturium swore again, singeing the thornbush. "I didn't do anything! I study necromancy, not disease. That sounds like Feliveg." She stepped around Uvdalf, who looked close to passing out from spell strain.

Rapunzel stiffened.

Jehoram stepped in front of Rapunzel, giving her a buffer. "Feliveg's dead."

"Oh, there's your problem right there. A good witch always sets kill spells for when she dies." Nasturium paused in her clipping. "It's usually something more immediate, though, like some kind of explosion."

"She'd been hired to create a spell, right before her death," Rapunzel said slowly, probably sussing out the details from memories she'd tried to bury. "Would she have made it to continue after her death?"

"Oh, yes, that's definitely something Feliveg would have done. She was always so conscientious about giving her spells a good anchor, so her customers would stay happy in case something happened to her." Nasturium absently whacked Thezzag with the ladle, and he slowly rose out of the mud pit. "Of course, you're out of the tower now, dear, so I suppose it's no wonder the spells are all out of whack."

When Thezzag was all the way out, Nasturium gave

Zach's tree a good sharp rap with the leg bone, and he tumbled down with a grunt. Uvdalf let his freezing spell go with an exhausted sigh, promptly slumped onto the thornbush, and yelped again.

"How does a spell get out of whack?" Jehoram sheathed his sword with more force than necessary. He'd almost gotten used to technical conversations, because they happened with increasing frequency when Rapunzel was around. He still occasionally found the need to gape like a fish and hope someone would show mercy and explain. "If a witch is dead, her spells are supposed to die with her."

"If you're being technical, it's the combination of the tower and her hair together that's the anchor, but since her hair is attached to her head, and her head is out in the world, all those spells are completely out of control." Nasturium snapped her fingers, and the traps reset. "It seems one of them is a nasty little plague. Probably a kill switch. Feliveg was always the vindictive sort."

"You're saying Rapunzel is causing this?" Jehoram asked incredulously. The words slipped out before he could stop them.

Rapunzel's face was dead white. Her breathing was rapid, and for a second, Jehoram thought she might faint, but she closed her eyes for a long moment. When they opened again, her face was utterly blank. He took her hand, but she didn't look at him.

Nasturium didn't seem to notice any of this. "Heroes and their educations. That girl's not what's powering the spells, she's what's containing them. Plague curses are chaotic, unless you can bind them and limit them. You're the binding, my dear." She faced Rapunzel, the only person in the group who apparently knew what was happening. "Feliveg's magic won't last forever, but there's no telling how much damage it'll do before it runs out of energy."

"Then how do I stop the plague?" Rapunzel asked,

her voice steady.

Since he was holding her hand, Jehoram was the only one who could tell how much she was shaking.

"You don't." Nasturium snatched a hair from Rapunzel's head and examined it. It turned blue and then burst into flames. "Nope. Can't manage it. Maybe Feliveg could have deactivated the spell." She paused and snorted. "Capable of it, but she'd never let go of her power like that. And since I'm not her, and I've really got no idea what she was thinking, I can't help."

"Then what do we do?" Jehoram spoke up when it was clear that Rapunzel was shrinking into herself.

"Move the lovely anchor here back to the tower. The plague will stop, and eventually, all the other nasty things Feliveg cooked up will run out of energy, even if they're not active. Good news is that you're young, sweetie. It probably won't take your entire life, and the rest of us won't have to worry about you dying and letting anything loose." She nodded, like everything was well and decided, and stumped back to her house.

Jehoram had one final question. "You're just letting us go?"

Nasturium clicked her tongue and looked back. "I'm not killing a prince if I can help it. That's a good way to get kicked out of any guild, evil or not." She slammed the door behind herself.

Rapunzel burst into sobs and ran off. Jehoram, not knowing what else to do, chased after her. Zach yelled something, but Jehoram ignored it.

He caught her and wrapped her in his arms. She didn't push him away. "Hey, it's going to be okay. We'll figure this out."

"We already have it figured out." Rapunzel sniffled. "Nasturium made it pretty clear what our only option is."

"There are other witches out there. And wizards who

are way better at this kind of thing than Uvdalf. We'll figure out something else. You don't have to go back there," he murmured into her hair.

"Even if there is a solution, I can't risk this plague getting any worse. Even a short detour could cost dozens of lives. This is the only way, Jehoram. I'm never going to find my parents, and I'm never going to be able to explore the world." Rapunzel pushed him to arm's length. "I just need a moment to adjust. By myself, please."

Jehoram did as she asked, heartsick himself.

***

The others stayed at the bottom of the tower as Jehoram took Rapunzel on the final stage of their journey, following her up the rickety staircase leading to the tower that had been her home for so long. And now it would be again.

As ramshackle as it looked from the outside, the inside of the tower was fairly sizeable and well kept. They hadn't even been away long enough for much dust to gather. There were various scars in the main room from that final battle with the witch, but most of it was repairable, and the kitchen table was somehow unscathed. Jehoram was pretty sure he remembered smashing into the solid wood at one point.

It was a decent space, but the dismal lighting almost had Jehoram escorting Rapunzel back down the stairs. He would have if not for the excited shouting out the window. He dashed over and looked down.

"I'm fine!" Zach waved up at him. He wasn't blue anymore, and he clearly wasn't at all sick.

This was a good thing. They had definitive proof that Rapunzel's presence in the tower was a cure. Too bad Jehoram's heart didn't agree with this victory, and it metaphorically twisted in his chest until it ached.

"Are you going to be okay, Rapunzel?" he asked, giving her plenty of space.

She smiled, and there was just a tinge of relief to it. "Oh, I don't mind. Not right now, anyway. This world, it's complete nonsense, but I can make my part of it good." She picked up a book and put it on the shelf with a loving pat. "It's easier to make a part of the world good if it's a small part."

"I'll keep looking for your parents," he blurted out. "I'll escort them here myself, make sure you get to meet them."

"Oh. Yes. Thank you."

Jehoram waited by the window, wondering what to do now. Did she want to be alone for a while, to adjust to her new—or old—surroundings? Did he need to pull her into a sweeping kiss to make her forget all about the hardship in the face of their overwhelming love? Did he even really believe they were in love at all? The rules weren't clear for this kind of situation.

"I haven't been completely honest with you, Rapunzel."

Rapunzel glanced at him and then deliberately looked away.

"During the battle with Feliveg, I hit my head pretty good, and try as I might, I'm having trouble figuring out the last few months. Pretty much the entirety of our relationship is a gigantic blur. I've been trying to get by on guesswork and the things you tell me, but I don't think I'm getting those memories back. Just thought you should know, before you end up stuck with someone who doesn't remember knowing you."

Rapunzel picked up a well-worn green book. There were slight indents on the cover where the gilt title had once been, but it was unreadable now.

"I know." Rapunzel's words put an icy fear into his heart. She looked him in the eye for half a second then back down at the book. "I haven't been entirely honest with you, either. We're not actually engaged." She tucked her hair behind her ears. "We kissed once, right before Feliveg showed up, but that was as far as we ever got. I just told you we were so you would do the things I asked, like help me look for my parents. Once it was obvious that you didn't remember, you just accepted whatever I told you as fact."

Jehoram didn't actually have a heart attack, but it sure felt like he might for a few minutes. Sweet, innocent Rapunzel had been manipulating him from the start. She'd trusted him even less than he'd trusted her. He put a hand on his sword, grip tightening reflexively.

And then he let it go, whatever anger he'd mustered fading as quick as it came. He knew she was cunning and clever, enough to get the information they'd needed for the quest. It didn't mean she wasn't still a decent person. Just a lot cannier than he thought.

"So you don't have to marry me," Rapunzel stated. Her tone was bland, but her hand trembled as she passed it over a knot in the wood of the table.

"I suppose I don't."

Rapunzel's eyelids fluttered shut, but not before Jehoram saw the glimmer of tears. She breathed, slowly, and when she opened her eyes, they were clear. There was nobility and strength in her posture. That hadn't been a lie. The kindness, the courage, that was in her too, and he could have seen the truth if he'd just set aside his own lies.

And then Jehoram knew the answer to the question he'd been asking himself through the whole quest, even if he didn't quite realize it was even a question. Did he really want to marry a girl he barely knew?

"Not yet, anyway. I'd like to get to know you first."

Her gaze turned in his direction, not quite reaching

his face but resting somewhere over to his left side. "What?"

"It's a good thing we're not getting married, with all the lying to each other. But I like you, and I know that what was between us wasn't all fake." Jehoram stepped closer to her.

Rapunzel picked up a small pile of books from the floor. "I just told you I spent the last month manipulating you. You can't trust anything I say."

Jehoram stepped even closer. "I can, though. Because you're the one who found Nasturium. You're the one who kept me from panicking about Zach. You're the one who saved me from that troll. Maybe I can't trust what you say with your words, but I can trust your actions. That's the part of you I like. And I'd like to keep getting to know you, if you're up for it."

"Why would you want someone like me?" Rapunzel put down the books she was about to reshelf, her hands finally going still, her gaze meeting his.

"I don't know if you've realized, but you're rather spectacular. Probably just as well you'll end up stuck in this tower, because otherwise you'd handle all the usual heroic troubles within a week, and I'd be out of a job. At the very least, I'm saying I'll visit regularly, and I'll make sure plenty of other people will come out and do the same. You're not going to be alone again." He patted her shoulder awkwardly. "Unless you want to be," he added quickly. "But even if it doesn't work out between us, I'm not going to abandon you to this tower. Now that Feliveg is dead, you're going to need someone to bring you food."

Part of him expected a sweet smile to put his guard down and try to keep him under her control. He wasn't sure what the rest of him expected. He knew what he wanted.

Rapunzel hugged him ferociously. Jehoram hugged her back. A damp patch grew on his shirt from her tears.

When they pulled apart, she gave him a watery smile.

"I'd like to give this a try." She sniffled and gave her head a tiny little shake, and just like that, the tears stopped, leaving behind just a trace of redness. "I can give you all the ointment you need."

Jehoram couldn't prevent the involuntary flinch. Rapunzel giggled. He grinned at her. "I promise I'll tell the tale of why I hate it. Eventually. But please, no ointment."

Jehoram held out his hand for Rapunzel to shake. She took it, and they held hands, suspended there between them as a promise for the future.

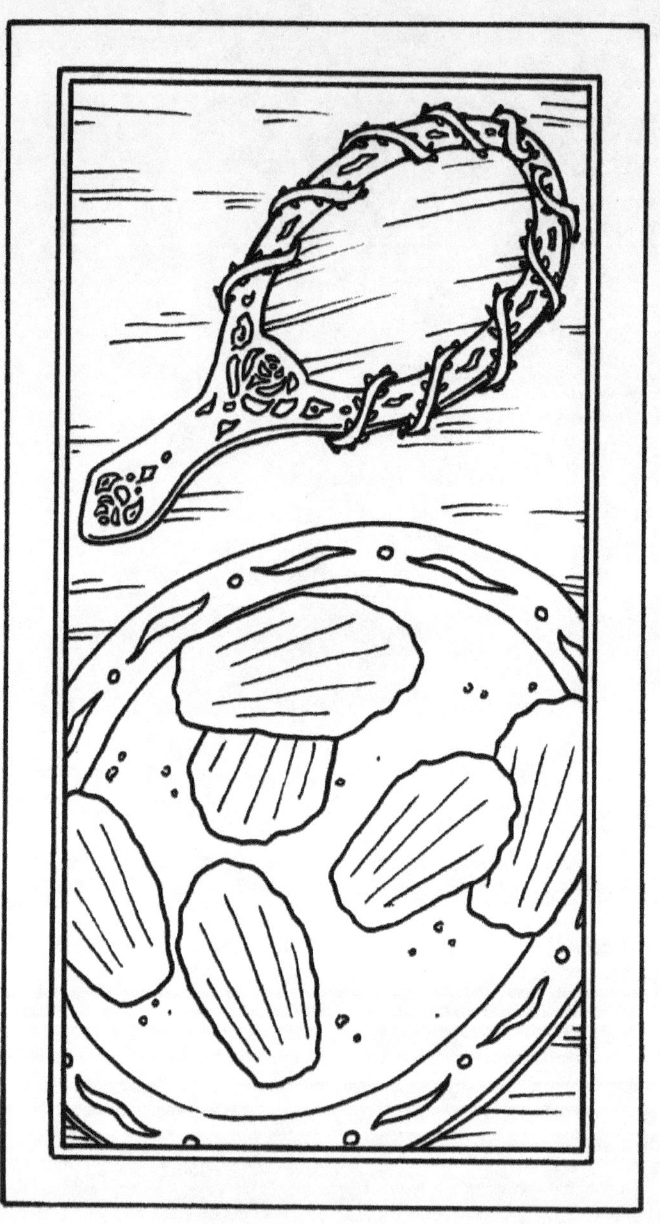

True Reflections

Matthew Dewar

Isabella tiptoed behind Madeline through the common room and into Isabella's sleeping chambers. The other princesses lounged on plush sofas staring at their handheld mirrors and were too busy catching up on the latest gossip to notice the girls sneaking back.

Closing the door behind her, Isabella turned to Madeline and hugged the full wicker basket in her hands with a giggle. "We just made it out of there before the cooks started."

Madeline nodded and stifled a yawn. "I can't believe it took all night. Another twenty minutes and we would have been caught. I don't think the head chef will be as lenient on us if he catches us a second time."

Isabella shook her head and untied her amber hair, allowing it to fall where it pleased. "If Geraldine sent me this recipe, it'll be worth it." Isabella plopped down on her bed and stretched, shoulders sore from rolling out the dough so many times.

"Who's Geraldine again?" Madeline asked.

"She's the royal cook back home." Isabella smiled. "She would wake me up early every morning and take me down to the kitchen." Isabella recounted Geraldine's sweet voice directing her to knead this and roll that, more sugar in this one, more spices in that one…

"Ah, that's right." Madeline nodded. "I remember

you talking about her now."

Isabella often forgot that Madeline wasn't a lifelong friend. They had met only at the start of the year when Isabella arrived at the castle ready to enter the competition to be the next Great Queen. Madeline was her assigned handmaiden hoping to win a twenty gold coin prize that she would use not to buy her freedom but to pay for medical treatment for her younger brother.

Every twenty years, St. Rosa's and St. Ivan's opened their doors to the royal families of the twelve kingdoms. Princes and princesses auditioned for one of five places in each school to learn how to be the next Great King and Queen. Throughout the year, they were ranked on a variety of scales. At the end of the year, a grand tournament was held where the winners were crowned. The prince and princess with the highest scores were married and became the next Great King and Queen, ruling over all twelve kingdoms for two decades until the next grand tournament was held.

Isabella reached for her polished silver hand mirror with etched vines wrapping the frame. "Hey, Mirror," she asked, glancing at her reflection, "Can you please save Geraldine's recipe as a favorite?"

"Certainly," Mirror replied in its hollow tone.

Turning her attention back to Madeline, Isabella said, "Just imagine opening a bakery together. People would travel from all over to taste our delights."

Madeline curtsied. "All hail Isabella, Queen of Breads, Pastries, and Cakes!" Tucking a blond curl behind her ear, she sat on Isabella's bed beside her and removed the cloth from the basket. A billowing cloud of steam escaped.

Each crescent moon pastry had hundreds of layers of flaky, buttery goodness. Madeline removed the lid from a jar of strawberry preserve while Isabella pulled out a small tub of freshly churned and chilled butter.

After smothering their pastry with condiments, they toasted each other. "To our final days together," Isabella said with a heavy heart.

Madeline sniffed.

Isabella glanced at her handmaiden. "Are you okay?"

"This is it." Madeline wiped her eyes. "Tomorrow is my last day with you. I'm going to miss you so much."

"Oh, Madeline. I wish I could take you with me when I leave." Isabella wrapped her coat around herself, feeling a chill that wasn't in the room a few moments ago. If the rankings didn't change, in two days she would be handed over to one of the princes as a prize. She would leave her home, family, and life behind and travel to the center of Alkamire to become the next Great Queen.

Isabella's heart panged at the thought, and she quelled the fear. When she signed up for the competition, she was more concerned with what everyone else wanted for her, so much so that she forgot to ask herself what she wanted.

"I wish I could come with you. When the school closes down for the next twenty years, I'll be forced to return home." Madeline's voice trailed off as years of pain sharpened her vocal cords.

Isabella winced. She had been brought up in a castle where everyone was treated with respect. But she knew there were some kingdoms out there that still acted like they had slaves. The kingdom of Borona—where Madeline was from—was one such place.

"When I become Great Queen, I will make it my life's mission to improve the lives of everyone, everywhere. Royal families in places like Borona had better watch out!" Isabella patted Madeline's knee.

Madeline wiped her eyes and cleared her throat. "Go on, check the rankings."

Isabella stuffed the last morsel of the golden, buttery

pastry in her mouth and wiped her sticky fingers on the cloth.

Madeline handed Isabella the mirror.

Isabella took it and winced at the dark rings and heavy bags under her green eyes. "Hey, Mirror. Can you please show me the most beautiful girl in school?"

"Isabella, it's more than that," Madeline chided.

"Is it? Because if you ask me, that's all this ranking system is." While the princesses were ranked on beauty, poise, grace, and diplomacy, the princes were ranked according to their strength of character, leadership skills, combat prowess, and general knowledge.

After a heavy sigh, Madeline said, "Hey, Mirror, please show Isabella the current ranked scores of the princesses."

"Of course," Mirror replied.

Isabella rolled her eyes then quickly scanned the surface. Her smiling face stared at her from the number one position. Her mother would be proud. "See, still at the top." Glancing further down the list, she spotted her stepsister, Eva White, had climbed from third to second.

Eva had a certain level of intensity about her that would serve the twelve kingdoms well. While Eva couldn't wrap her head around relationships with friends or family, she certainly knew how to act as a queen and had been bossy and conniving since the day Isabella met her. Isabella had often indulged the fantasy of letting Eva win so both girls would get their happily ever after, but it was merely that. A fantasy. Isabella had to win to continue her mother's legacy and prevent Eva from using her position for personal gain.

"Is Percival still leading the princes?" Madeline asked.

"Last I checked, yes." Isabella sighed. "If you remove his arrogance and cockiness, he will make a great king."

"You've never told me before, which prince do you hope wins?" Madeline pinched her bottom lip between her teeth, and her eyes sparkled.

Isabella's chest tightened, as it always did when she was asked a question like that. It was the one secret she had kept from Madeline. Why wasn't she as obsessed with boys as the other princesses? Why did she never dream of boys the way Eva recounted hers? When would that prince walk into her life and sweep her off her feet?

Madeline sat there expectantly, waiting for Isabella's response. Isabella prepared a lie to divert suspicion, but something about Madeline drew the truth from her lips before she could catch it.

"I don't like any of them." Isabella's heart thundered, taking away her breath. "I, I don't think I like boys at all." She had hoped this competition would open her heart and fix her. She longed for the other princesses to rub off on her, that their lusting over boys would be contagious, but it only confirmed just how damaged she was.

Madeline's eyelid twitched, but she smiled warmly. "Is there a princess?"

Shaking her head, Isabella picked at a fingernail. Her throat constricted. "I'm broken, Maddi. My heart doesn't work. I don't love anyone." She didn't yet know whether she felt better or worse for admitting it to someone.

"You're not broken." Madeline placed a warm hand on Isabella's knee. "You just haven't found the right person yet."

Isabella stood and paced. It wasn't just a matter of finding the right person. Deep down, somehow, Isabella knew that there wasn't a someone out there for her. "All that my mother has ever wanted for me is to fall in love and start a family, and it's the one thing I can't do for her. Even though I don't really want the responsibilities of a Great Queen, at least it forces me into a marriage. I won't be happy, but I won't be a disappointment either."

Madeline took Isabella's hand and massaged it. "I hated my life as a handmaiden, and then I met you, and this past year has been wonderful. You are capable of so much love, of bettering the lives of everyone you meet. I truly believe happiness will find you one way or another. Maybe not straight away, but one day."

Isabella squeezed Madeline's hand in return. "Thank you for your hope-filled words, but forgive me if I don't jump for joy."

"If I'm honest, the selfish part of me is very happy that you're the top ranked princess. With you as the next Great Queen, I know that the twelve kingdoms are in safe hands."

Isabella smiled and stared past Madeline and out her window where a few fluffy white clouds floated on a gentle breeze. It was what her mother wanted. It was what everyone wanted for her. It was what she was born to do. Despite how unhappy it made her, she would show the world that she was not broken. She needed to stop indulging her fantasies and daydreams and wake up to the reality of her life and future.

***

After her final day of classes, instead of sleeping like her body wanted, Isabella snuck out of her sleeping chambers and crept through the common room where she spotted Eva sitting in an oversized armchair by the fire, mirror in hand. Her hair, as black as ebony, fell across her face.

"Good evening, Eva. You're up late."

Eva jumped and quickly turned the mirror over so Isabella couldn't see the reflective surface. "As are you."

Touché. "Congratulations on moving up to second

place."

"Congratulations?" Eva's red-as-rose lips pulled back into a snarl. "Don't rub my face in it. It's an embarrassment."

"I didn't mean—"

Eva's eyes narrowed as she stood. With a flick of her hair, she stormed off.

Isabella shook her head. The day she met Eva was seared into her memory as the first of many sour interactions. Isabella had been eating an apple outside on a swing when her mother introduced her new husband and his daughter, Eva. When their parents left to allow the girls to bond, Eva held out her hand, and Isabella was only too happy to share her apple; after all, they were sisters now. When Eva took the apple, she dropped it on the ground and stomped on it, mashing it into the mud. "Oops," she said, with a tilt of her head and a saccharine smile. She ran back to her father in tears, saying Isabella had thrown the apple on the ground instead of sharing.

Isabella tore her eyes away from the armchair Eva had just been sitting in and proceeded out the common room.

Cooking with Madeline made her forget her worries, and what better way to finish the year than to tie the last cake back to her fondest memory when Madeline and she spent an entire summer's day at the beach.

To make their last midnight kitchen adventure extra special, Isabella planned to invent a cake for Madeline. Something to remember her by.

Madeline loved almonds, sponge cake, and lemons. Maybe she could come up with something that incorporated all three?

Isabella reached the school's kitchens with her stomach in knots. When she was sure that the kitchen was truly unoccupied, she pulled out a mixing bowl, set a pot on the fire, and found all the necessary ingredients. She opened her bag and withdrew four scallop shells that she and Madeline had picked up from the seaside on a lazy weekend at the start of the year. After cleaning them, she lightly covered them in butter.

Soft hands wrapped themselves around Isabella's shoulders. Madeline's voice whispered in Isabella's ear. "What are we making tonight?"

Isabella turned around to face her friend. "Something extra special."

Madeline's eyes sparkled. "Well, don't hold out on me, what is it?"

"You'll see." She grinned.

Isabella melted some butter over a flame while she instructed Madeline to measure out flour and sugar and grind several almonds into a powder. Isabella then added eggs, lemon juice, and lemon zest to the dry ingredients before adding in the butter.

"This recipe looks similar to the sponge cake we made a few months ago." Madeline beamed. "That's my favorite cake we've ever made."

"I know," Isabella replied. "But there's a little twist." She inclined her head to the shells.

Madeline smiled. "I remember that day. What are they for?"

Isabella spooned the batter into the shells and cooked them in the oven for ten minutes. Once the cakes had cooled, she removed them from the shells.

Each small cake had the indents of the shells on it, so the cake itself looked like it belonged on a beach. Isabella sprinkled them with powdered sugar and handed one to Madeline.

"I can't believe you made this. This is incredible!" Madeline remarked after taking a bite. "What do you call it?"

"This was inspired by someone I deeply admire, so

it's only fitting I name it after her. This is what I call a Madeline cake."

"You're the best." Madeline enveloped Isabella in a tight embrace. "Now you need to get some sleep. Tomorrow is the grand tournament, and you have a crown to win!"

As tempting as it was to allow one of the other princesses to win, Isabella knew Madeline was right. Not everyone was born to be happy. Some people were put on the earth for a bigger purpose. She needed to win that crown. And Eva needed to keep her narcissistic hands away from it.

The girls said their goodbyes, and Isabella quickly made her way back to the sleeping quarters. As she neared the common room, she was surprised to find everyone up and huddled in a corner.

Giselle, the tallest of all the girls, pointed a long finger at Isabella as she walked into the room. "How could you do this to her?"

The princesses turned to glare at Isabella, parting enough to reveal a sobbing Eva, clutching a bald patch on her head.

Eugenie, a skinny girl with long red hair, stormed forward. "What did poor little Eva do to deserve such a despicable act of jealousy?" She poked Isabella in the chest. "And to think I used to admire you." She shook her head and slunk back to the other girls.

Harini folded her arms. "Are you going to say anything?"

Eva glanced up through watery eyes and smirked at Isabella. Then she put on the waterworks again. "Why do you hate me so much?"

Heat rose from Isabella's chest and spread up to her cheeks. "What? I didn't do anything! I was in the kitchen baking a cake."

"So if we go down to the kitchen right now and ask

the other cooks, they'll say you were there?" Giselle asked, clearly distrustful based on her tone.

"Well, no. I was there…" If Madeline got into trouble, she would lose her twenty gold coin prize. Isabella dropped her gaze to her shoes. "…alone."

Eugenie crouched beside Eva. "Do you want me to go get the headmaster?"

Eva shook her head and wiped her nose. Her skin seemed a few shades paler than usual. "No, that's okay. I think we can sort this out ourselves. Just keep an eye on her so she doesn't send another huntsman after me."

"What are you talking about?" Isabella cried. "I never sent a huntsman after you!"

Eugenie growled, aggressively thrusting her finger at Isabella's face. "What about the rest of us? Are we threats too? Who's going to be your next victim?"

"No one! I—"

Harini stormed to the door. "If there's a huntsman around here, the headmaster needs to know about it."

"No!" Eva shouted. "The huntsman was ordered to make me ugly, but when he saw me, he fell in love and couldn't permanently disfigure me. He tore out a chunk of my hair and warned me of Isabella's intentions to win at any cost." She took a moment to dry her eyes and breathe deeply. "He promised he'd come after anyone who snitched on him."

Unable to stand the attack any longer, especially when she had nothing to do with it, Isabella pushed past Harini and ran out of the room. She could hear the other princesses fussing over Eva, promising her they would compensate for her hair and make her more beautiful than ever.

Isabella was breathless by the time she reached the headmaster's office, and her tears had dried up. It was the middle of the night, and he wasn't in his study. She clenched her fist and pounded on his door until she turned around, leaned her back against it, and slid to the floor. She hugged her knees to her chest and buried her face. What was she going to do about Eva?

After several minutes, Isabella pulled out her mirror. The screen was full of angry, hateful messages from the girls. "Hey, Mirror, can you please block all incoming messages from the princesses, and please show me the rankings."

"Certainly."

A new princess held the top rank. Eva White. Isabella scanned the faces and found hers had dropped to third place. She pressed the image of her face, and the screen changed to show a breakdown of the ranking system. She still had high scores for all her subjects and from her teachers, but the bar showing her popularity amongst the girls had completely fallen flat.

A hot tear trickled down her face. A mixture of relief and shame washed over her. If she wasn't in first place, she wouldn't have the pressure of being the next Great Queen and spending her life with a person she could never love. She would have more freedom to be her own person, but could she allow someone as sick and twisted as Eva to rule the twelve kingdoms?

No.

Taking several deep breaths and gripping her mirror, Isabella decided it was time to accept her fate.

***

An incessant trill woke Isabella up.

"Hey, Mirror. I'm awake now."

The alarm setting on the mirror switched off, and Isabella stood and stretched. She massaged the back of her neck. Falling asleep in an empty classroom was not a bright idea. But she didn't want to face the girls in the common room or have the headmaster ask why she was sleeping outside his office.

Exhausted, she shuffled back to her room, hoping the common room would be empty at this hour in the morning. It was the day of the grand tournament, and all the princesses would likely be preparing for their parade and talent show, while the princes would be warming up for their day of jousting, hand-to-hand combat, horse riding events, and exams.

After Eva's stunt the previous night, Isabella became more determined than ever to win. She wasn't just doing it for her mother's pride anymore or to prove to the world—and more so herself—that she wasn't broken. She would learn how to rule well, and her insecurities would soon become her strengths. Eva would leave the twelve kingdoms in ruins.

As she entered the common room, the gossiping princesses fell silent.

Isabella kept her head high as she crossed the room, ignoring the stares she could feel burning into her.

"You failed. She's still alive," one of the girls hissed.

As a Great Queen, Isabella would constantly be faced with those who opposed her. The girls could test her all they wanted; it would only make her stronger. She would prove Eva to be the liar that she was and regain the loyalty and friendship of the others. If she couldn't handle Eva, how could she ever hope to stand up against the slavery in Borona? Or the heads of state that would refuse to budge on their crippling tax hikes? Or calm a room of bloodthirsty rulers when territorial disputes threatened a war?

Harini got up from the cushion she was sitting on by the window and approached Isabella, placing a hand on her arm. "What has gotten into you?" she whispered. "Do you need to talk about it?"

Isabella stared into Harini's hazel eyes, begging her

to see through the deception. "She's lying. I promise you I had nothing to do with it. I'm her biggest threat, she's trying to ruin me." There was a flicker of doubt on Harini's face, and Isabella pushed harder. "I was already beating her. What did I have to gain from cutting her hair?"

Harini chewed on her lip before holding up her mirror. A recorded message of Eva in a hospital bed played. Weak and pale, Eva tried to talk, but her voice cracked and her breath rasped. After a sip of water, she tried again. "Please, girls. Watch out for Isabella. She came for me again. I stupidly trusted her, thinking she wanted to apologize for the hair incident. Isabella gave me a lace bodice to try on for the tournament. Then she tightened it and tightened it until I passed out." She wiped her eyes and took another sip of water. "She left me there for dead."

Isabella gripped the mirror so hard it dug into her skin and her knuckles whitened. "Please, Harini," she whispered. "You have to believe me. I've done nothing wrong."

"You could have killed her," Giselle cried. "Eva trusted you enough to meet with you alone. I knew I should have stayed with her. This is my fault." Giselle buried her face in her hands, and Eugenie shuffled over to wrap an arm around her.

"Your beauty is only skin deep. Inside, you're as ugly as a toad," Eugenie spat.

"I'm now ranked above you," Giselle called out. "What are you going to do to me?"

"I didn't do it," Isabella exclaimed. "I swear to you all I had nothing to do with this. She's lying. I'll prove it."

"Oh sure. First she cut her own hair to make herself ugly, and now she's tried to kill herself," Eugenie mocked.

Harini shook her head. "I don't know what to believe."

Scanning the room for any glint of empathy, Isabella

came up short. Truthfully, she wouldn't believe herself if she were in their shoes. None of the girls truly knew what Eva was like. Isabella always hoped things would improve as Eva matured, but if anything, she was worse now.

Isabella kept her head high until she closed her bedroom door behind her. Only then did the tears gush from her eyes. Her mother had always comforted her after Eva got her in trouble with her stepfather. As much as she needed her mother right now, she would be a queen soon, and she couldn't run to Mommy every time she needed help. She picked up her mirror. "Hey, Mirror, show me the princess rankings."

"Where are your manners?" Mirror's hollow voice echoed.

"Please, Mirror."

"Okay, someone's in a grump." Mirror displayed the rankings: Eva, Giselle, Harini, Eugenie, and Isabella in last place.

She pressed her face and was shocked to see the only high score was from her classes. Both her popularity amongst the princesses and teachers had plummeted. The teachers had obviously heard about her "attempted attack" on Eva.

A message appeared on her screen from the headmaster: "Isabella Grimhilde. You are summoned to an urgent council meeting at 9 a.m. in my office."

Straightening her shoulders, Isabella wiped the tears away and paced in her room, debating what to do. She told herself she could face this alone, but even the wisest rulers required guidance at times, and there was no one wiser than her mother.

"Hey, Mirror, please connect me with my mother."

"Connecting you with the queen of Aleerya now."

After a few short moments, her mother's face appeared on the mirror's surface. Her cheekbones glimmered with sparkling bronze which matched the shadows around her chestnut eyes. "Hello, sweetie, what's—"

Seeing her mother's face broke down the wall holding back Isabella's emotions. Tears ran down Isabella's cheeks, and she couldn't stop sniffing back the anguish.

"Oh, honey. Please tell me what's wrong."

"It's terrible, Mom. Everything is so wrong."

The queen dabbed at her own eyes which had begun to glisten. "That's what happens when you're at the top. They all come for you. I had the same thing happen when I was—"

"I'm so sorry. I'm not, I'm not at the top anymore."

"Oh, honey. Take a few deep breaths and then tell me what's happened."

They sat in silence for a moment while Isabella composed herself.

"There are rumors and gossip, and none of it's true, but no one believes me. They say I've attacked Eva and I tried to kill her. But I didn't. I wouldn't."

The queen's eyes hardened. "Is she okay?"

Isabella nodded. "She faked the whole thing to get sympathy from everyone else."

"She's still up to her old tricks." The queen stared off into the distance for a moment before facing Isabella once more. "I can come to the school and talk to—"

"No, definitely not. Thank you, but I need to do this myself." Isabella tucked a wisp of hair behind her ear.

"Very well, my child. You've always been very resourceful and independent, but you don't always have to do things by yourself. One day, you'll have a king by your side. You need to learn to share your pain and accept help."

The word "king" ripped Isabella's soul in two. The mirror shook in her hands. "Mom, I…" A monster clawed at her throat to stop the words from coming out. She feared her mother's disappointment or, worse, her abandonment, but she couldn't continue to live her lie. It was killing her.

"Honey." The queen's voice was sharp, clearly sensing something was wrong. "Tell me what's wrong now, or I'm coming to the school whether you like it or not."

"I'm sorry. I'm not, I don't love any of the princes. I know you eventually fell in love with Dad, but for me, it's different." She hung her head in shame. "It will never happen."

The queen nodded slowly. "It is not you who needs to apologize, it is I. I should have connected the dots sooner. Two queens would certainly cause some waves, but I guess—"

"No, Mom. No one. I'm broken. I've never felt love for anyone. I'm incapable of it."

The queen's mouth fell open. "How can you say that? You are the most loving, kind, and sweetest child I ever could have hoped for. You are certainly not broken. Unique? Yes. Special? Yes. Loving? Definitely." She said the last word with such conviction Isabella couldn't deny it.

Isabella's heart thudded. She had dreamed of hearing those words for an eternity but feared they would never come. After years of pain, fear, and self-loathing, she wished something had been said earlier.

Her mother continued, "I didn't realize I needed to say this, but I will right now. All I have ever wanted is for you to be happy. If that means you want to abandon the crown, you should have done it long ago."

A loud sob came from Isabella's mouth. "You're not disappointed or angry with me?"

"To be honest, I'm angry and disappointed at myself for making you feel like you couldn't tell me this earlier."

Tears fell freely from happiness and a sense of freedom that she hadn't felt since she was a child.

As the tears began to subside, Isabella choked out, "I

love you so much, Mom."

"Oh, do you? I thought you were incapable of love." There was a twinkle in her eye as her lips twitched upward into a smile.

Isabella laughed as she ended the call.

***

Just before 9 a.m., Isabella began making her way to the headmaster's office. A thousand scenarios played out in her mind, and in each one, she was the villain. She just didn't have any proof of Eva's trickery.

Soft footsteps rushed up behind her. Isabella spun to see a red-eyed Harini chasing after her.

"Isabella!" She wrapped her arms around her tightly, and her body trembled. "I didn't know what to do."

"What's wrong?"

"I just heard you were on your way to the headmaster's office." She wiped her puffy eyes. "I'm scared, but I want to help you."

Isabella found it difficult to swallow. "Why are you scared?"

"It's Eva. I think you're telling the truth. A few weeks ago, I ordered the most wonderful silk. It shimmered a thousand different colors and truly was one of a kind. Eva saw me working it into a dress for the tournament and commented on how lovely it was. She came back a little while later with a cup of mineral acid and poured it over my dress. She threatened to pour some over my face if I ever told anyone about what she did."

Isabella squeezed Harini's shoulders. "I'm so sorry."

"Don't be. I knew what Eva was capable of, and I should have stood up for you earlier. I was scared."

"It's fine." Isabella nodded. "But I need you to tell the headmaster about this. He needs to know what Eva is really like."

Harini took a deep breath. "Of course."

Isabella pulled her lips into a thin smile. "Thank you."

***

Isabella's hands trembled as she waited outside the headmaster's office. With a click of her heels echoing along the corridor, Eva approached.

"I promise you I'll kill myself if you tell them the truth," Eva hissed. "Do you want that on your conscience? Do you want to be responsible for my death?"

Isabella ignored Eva. It wasn't the first time Eva had threatened to end her life. And it wouldn't be the last. Eva couldn't emotionally blackmail herself out of this predicament. And if she did become the Great Queen, was this her grand plan? Every time someone didn't do as she wanted would she threaten to kill herself to get her way?

"Did you hear me?" Eva replied. "I'll jump out a window, and it'll all be your fault."

"You're sick," Isabella spat. "There is something seriously wrong with you."

Eva began to cry. Fat tears fell down her cheeks as she sobbed. "Why did she leave me?"

Isabella clenched her jaw and ignored her. Eva always used her mother's abandonment as an excuse for her actions, but she'd gone too far. There was no more forgiveness. There was no more sympathy for Eva regardless of what she had done or what she threatened to do. Isabella shook her head.

The headmaster's booming voice called them into his office to face the school council. The grand headmaster of both schools sat in the middle of the panel. On his left were the three female teachers of St. Rosa's, and on the right were the three male teachers of St. Ivan's.

Sighing, the headmaster rubbed the indent on his forehead gained from decades of wearing the crown of Alkamire. "Isabella, there are some strong allegations against you. What do you have to say for yourself?"

Isabella stood before the council and straightened her dress. She spent a moment looking each teacher in the eye. One appeared overly happy to be there, another seemed grumpy. One teacher sneezed, and another looked like he had been dozing. Isabella finally settled her gaze on Eva who wormed in her seat under Isabella's glare. "Days ago, I would have taken the blame and pretended what Eva said was true. I didn't want to be the next Great Queen, and Eva's actions gave me the perfect excuse to run away. But Eva has pushed me to see my strengths. I've come to terms with the fact I'm not perfect, and I'm okay with that. I will prove to you today that I am innocent, and I will also prove that Eva is unfit to be the next Great Queen."

Eva jumped to her feet. "Lies!"

Isabella laughed. "Do you honestly believe yourself?"

"Girls. Enough." The headmaster clapped his hands, and the girls fell silent. "There are ways for me to gather information that students are unaware of in case of moments like these, and I'm afraid, my dear, that you've been caught."

Eva smiled triumphantly and folded her arms.

"Isabella," the headmaster began, "I need you to await your punishment in this room. The council and I are going to take Eva to the tournament where she will be crowned."

"What?" Isabella sputtered. Surely they didn't believe her? "I have a witness. One of the other princesses can vouch for me."

The council filed out with an arrogant Eva strutting her way after them. The door clicked as the headmaster left. She was locked inside.

Time slowly passed, and Isabella grew angrier and angrier by the minute. Had Eva manipulated Harini into framing her? She paced by the window, furious at how easily Eva manipulated others and how unfair it was she always got away with it. Just like the apple when they first met, and the hundred other times since then.

The door opened, and Isabella rounded on the headmaster, ignoring all manners and etiquette. "How could you—"

He raised a hand to silence her. "Isabella, I'm sorry I misled you. These competitions can bring out the best and worst in us, and through your mirrors, we monitor you all closely to see how you adapt to different situations. Unfortunately, I have seen some disturbing character flaws in Eva. I consulted with one of the best physicians in the twelve kingdoms, and he agreed that she required immediate attention."

Isabella inhaled sharply. "Is she going to be okay?"

"The truth? Yes and no. Physically she's fighting fit, but mentally she's unwell and certainly unfit to rule the twelve kingdoms."

Isabella nodded. "What will happen to her now?"

The headmaster smiled. "She's going to be well looked after." He stroked his chin for a moment as old wise men often do. "May I ask, why are you so concerned about her well-being?"

"I…" Isabella's voice trailed off. She tried to think of a reason, but she couldn't. She just wanted everyone to be happy. Even if they were horrible people, they still deserved to be happy and healthy. "I don't know, I just am."

The headmaster smiled. "Of course there is no reason. It's just who you are." He cleared his throat. "Now it's come to my attention that you might not want the title of Great Queen?" He raised an eyebrow.

Isabella thought of the life that she could have. With

Eva out of the question, she didn't need to worry about the fate of the twelve kingdoms. She didn't need the title to gain her mother's approval. For the first time in her life, Isabella felt free to follow her heart. A warm tingle spread across her cheeks as she smiled.

***

Isabella waited backstage with the other girls before their fashion parade. A light sheen of sweat threatened to ruin her makeup, but the mad scramble to try and snatch the crown would be worth it. There had to be enough time.

"I am so glad everything worked out." Harini smoothed her ruffled sunflower hoop dress and adjusted the large yellow bow nestled in her curled hair. Golden chains hung from her neck, and caramel glitter sparkled around the tight bodice. "I wish I had said something sooner."

"You said something when it counted," Isabella said.

Eugenie sidled next to Harini. Her slim-fitting asymmetrical violet gown was studded with shimmering amethysts and lavender sapphires that, when they caught the light, sent a disco of purple reflections around the room. "I had no idea Eva was capable of all that. I'm so sorry you went through it alone."

"As am I," Giselle added. Her tight sky-blue bodice exploded into a tulle skirt at her waist, and her oversized sleeves had the elegance and movement of a river as she moved.

"It's fine," Isabella said. "I'm just glad everyone is okay now."

A breathless page boy hurried into the room. "Ladies, it's time."

Isabella nodded to Harini as they filed out onto the runway to the applause of the dignitaries and family members from the twelve kingdoms.

Isabella took up the rear as she stalked down the runway in her ruby-red gown. When she reached the end of the catwalk, she pulled at the fabric and twirled. In a flurry of movement, she revealed the costume underneath.

The crowd fell silent as they drank in her vulnerability. She wore a simple light gray dress that any commoner would wear, tightened around the waist with a rope. She had spent the last hour marking the dress with every word that defined her: strong, scared, broken, hopeful, baker, queen, loving, friendly, and so many more words. She was more than a pretty dress, and she needed the people to know that she was just like them.

Cheers erupted from the crowd as Isabella draped the red dress over her shoulder like a cape. She spun once more before returning backstage with the other princesses.

One by one, the girls took to the stage to perform their talent. Giselle sang, Harini danced, and Eugenie played a flute so beautifully Isabella felt the emotion in every note. Finally, it was Isabella's turn.

She gazed about the sea of faces staring back at her. She took a steadying breath and glanced about. Madeline and the other handmaidens weren't anywhere to be seen. Her fingers trembled. Maybe Madeline hadn't been able to convince anyone else to help? Every set of eyes bored into her, expecting a dance, or a song, or a show.

The audience seated in the left section of the stadium started shouting and begging, hands raised to draw attention to themselves and their want.

And then a similar commotion started on the right side of the stadium. And then the center.

That familiar sweet vanilla scent wafted on the air, sharpened by a tangy lemon undercurrent.

Isabella grinned. "Noblewomen and men, Queens and Kings," Isabella began. "I have created for you today a small citrus cake with vanilla cream. Simple yet delicious."

The dignitaries in the stadium gobbled down their sweets before applause washed over the crowd. Isabella couldn't wipe the grin from her face as she curtsied.

"Are there seconds?" someone shouted as the cheering began to soften, which sparked another surge of cheers and whistles.

***

Isabella had been Great Queen for three months, and already so much had changed.

Her first task was to abolish slavery in Borona. Once Madeline was safe, Isabella helped her set up a bakery. Royal Pastries and Cakes was a huge success with the people, and Isabella ensured she made time every day to help Madeline. She was going to need to expand soon, as the daily orders for her sweets and pastries increased. It seemed every noble person in the twelve kingdoms wanted to feature Isabella's fare at their royal feasts.

Her second task was to seek the Great King's consent to change the laws requiring the Great Rulers to be married. Percival was only too happy to agree, and shortly after, he wed his childhood sweetheart. Isabella and Percival lived in separate towers and convened in the Great Hall each morning to hear the concerns of the people and in the afternoon to discuss the state of affairs with various diplomats and advisors.

Through all the celebrations and kingdom-wide changes, Eva continued to dwell in Isabella's thoughts, and Isabella took the journey back home to visit Eva where she was being cared for by a team of physicians.

"How is she doing?"

The ancient physician tucked a vial of clear liquid in his pocket before walking surprisingly briskly down a long stone corridor. "Unfortunately, she's not as well as we'd like.

It seems that her childhood trauma has fractured her psyche. It's utterly fascinating." He ruminated for a while, humming to himself. "Since being separated from human contact, she has worsened, so we're working on reintegrating her with society, albeit under careful supervision."

Isabella's heart panged for Eva. Maybe she shouldn't have come after all. Some guilt attempted to wedge itself in the forefront of her mind, but logic pushed it aside and replaced it with sympathy. "Will she get better?"

The physician took in a long, slow breath. "I have only ever cared for one other with this condition, and I must say it poses many challenges. She will get better, but it will take some time."

They approached Eva's room, and the physician opened a window on the door where Isabella peered inside.

Eva sat on the edge of her bed, giggling and clapping loudly. A beautiful doll sat on the middle of the floor. "Keep dancing! Keep dancing!" she cried.

"Eva, are you okay?" Isabella whispered.

Eva looked past Isabella with unfocused eyes.

"Look at her!" Eva pointed at the doll. "That's evil Isabella. She tried to kill me. She looked in her mirror every day, and when I became more beautiful than her, she tried to kill me. She poisoned an apple, but I knew it was poison, so I didn't eat it. A huntsman tried to take my heart. The animals in the woods led me to safety. They made me beautiful again as they danced and sang around me. Then seven dwarves found me. They cared for me. They knew she was evil, and they took me away to be their queen. And then my prince came." She turned to the teddy resting against her pillow on her bed. "Today is my wedding day. And on my wedding day, my prince brought the evil Isabella to me and put her in these enchanted shoes. She's going to dance until she dies." Eva's glassy eyes met Isabella's. "I win. I always win. Dance for me, Isabella."

Beauty

LB Garrison

Jon stopped in the cold shadow of a Tumtum tree near the forest's edge and unbuckled his squirming pack. He laid it against the scaly bark. The sun sat low on the horizon, casting amber light through the fall shades of the Fay Woods. This would be the last dragon cocoon of the day.

His goal hung in a sticky, leaf-covered web among the swaying branches. The tree split into three major limbs just five feet off the ground. Getting to the tangled ball of dragon silk shouldn't be too difficult. He donned his pigskin gloves, grabbed a frost-covered branch, and climbed.

The breeze was colder fifteen feet from the wind-swirled grass. The distance seemed greater looking down than it had from below. Jon used the branch above to steady himself. His stomach squirmed. He needed to focus on the goal, not the height. Jon waited for the wind to calm and inched his way to the cocoon.

Something flashed in the distance. He stepped back, turning from the glare. His boot slipped on the icy branch, and he dropped. The world tilted. Jon seized the upper branch, leaving him dangling in the air. He blinked away the black and purple blotches left in the wake of the flash. His pulse thumped.

Another shimmer of light.

Something in the Murk reflected the setting sun.

That couldn't be. The Murk was a grove of tangled trees and twisted thornbushes in the midst of the Fay Woods. Nothing else existed there but bad luck, or so the stories went. The branch above him cracked.

Jon scrambled to recover his footing before the limb supporting him split. He dropped to the rocking branch above the cocoon and gripped it with conviction. It took a moment for his heart to slow.

Where had the light come from? He dug into his pocket and retrieved his bauble. The sphere of crystal nestled in the palm of his hand. With a few flicks of his thumb, he found the photo rune and held the bauble up, zooming in to scan the shadowy stand of ancient trees. A window hid among the leaves.

"In the Murk?" Jon mumbled.

If not for the sun's low angle, he wouldn't have seen the reflection. He captured the image and cupped the bauble in his hand. The image floated in the crystal.

Fading light fell through the window, illuminating a smudge in the picture. He adjusted the contrast. It was a girl with blond curls and a button nose. She was prettier than any girl in the Croft for sure. She lay on a bed of dead lilacs by the window, her face covered with a gray layer of dust, except around her nose, where her breath kept the dust from settling. Pinpricks played down his spine. It took real magic to do something like this. Fay magic.

If there was a window, there must be a door. His heart did a flip. This was just like a story from Magical Adventures.

Jon shoved the bauble in his pocket and retrieved his pocketknife. He kept the blade sharp, but the dragon silk was tough. It took a few minutes of sawing before the cocoon plunked to the ground.

He shimmied down the tree, a little faster than he should. The cocoon wiggled its way across the dead grass toward the trees and freedom. Orange and red leaves stuck to it.

"No, you don't." Jon grabbed the newt and stuffed the wiggly bundle into his pack with the other three. Hunt Master Vass could arrive at any time to pick him up. He had to hurry.

He shouldered the pack and climbed down the steep hill to the flat ground below.

The Murk lay about a half mile away, surrounded by a broad ring of barren land. Jon jogged most of it, crunching through the leaves until he neared the stand of brooding trees. He slowed at the border.

Scarecrows ringed the Murk, spilling moldy straw from torn clothing across the ground. Sightless button eyes dangled in the wind. A warning to all of the dangers within the barbs.

People vanished in the Murk, they said, but no one could name a person who had. Jon wouldn't be long, and they were just stories. If he shivered as he passed the scarecrows, it was only because of the cold.

A jumble of black thorns grew between the trunks. The darkness beyond went on forever.

Jon tried his pocketknife on the black vines, but they were tougher than they looked. Cutting them would take more time than he had. Hunt Master Vass wouldn't be happy if he knew where Jon was.

Jon walked around the wall of trees. Much of it appeared the same, but a hundred feet further, he came upon an opening. Fitted stones with tufts of grass growing between them covered the ground, possibly the remains of a road.

He walked into the deep shadows. Thirty feet down a stone passage, thorns wound around a steel-reinforced oak grate. It was a gatehouse. Past the thorn-tangled gate, shadows of swirling leaves fell over the stone floor of a vast open space, the bailey of a castle. Cold air, dank with a trace of sulfur, ebbed and flowed, like the breath of a great beast. Jon leaned closer to the gate. Derelict buildings of stone and wood crumbled across the shaded bailey. He tightened his grip on the gate and concentrated to slow his excited breathing. He was an unrepentant nerd. Quinn would have teased him without mercy.

Barbs tore flesh. He yanked his hand back. Had the thorns moved? His skin was pale, covered with tiny wounds. He stepped back.

Beads of bright red blood speckled the thorns. The vines drank the blood dew and grew thicker, creaking and winding around the gate.

His breath caught in his throat.

The bauble vibrated in his pocket. "Jon!"

Great. He hurried to the tunnel's entrance. In the distance, Vass's wagon sat near the hillside cliff. The ebony horses swished their tails. Vass must have traced Jon by his bauble. How long had they been there?

Jon adjusted his pack and ran the distance to the wagon. Panting, he had to slow and climb up the hill. His breath turned to mist in the evening air. The other young newt wranglers whispered and snickered from their seats in the wagon, stealing quick glances at him. He hated being the center of attention.

Vass stood with his hand on the wagon and frowned. "You're out of your section."

Should he tell Vass about the girl? He shouldn't have been near the forbidden area at all, and he needed the job for the other orphans' sake. Jon took a moment to catch his breath and chose his words. "Sorry, Master Vass. It's the end of the season, and the newts are getting scarce. So, I worked my way over here."

Vass looked past Jon to the dark grove. "Stay away from the Murk. It's ill fortune."

Jon rubbed his hand. That might actually be true. "Yes, sir."

Vass climbed into the driver's seat. "Get aboard. I don't fancy being caught in the woods at night."

"Yes, Jon, some of us have homes to go to," Barkly quipped from the wagon.

The other guys laughed.

"Settle down, boys," Vass snapped.

Jon clenched his jaw. Any retort would just encourage more heckling. He set his pack in the wagon and climbed on the tailgate, preferring to stay alone. The wagon lurched forward. Jon turned his coat collar up against the cold.

The others' talk soon turned from the day's hunt to the Samhain festival and ranking the Croft's girls from most to least desirable. Jon didn't join in. Strangely, it vexed him no one mentioned Quinn, though he would have objected if they had. Sometimes, his feelings about her got jumbled up.

He took his bauble out and stared at the beautiful girl's image. Her clothing differed from the everyday kind, but he didn't know enough about fashion to guess the period. She must be from the Time of Lore, near the end of the fay era. Jon could only dream about the things she must have seen.

Miles passed. The horse's hooves clomped onto a cobblestone road. Rarely, dragon-scorched ruins peppered the hilltops, but only because Jon knew where to look. He might never know which had belonged to his family.

The sun set, and the buildings grew more numerous. Eventually, the wagon stopped by Jasper's Clothing and Dry Goods. Vass partly owned the store, and he used it as a base when he was in town. The wagons of other newt harvesting teams crowded the street.

While the other wranglers were occupied turning in their harvests, Jon snuck into the store. It smelled of tobacco, sandalwood, and linen. Oil lamps added their glow to the dying sunlight. A woman and her daughter picked through a sales rack of summer dresses.

He moved past the canned vegetables. In the back, where few ventured and shadows dwelled, dead eyes watched from jars of alcohol and muttering books lay bound by heavy chains.

He took the Omni from the bookshelf and ran his fingers over the black cover. The patchwork of mismatched leather had the spongy feel of chicken skin and the warmth of a handshake. It was supposed to be human flesh. Probably a story to enhance its reputation and price. Someday he would save enough to buy it, but that would take years.

A hush settled over the store. Even the books stopped talking.

"Sleeping girl," Jon whispered.

The Omni opened. Pages fluttered. It stopped at a point near the end.

"*Beauty*," Jon read the title. The drawing looked like the girl, but the story came from back east, beyond the Broken Mountains. He scanned the pages: evil fay, sleeping curses, and a kingdom lost. Many doubted the old tales, but the proof of this one slept in the Murk, and Jon had seen her.

Dragon scraps were orphans left behind in the wake of a dragon attack. They were never expected to amount to anything. But he was more than just a dragon scrap, and this could be his one chance to prove it.

"Jon?" Vass's voice boomed like thunder in the quiet shop. He stood at the end of the aisle, holding Jon's empty backpack.

Jon snapped the Omni shut. "Just checking on my book."

Vass dangled a black coin purse by its drawstrings.

"I'd advise you to forget about old magic and stick to tangible things, like food."

Jon wedged the book on the shelf between the others. "That only feeds the body, not the soul."

"You're a strange kid." Vass tossed the coin purse.

"Yes, sir." Jon caught the purse. Coins clinked inside. "This seems a little heavy."

"A thank you. You went over your quota again. Dedication. I like that. Tomorrow, I'm going back to Capper's Town until the next newt harvest." His eyes narrowed. "I know you went to the Murk today. If the bad luck stains you, it'll spread to the rest of us. Don't go there again, or it won't go well with you. I'm not just talking about the job either. You understand?"

"Yes, sir." The Hunt Masters had money, and that bought influence in the town. A change of subject was probably called for. "Oh, did Magical Adventures twenty-eight come in yet?"

Vass shook his head. "Kids. It just came in today. Don't take long, I want to close up."

Jon had a list from Quinn. A sack of oats for the old mare and their breakfasts, turnips, salt, and a few other staples. Turnips tasted like dirt, but they were cheap. After all that, the little coin bag was nearly empty. He barely had enough for Magical Adventures. The slick cover sported a picture of a hero fending off a blast of fire with his shield.

"Do you want it, or don't you?" Vass asked as he stuffed the other items into Jon's pack.

On the counter stood a little pyramid of boxes in gold foil. Inside each lay twelve pieces of the chocolate mist candy Quinn loved but they could rarely afford. Jon put the book away and took a box of chocolates. "I'll take these."

Lantern tenders walked the streets with burning wicks on long brass poles, lighting the streetlamps on Central Avenue. Banners for the Samhain festival hung over the streets. The town square had been cleared for dancing. At dawn, the harvest festival would begin. With everyone occupied, it could be Jon's best chance to explore the Murk without being caught.

The lanes were mostly empty. The Croft was still a farming town, and most people went to sleep with the sun. Only pale moonlight lit the street where Jon lived. The Glass House sat on a hill at the city's edge. A failed winter vegetable farm, the old building had stood vacant for decades before the Croft set it aside for orphans. Newt harvesting controlled the dragon population, which reduced the number of orphans. Currently, there were only five.

The door creaked. A red brick hallway ran down the center of the complex, lined with doors leading to the large glass and iron growing rooms on either side. They had converted the storage in the back into bedrooms. Magic in the walls, intended to protect young plants, still warmed the building.

Mismatched candles smoldered in wall brackets, spilling amber light down the length of the hall, filling the air with the aroma of hot wax. One of the girls had probably left them burning for him. He took a candle and went to the green tiled kitchen, placing it in a holder next to the door. It didn't take long to put away the few groceries.

The door squeaked open.

"Jon?" The candle glow from the hall outlined a short, lithe figure through her nightgown.

Jon didn't quite look her way. Quinn had matured in the past year, and he shouldn't notice such things about his best friend. "Hey, Quinn. Sorry, we ran a little late tonight."

She slipped through the door and leaned against the wall with her arms crossed. "We have some hash leftover. I can warm it up for you, or are you just going to read all night? Your latest picture book came out today, right?"

A smile tugged at the corners of her mouth, ruining

an otherwise perfect deadpan expression.

"It's a graphic novel, and what's wrong with a little adventure and romance?"

"Romance." Quinn gasped.

"What?"

"I thought you were a boy."

Jon sat in one of the rickety chairs around the dining table. "Shut up and come here. I saw something today."

Quinn sat close beside him.

He pulled up the girl's image on his bauble and handed it to Quinn. "There's a window in the Murk. I took a picture of it."

Quinn squinted at the image and nudged him with her shoulder. "So, you're a peeper?"

"I'm serious, Quinn. Look at the dust on her. She hasn't moved for years. This kind of magic hasn't been seen since the greater fay left." He leaned closer. "Beautiful, isn't she?"

Quinn fiddled with the image. "Yes, in a conventional way, if you like that sort. Who have you told about her?"

He sat back. "I can't trust anyone else."

She smiled. "And rightly so."

"There's a legend about a sleeping girl in a castle. It must be her. I'm going to try to get into the Murk tomorrow, while everyone else is at the festival."

She looked from the image to his eyes. "It could be dangerous, Jon. And supposing you could get in, what would you do?"

"In the Omni, it says this is a standard kind of curse. Usually, the hero is a prince, but anyone who wakes her would be a hero."

"Wakes her, how?"

Jon's face warmed. With any luck, the room was too dark for Quinn to tell. "With a kiss."

Quinn frowned. "Is that how it's done? Have you ever kissed a girl, Jon?"

"Uh…no. I'm only seventeen summers and a dragon scrap besides. No girl in the Croft would want a guy with my social status."

A smile crawled across her lips. "True. Your one hope lies in finding an unconscious stranger."

"You have a deviant little way of twisting things. I know the chances are remote, but there's still a chance." Jon frowned. Now she had done it. If he didn't ask, he would just keep thinking about it. "Have you kissed?"

Quinn paused a moment. "I'm a year younger than you, technically marrying age, and haven't ever been asked to a festival."

Quinn's dark curls, tan skin, and boyish looks weren't fashionable, but she deserved more attention than she got.

"Have I something on my face?" Quinn asked.

"What? No. I was just thinking, it can't be very hard. Kissing, I mean."

Quinn tilted her head to one side. "Well, I suppose I wouldn't know. My, this has become a lively conversation."

"Anyways, my original point was that magic hasn't always been baubles and cooking stones. Golems and wizards were real back then. There is so much we could talk about."

Quinn dropped the bauble into Jon's hand. "She's still a stranger. There is no assurance you two would get on with one another."

Jon spun the crystal sphere on the table. "Have I told you I find your pragmatism annoying?"

Quinn propped her elbow on the table and rested her chin on her palm. "Often."

Jon looked at the image again. The girl was a stunning beauty. "Regardless of anything else, she is trapped in the Murk. Don't you ever think of being something more than a dragon scrap? Of doing something important?"

Her eyes shifted, focusing beyond the walls for a moment. "I understand the appeal of adventure and being a hero, but I wish you could see what you have as well."

"Whatever happens, this place and all of you are part of who I am. I won't forget. Oh, I got you something." Jon dug in his pack and pulled out the box of chocolates. He gave them to Quinn.

She clutched the box to her chest. "These are expensive, Jon. You shouldn't have."

He shrugged. "You like them. I saw them sitting on the counter, and I thought of you."

She ran her finger over the foil. "Jon—"

"I'm not taking them back. What's the point in surviving, if you don't have a little joy now and then?"

Quinn sighed. "You're terribly impractical…and sweet, when you're not being obtuse."

"I'm being obtuse about something?"

"Yes, like that exactly. Good night."

Quinn hesitated, then kissed him on the forehead and hurried out of the kitchen.

✳✳✳

Jon woke, panting and sweat soaked. The dream of cowering in the cramped, smoky box faded. He shouldn't be anxious about the Murk, but that was the only reason he had the box dream. Yellow morning sunlight peeked under his door. There was no time for doubt. He rose and got ready.

Jon crammed his heavy pigskin gloves into his pack, along with rags to hold the thorns. They didn't have a saw as such, but his collector's edition sword of Damocles from Magical Adventures eight was made of iron. The fay hated iron, so it should work on the thorns. He packed it as well.

He shouldered the pack and checked the time with his bauble. A little before eight. The laughter of the twin boys, Abel and Case, echoed in the hall. Typical morning chaos filled the kitchen. The twins chased each other around the table.

Quinn fished cooking stones from a pot of porridge. The little black stones stayed hot but shrunk over time. The largest stone was about the size of Jon's thumb, and they would need to replace them soon. Now that the newt harvest was over, he could work full time at the apothecary again.

"Morn', Jon." Anabel brushed her blond curls against his arm. "Thanks for the chocolate."

Jon glanced at Quinn.

"I couldn't keep such fortune to myself, could I?" Quinn asked. She drizzled the porridge with golden syrup and handed Jon the hot bowl.

"You're welcome, Anabel," Jon said. He sat at the table and sprinkled poppy seeds on his breakfast. Wisps of steam hovered above the lumpy oats.

"Hurry, Jon. We're going to the festival," Case said as he rushed by.

Quinn filled the sink with the hand pump. "Abel. Case. No one is going until you clean up."

"Aw," the boys complained in unison, but they did as they were asked.

"Will you be working today?" Anabel asked, resting her elbows on the table. Her feet swung back and forth. The twelve-year-old girl had as much energy as the twins, though she channeled it more constructively.

"In the drying rack, you two." Quinn cleaned the cooking stones and separated them to slow the reaction.

The twins stood on tiptoe to wash their dishes.

Jon took a cautious taste of the bland porridge. The poppy seeds crunched between his teeth. "I don't have to work, but there is something I need to do in the woods. It may take all morning."

"That's no fun." Anabel pouted.

Quinn sat beside Anabel and passed a checkered coin purse to her. "I've saved money from my sewing jobs. Take the boys to the festival and make the coin last. I shall be going with Jon to keep him grounded."

Jon swallowed. "You are?"

Anabel took the purse. "Are you sure, Quinn? This must have taken forever to save."

Quinn peeked at Jon through her bangs. "It didn't take so long. Someone once advised me we should enjoy ourselves, and Samhain comes but once a year. Mistress Tayler will meet you at the end of the lane to take you to the festival. Be sure to mind her. Come, boys."

She wiped a smudge of chocolate from Abel's lips and tousled the boy's hair. "Now, you're presentable. Off you go."

Quinn fussed over the young ones and saw them out the door with a kiss for each. The boys feigned disgust but smiled all the same. Jon scraped up the last of his porridge.

He washed his bowl and put it in the drying rack with the others. "I didn't think you approved."

She packed sandwiches in a paper sack without looking his way. "You shouldn't go in the Fay Woods alone. A sprite might invite you to dinner, and you wouldn't return for a hundred years."

"That hardly happens anymore, and you know it."

Quinn folded the top of the lunch sacks closed and rested her hands on them. She still didn't look at him. "I stayed up thinking. If this will make you happy, I should be supportive. Besides we never spend time together without the children."

"You didn't mean to say that last part out loud, did you?"

She rolled her eyes. "I simply meant it should be great sport to watch you attempt to rescue this princess of yours."

"That's more like it."

***

A worn, gray quilt served as a saddle for Beasley, the abandoned gray mare that grazed the lawn around Glass House.

Jon sat in front and pulled Quinn up. She took a moment to adjust the lunch pack, and Jon urged the horse into the street.

A haze of smoke from flame-seared mutton filled the air. Dried flowers adorned whitewashed doorways, and people in white linen robes filtered through the streets. Jon took the back roads out of town. Hunt Master Vass would be leaving about now, and he did not want to chance an encounter.

Beasley faltered on the downward sloping road beyond the town's borders. Quinn slipped around on the blanket. They had never ridden together.

"You can hold on to me if you want," Jon said.

"Would you mind?"

"Well...no."

Quinn slid her arms around Jon's waist. Her warmth seeped through his clothes. Jon tried not to notice and urged Beasley into a trot, which was the best pace she could manage. They passed the decaying ruins of a farmhouse.

"Do you remember before?" Quinn asked. "I don't. Not really."

"I remember pieces. Mother's touch. Father's voice. Mostly, I remember huddling in my toy chest and the taste of ash." Mother had hidden him in there to keep him safe. He cowered while his family died, and he couldn't even remember her face. The silence had gone on too long. "Anyway, when it was over, someone found me, but I don't know who. Maybe I blocked it out. I recall more about the indentured apprenticeship with the Masons than home. You never wanted to talk about it before."

Quinn squeezed tighter. "I don't want to dwell on my younger days. Being shuffled from family to family as if my misfortune was contagious. Living on the streets like an animal until we met. I suppose that's why I don't light candles for dead relatives on Samhain Eve. I don't know my past, and of late, I fear life is about to change again."

"For the better. You'll see."

"I hope so, Jon. I do."

They rode in silence most of the way through the woods. The Murk loomed ahead, casting a vast shadow over the forest in the cold morning sun. Jon guided Beasley around to the opening from the day before. He helped Quinn down and tied Beasley to a tree near the entrance.

Quinn stared down the dark stone tunnel. "What is this place?"

"It's a castle," Jon whispered, though he didn't know why. Something about the ancient stone demanded reverence. He pointed to the brick-lined holes in the ceiling. "See those? They're called murder holes. When the castle was invaded, they would close the gates on either side of the entrance, trapping the enemy in here. Then they would pour hot coals or boiling oil on the enemy soldiers. This wasn't made for show. It was a real functioning fortress once."

Quinn's eyes slid from the ceiling to his face. "Thanks, Jon. And I was concerned about spiders."

Jon walked to the second gate. "There hasn't been anyone here for a long time."

Quinn followed in a zigzag path, avoiding the murder holes.

Jon set his pack down and pulled out the replica

Damocles sword. It was an indulgence he shouldn't have purchased, but it would be useful here. He hesitated then broke the wax seal. Sacrifices had to be made.

"You've never once used it or even looked at it? What about enjoying the moment and all?" Quinn asked.

Jon slid the dark gray blade from its scabbard. It didn't look particularly sharp, but it didn't have to be. "If you remove it from its original packaging, it lowers the value."

Quinn rolled her eyes. "Well, yes. Obviously."

"Stand back. Fay magic and iron don't mix. There may be sparks or even fire."

Quinn took a couple of steps back. "Be careful and mind your eyes."

Jon leaned back. He tightened his grip and touched the blade to the thorns.

Nothing.

He swung and hacked at the tangled barbs. Thick goo, like congealed blood, oozed from the vines, but no sparks lit the shadows.

Quinn stepped closer. "What's wrong?"

Jon ran his thumb along the side of the dull blade. It made worms crawl in his stomach to think of how he wasted money that could have gone for new cooking stones. "It's hard to tell in this light, but I think the metal has a bluish tint."

"I don't follow."

He sheathed the sword in its decorative scabbard. It looked good, at least. He shoved it into his pack. "It's pewter. Cheap pewter. Not iron."

Quinn put her arm around him and rested her head on his shoulder. "Jon, I brought apples."

"Random. I like apples, but they aren't exactly…oh, you don't like the skin. You brought a knife."

Quinn rummaged around in the lunch bags. "A

couple. They're steel as well. Will that do?"

"They have to be pure iron to be anti-magic, but if they're the serrated ones, we can saw through the vines."

Quinn took knives from the pack and handed a steak knife to Jon. "These should work then."

Jon emptied his pack and gave Quinn one of the gloves and the majority of the rags. The thorns were painful, and he would rather he got hurt than her. They wrapped the rags around the vines to hold them and carefully began sawing. The vines were tough, but working together, they cleared the thorny bush away from one section of the grating.

Jon ran his hand along the chipped wooden gate. "The openings between the bars aren't as big as I thought. I don't think I can squeeze through."

Quinn knelt beside him. "I can."

"I doubt any large animals could have gotten inside to make a home, but the building itself might be dangerous after so many years of neglect. I'm not sure you should go by yourself."

She gave him a smile. "Aw, I'm not so delicate. Besides, if you turn 'round, you'll always wonder what could have been. I don't want that happening."

Adventure beckoned. Somewhere in the castle was the beautiful girl. "You know me well. I guess that's why we're friends."

Quinn broke eye contact and stared into the heart of the castle. "What do I do?"

Jon leaned against the gate and peered as far into the castle as he could without touching the thorns. "There must be a winch and maybe some counterweights to raise the gate. It would be close by. It should look like a wheel with chains or rope around it. Hopefully, chains. Ropes would be in poor shape after all this time. If they survived at all."

Quinn grabbed the grating and pulled herself

through. "Okay. I'll call you when I find it."

"Be careful."

She glanced back, nodded, and disappeared around the corner.

Jon took out his bauble and sat down to wait. He brought up the picture of Beauty. It seemed incredible that he sat in the same castle where she slept. A girl so appealing she was legendary. Strange that nothing else about her had survived.

The bauble vibrated. "Is this it?"

A picture floated across the bauble's surface. A chain-wrapped wheel squatted by a wall. The spokes of the wheel extended out past the rim. Gear teeth and a ratchet system kept it from turning backward.

"Yes. That's it."

"It'll take a moment," Quinn replied.

Jon stood.

The gate creaked and moved up an inch. Then another. Bit by bit, the gate rose until it hung a couple of feet from the paving stones.

"That's enough. Let go of the wheel for a moment."

The gate squeaked and dropped a fraction. Dust drifted down.

"It looks stable. Meet me by the gate."

Jon pocketed his bauble and took a shaky breath. Of course, if it wasn't stable, he would be crushed to death and then some. He pushed his pack through first. Sliding onto his back, he inched under the gate, careful not to touch it. By the time he had wormed his way through, Quinn stood beside him. He slipped his pack on.

"Where to?" she asked.

Buildings were scattered across the huge bailey. The one with a smokestack had probably been a blacksmith shop. One had a cross on its roof. A chapel. The others had no obvious purpose, though there must be a stable, an armory, and other military-related structures. Trees grew high above the battlements, surrounding the castle like a second wall. Flickering shafts of sunlight fell through the wind-troubled leaves. They filled the air with a static rustle. The window had been about where the tallest tower stood. Stairs wound around its walls, leading to a door in the side.

Jon pointed to the tall structure. "I think she's at the top of that tower. Because it's easily defended, that's typically where royal living quarters were. So it makes sense."

The dizzying reality of the situation crept over him. He had spent most of his free time playing adventure board games. Now they stood where no one had for centuries, and he was about to meet a legend. What would the princess think of him? He had hardly ever talked to a girl, let alone kissed one. What if he was no good at it? He wiped his sweaty palms on his pants.

"Jon. Relax." Quinn looked up at him.

"It's just, uh, girls make me nervous. I guess."

"Really? I'm quite sure they're just like people, once you get to know them."

"You know what I mean. She's beautiful and royalty. I'm just a dragon scrap."

Quinn squeezed his arm. "Jon, you're one of the nicest blokes I know. You're hardworking and caring. You are worthy."

"I suppose I'm no worse off for trying. It's just…well…it would be her first impression of me."

Quinn let go of his arm and stared at the tower. "If it's the kiss you're worried about, you could practice on me. If you want. I wouldn't mind. And it wouldn't be a first kiss, since it's just practice."

It wouldn't hurt to get a better understanding of the mechanics. He really wasn't sure where the noses went, and it was just Quinn. "Well, okay. If you don't mind."

She stepped in front of him, tilting her head up. "No,

I don't mind. Terribly."

"Could you, maybe, close your eyes?"

She did. "Oh. Like this?"

"Yeah, like that." He leaned in. This didn't seem less nerve-racking than the real thing with the princess. He closed his eyes too. His lips touched Quinn's. She was so soft and warm. Pin prickles spread down his spine.

He pulled away. A breeze ruffled her curls. He reached toward her tawny skin and paused. This was still Quinn.

Her eyes fluttered open.

His fingers curled back, and he dropped his arm. "I…think I've got it now."

She touched her fingers to her lips. "That was nice."

A metallic ping echoed from the gatehouse. The gate slammed against stone. Dust billowed from the entrance.

Quinn stepped around Jon. "What happened?"

"The retaining pin must have come off the wheel. If the pin broke, there will be nothing to hold the gate."

Quinn's eyes grew wide. "You can't fit through the gate."

Rubble was scattered about the bailey. "We could open the gate and put bricks under it to keep it open. I think—"

A roar rolled through the ruins like a rumbling waterfall. The ground beneath Jon's feet trembled.

Jon grabbed Quinn's hand. They ran. The blacksmith's was the closest building. They ducked behind it. Jon pressed against the pockmarked wall.

"What is it?" Quinn whispered.

Jon peeked around the corner of the building. "I don't know. In stories, magical places are sometimes protected by a guardian."

She was as rigid as stone. "Ah. Seems like something one might mention."

A cloud of dragon newts, like baby pythons with glittering teal and black butterfly wings, flittered around the buildings. They were half the size of the ones Jon harvested in the cocoons. With a crunch and a puff of smoke, a dragon slithered into the open on stubby legs. It looked like an ordinary horned lizard, except for its size, wings, and protruding fangs. Lots of fangs.

Jon withdrew and pressed against the wall again. "It's a black dragon."

Quinn stared straight ahead. "Dragon, you say? Fire?"

"I think so."

Quinn swallowed audibly. "Outstanding."

"You're taking this well."

"It helps if I focus on not wetting myself. What do we do?"

The slow cadence of booming footsteps came from the left. Fortunately, the cold-blooded beast would be slow in the frosty morning air.

Jon took Quinn's hand. "We have to go."

They snuck along the wall to the far corner of the smithy. The dragon's belly rasped against the cobblestone. Its massive shadow flooded the narrow alley between the buildings.

The shop shuddered. Quinn squeezed Jon's hand. Bricks from the furnace chimney clattered on the roof and dropped, shattering on the street. A low growl, more felt than heard, came from near the gate.

On the narrow side of the shop, the door stood open. Wood and plaster couldn't stop a dragon, but it hunted mostly by sight and sound. Staying hidden was their best bet. Jon stepped inside with Quinn close behind.

They crouched behind the door, next to a counter, and waited.

Footsteps pounded the earth. Jon held his breath.

Quinn pressed against him.

Iridescent black scales flowed by the doorway. A tail thumped the wall, and a swarm of mini-newts fluttered past.

The footsteps receded, circling around the bailey. Had it noticed the thorns they'd removed? With the gate closed, it might think they were trapped. How smart was it?

"Why so many?" Quinn asked. "Aren't newts solitary?"

"There's never more than one in a tree." They followed this dragon like a mother, and they were so small. They must be newly hatched. His stomach tightened.

"Jon?"

He shook himself. "I'm sorry. What?"

"I asked if you could see it," Quinn said.

"No. I think we're safe for the moment." But for how long?

Quinn huddled by the wall. "What shall we do?"

Jon sat beside her. "I have an idea. You can get through the hole we made in the thorns. If I distract—"

"No. Try again."

"Quinn—"

"No. I won't leave you. The gate may not be a possibility, but perhaps we can find another way out."

"You are so stubborn."

She grinned. "Guilty, I'm afraid. Find another way to be a hero, if you must, but we'll leave together."

"I can't leave. Not while the dragon stays." Jon stared at the dusty floor. Vass had threatened him. The more he thought about it, the more the pieces fit and the more broken the world became. "The newts follow the dragon like goslings. I think it's a queen. If so, it's the source of the newts."

Quinn stared into his eyes for several seconds. "No, Jon. The Croft lies on the newts' migration path. You know that."

Jon swallowed. "The unsociable newts wouldn't be massed here if they were just passing through. Who tells us the Murk is bad luck, and who profits from the newt harvest?"

"Vass and the other traders." Quinn chewed her lip a moment. "If you're correct, we've been lied to. As infuriating as that may be, there are hardly sufficient flintlocks in the Croft to take down a dragon. Collecting the newts would still be our best option."

"We don't need flintlocks to end this. A dragon guardian and the thorns would keep suitors away, perpetuating the curse. The dragon was probably summoned or created by the spell. If the curse was lifted, it might leave or even vanish. Maybe I'm wrong, but it's our best shot."

The rumble of scattering stone and the splitting of wood echoed in the bailey. Was it attacking the buildings?

Jon walked to the door and ventured a peek outside. The dragon had smashed one of the buildings on the far side. It gobbled the wooden beams to stoke its internal fire and heat up its metabolism. The monster was preparing to hunt. They couldn't hide for long. "I've always wondered why I survived when my whole family died. I think, maybe, it was for this moment. That's why I can't leave. I'm going to wake the girl."

Quinn was silent for a moment. "I'll help."

"I don't want to put you in danger."

She rose and dusted off her backside. "I don't fancy either of us being in danger, but we're stronger together."

That had always been true. "There is something you should know. In the story, it's a hero or a prince that breaks the curse. I'm just…me. It may not work. If it doesn't, promise me you'll get out."

Quinn joined him at the door. "Would a castle wall stop a dragon?"

Jon glanced at the dark stone. "It's thirty feet thick,

and castles were often reinforced with iron to withstand war dragons. Why?"

She pointed to a cluster of buildings nearby and an open passage in the wall. "I'm fast. I can use the buildings to keep out of its line of sight. When I'm near the wall, I'll get its attention and then dodge into the doorway. It's too large to follow. You run the other way and get up the stairs to the tower."

"Quinn, didn't you hear me? I may not be able to wake her."

Quinn seemed unsure where to look, but she avoided his eyes. "I heard. You lost your apprenticeship sneaking food for me. On the street, you protected me, kept me from doing what other girls had to do to survive. You are a hero. You're my hero."

Her hero? She must be trying to relieve the tension. Jon waited the space of several breaths for the punch line.

Quinn leaned out as if measuring the distance she would have to run. She drew trembling fingers through her hair. "You don't know what to say, do you? The truth is, I came here to help you find happiness with this princess because you will never look at me the way I look at you, and my flirting is abysmal. Go to her, Jon, and take your best shot."

She bolted.

Jon reached for her and missed.

"Dagda's beard." They had grown up partners in a world that didn't want them. He had misunderstood their whole dynamic. Now things were complicated, and he had no time to sort them out.

***

Jon ran to the squat building across the alley. The stair to the tower lay several hundred feet away. He couldn't get closer without stepping into the open. His bauble vibrated.

"Jon," Quinn whispered.

He looked at his bauble. "I'm ready. Be sure you're close to the wall."

She broke the connection. Did that mean she was going?

Quinn screamed.

Jon knew it was just to gain the dragon's attention, but he cringed all the same and had to fight the urge to try to aid her.

The dragon's head swung toward the sound. It snorted. Newts swarmed into the air. It raked its claws against the stone and pulled itself around. Its tail slammed against the chapel, taking a chunk out of the wall. Fire hissed between its fangs. The dragon's temperature would ramp up quickly. It wouldn't be slow for much longer.

Jon sprinted to the tower stairs.

Thundering footfalls shook the ground. Smoke engulfed its head.

Quinn was nowhere to be seen, but at least the dragon still charged toward the wall. It must be chasing her.

Jon took the steps two at a time. The stair wound around the tower, ending at an oak door. He grasped the metal handle and yanked. The door opened. Thankfully, it wasn't locked. He hadn't even considered that. He plunged inside.

He stumbled into a table and felt his way through the room for a few agonizing seconds while his eyes adjusted to the darkness. The beast bellowed in the courtyard.

A circular statue-filled room took shape around him. Blue tapestries covered the wall. Two sets of stairs led up and down from the entry room. The statues wore clothing and stood clustered together in groups, like a party. He darted through the stone crowd. They were so lifelike.

By the stairs, he brushed against one sculpture. It was warm!

The face wasn't stone but skin. All of them were people. His heart thumped in his chest. He had never read about something so bizarre.

A roar rumbled through the tower. Quinn.

He dashed up the stairs past broken windows and closed doors. The stairs ended at a broad oak door with gold inlays. He pushed the door open.

Bright dust motes floated through the shaft of light from an oval window. It fell on the perfect girl. A halo of golden hair radiated from her and spilled across the faded lilacs carefully arranged around her. She had a heart-shaped face, rosy cheeks, and full lips. She was beautiful, and all he could think of was Quinn.

The dragon roared.

He knelt beside Beauty. The flowers crumbled at his touch. His mouth went dry. This was just the same as it had been with Quinn. He just had to lean in. Their lips met.

She was cold.

Slap!

He stumbled back before he realized his cheek stung. He touched his face with his palm. The skin burned.

The princess sat on the bed, glowering at him.

Jon dropped his hand. "You hit me."

"Commoner," the girl spat. "How dare you put your foul lips upon mine!"

He had thought it might not work, but this wasn't what he expected at all. "I'm here to rescue you."

She virtually jumped off the bed, leaving a deep hollow in the mattress. She paced. "And what is it you're expecting? A happily ever after?"

"Well…I guess I was."

She stopped in mid-stride. "Dolt. A single stolen kiss is no basis for a lasting relationship."

Strange. Awake and with her personality in full view, she lost her beauty. "It isn't just a kiss. We risked our lives to fight our way here to break your curse."

She threw her hands in the air. "What curse?"

"The sleeping curse."

"I had grown weary of ball gowns and idle chatter. It was a gift." She waved toward the bed. "I've spent all this time in a lucid dream, doing anything I bloody well please with one perfect prince after another. Do you think you can compete with that? Do you?"

All sound outside the tower had ceased. Had the dragon gone?

Jon's stomach clenched. What had happened to Quinn? "For what it's worth, I am sorry I woke you. If you'll excuse me, I have to check on someone important."

"Important?" she huffed. "I have not dismissed you."

Jon touched his finger to his cheek. "You have a little something right there."

She touched her cheek and stared at the dust on her fingers.

Jon pulled the door shut behind him. Something thumped against the other side and shattered.

Hands twisted Jon's arms and pulled him off the top step. A man in blue silken robes pushed by Jon. He was one of the statues.

With a soft click, the man turned a key in the door's lock and leaned his back against it. "You kissed her?"

There seemed no point in denying it. "I didn't know about the gift."

"Gift?" the man repeated. His eyes slid to Jon's. "That was a ruse. A fatal accident made her queen. That spoiled brat is not fit to rule."

"It was supposed to be just her that slept, wasn't it?" Jon breathed. "The thorns, the dragon, they weren't supposed to happen?"

The man frowned. "Thorns? What dragon?"

"Wilfred?" came the girl's muffled voice.

The door rattled as small fists beat against it. "You old goat. Let me out!"

"Take him," the man grumbled.

The two men behind Jon jerked him around. He yanked back, but the two soldiers dragged him to the first floor, his boots thumping over the steps.

People in silk and lace wandered about, mumbling. Had they been in lucid dreams too?

The men pressed Jon against a wall and released him.

"Jon!" Quinn yelled. A man held her. She struggled and kicked at any shin that dared come into range.

Jon's heart bumped in his chest. "Quinn!"

Wilfred stood on the last step. "Joy, another one. Put her with the first."

The men hauled Quinn through the crowd and deposited her by Jon.

She brushed against him. A smudge at the corner of her mouth might be blood.

"You, okay?" he asked.

"I've a few scrapes, but nothing major to report. You?"

Jon nodded and concentrated on reading the crowd. "Fine. Be ready to move."

The crowd's faces ranged from perplexed to angry. One portly man with ring-encrusted fingers pushed his way forward. "What happened to your plan, Wilfred?"

Wilfred ascended a couple steps to stay above the others. "I assume you had the same dreams as I, Percival. We paid the dark fay to give the spoiled brat a nap. Instead, the fay put the whole bleeding castle asleep and made us the imp's dream-servants. The fay thought it amusing, I'm sure."

"Twisted witch," someone shouted. Murmurs of the

fay rippled through the people as they crowded Wilfred, talking over each other about the fate of their families and their lands. Confusion shifted to anger. The men near Jon streamed forward with the rest.

"I expected you to be alone or with the girl at the very most," Quinn whispered. "Who are these people, and why are they so grumpy?"

"They were caught in the spell." Jon studied the door to the downward stairs. Iron bar latches on it allowed it to be locked from either side. He nudged Quinn toward it. "When they discover the kingdom crumpled while they slept, I'm not sure what they'll do. I don't think we should stay while they work this out."

Voices grew louder, echoing in the stone room.

Jon reached for the door handle.

"They know how long it's been," Wilfred shouted, pointing at Jon.

The people turned.

Jon pulled Quinn through the door as the mob surged. He shoved the door closed with his shoulder and slammed the bar into place. The door rattled with impacts from the other side.

Jon summoned light with his bauble and sprinted down the stairs with Quinn beside him. Deeper into the darkness they went.

"Isn't this where they keep the dungeon?" Quinn asked.

Above, the door clattered. Wood cracked.

They should be near the ground level. "I'm betting there's a postern."

"I don't speak nerd."

"It's an escape route for royals. The royal quarters are here, this is where the postern would have been."

Jon reached out to a shadow to the left. His fingers touched nothing. His pulse quickened. "Here."

They scooted into a cramped passage so narrow, Jon had to crouch and turn sideways. The tunnel ended in a wooden door with a rope-wound wheel to one side. He wrenched the door open.

Blinding daylight shone through a metal gate.

Shouts echoed in the stairwell.

Carefully, he turned the wheel, raising the gate. The rope creaked, and strands of it popped loose. Jon cranked on the wheel until the gate was a couple of feet above the floor. He latched it.

"Go," Jon said.

Quinn wiggled under the gate. He followed.

"Stop!" someone yelled from down the tunnel.

Jon pulled down on the gate. His arms trembled with the effort. He leaned his weight on it. The decayed rope snapped, disappearing through a hole in the ceiling. The gate fell, slamming into the stone floor. Jon pulled out his sword and jammed the blade into the gate's track, snapping it off. There was only room for one person in the doorway. Between the weight and the blocked track, the gate wouldn't move now. He tossed the blade aside. At least it was good for something.

Jon followed Quinn into the morning light and pulled her to the side, just in case they had crossbows.

Birds chirped in the trees around them.

The Murk and its thorns were gone, leaving the crumbling castle behind. The scope of the ancient fay magic ran icy fingers down Jon's spine.

Quinn glanced along the stone walls. "The dragon vanished as well. Literally went poof. It's really and truly over, isn't it? No more alarm bells or burning homes."

"No more orphans," Jon said. What the newt traders paid had never equaled the cost of living under the dragons' reign. Vass wouldn't be welcome when he returned in the spring. At least it was over. "It will be a Samhain to remember. Speaking of that, we had better start back. As slow as Beasley is, we'll be lucky if we get to the Croft by sunset."

Jon led the way to the horse.

Quinn tarried for a moment as if she couldn't leave the castle's shadow for the sunlight. "What of the royals?"

"The elders can decide, but I doubt anyone will want to risk crossing the woods after dark. It may not have been intentional, but the royals' squabble caused considerable trouble for the Croft. One night in a cold castle is the least they deserve."

Quinn hurried to catch up and walked beside him, but not as close or comfortably as usual. "So, I assume you did the deed with the princess, but mucked it up somehow."

"You sound happy about that."

Quinn looked down a little more than necessary to watch the rough path. "Not happy especially. Honestly, I do want you to find the joy you deserve, because…I think I'll stay quiet now."

Jon managed to steal a glance at Quinn while she focused on not looking his way. Really, the princess didn't compare, not to actual beauty. "One kiss is no basis for a relationship."

Quinn glanced at Jon. "That's mature. The princess said it, didn't she?"

"Yes. The constant teasing. Is this how you flirt?"

"Awful, isn't it?"

"It's kind of cute, now that I'm watching for it."

They walked in silence for a few paces. The air between them lay heavy with unsaid words. So many things had changed today. His job. The fate of the royals. Quinn. She seemed embarrassed at her confession, unsure about what to do next, and she was hurting. Jon had known her long enough to tell. He stopped. "You said something before we parted, and I didn't have time to react."

She rolled her eyes. "Yes, well, I wasn't sure I would survive playing tag with a dragon. Right about now, I wish I hadn't."

"Not knowing what would happen to you—I've never been so scared, Quinn."

"I didn't know I could keep its attention, and you were in the open, so there was danger enough for both of us." She brushed her hair with her fingers. "Jon, you feel the way you feel. Unrequited love is difficult for both. Awkward."

"It's not unrequited."

Quinn finally looked at him.

Her green eyes had flecks of gold. It was his favorite thing about her. "I've always thought we were friends. Partners. I didn't know where the boundaries should be. I was afraid to feel anything else. Of ruining what we had, but other feelings were there, and they've been growing stronger."

"What are you saying?"

Jon stopped and took Quinn's hand. "Let's start over. Would you do me the honor of being my date to the festival dance?"

Quinn jumped up and wrapped her arms around him. "Oh, Jon, I would, but you're a dragon scrap. I have a reputation to consider."

"Just say yes."

Quinn giggled. "Yes."

An Empire of Fools

Shannon Yukumi

Act I
"The Boar's Hole"

"This is an empire of fools." Emperor Truviar Black fiddled with his lace cuffs as his wife's slippered footsteps ascended the eastern stone tower behind him. "The politicians would have me a pauper, if not my head on a spike, by the end of the next harvest."

The blue sky opened up above as Truviar exited the pitted stone staircase to a balcony overlooking the lands. He crossed to the edge and leaned over with a great sigh.

Fixing his gaze on the horizon, he swept his hand over the thatched cottages sprawling below his great keep, the rolling fields beyond, and the thundering mountains in the distance. "All of this, swept out from under me. Everything I have worked for."

Truviar, once mighty and muscled, sagged, the stresses of age and politics heavy in his heart. The empress sidled up to him, pushed his curly gray locks to the side, and placed a soft hand on his shoulder.

She massaged him lightly with her thumb. "Has there ever been a time when the council hasn't troubled you, dear?"

Truviar dropped his gaze to the council's longhouse,

built nine harvests before in the castle gardens. A horrid building filled with bickering lords and pomposity. "The former kings still squabble but are keen to set laws to undermine my authority, and I hear their whispers in the halls. Plotting against me. *Me*, the conqueror of these lands and *creator* of a great nation. They should grovel at my feet for bringing peace to our kingdoms." He grimaced at the rose garden, once full of red and white blooms and robust thorns, now withered and blackened to shriveled vines like dead snakes. The politicians couldn't agree to a gardening budget or even find a single shred of time to water them between their infighting and petty scandals.

"Dear… has something new come to light?" Martha whispered.

Truviar drew himself up, throwing out his chest. "The lords now claim that having no heir is grounds enough to have me abdicate the seat of the lands this year. I of course refused—I have much yet to give back to this empire." His hands shook, and he balled them into fists to quiet their tremors. "The politicians are claiming Hunter's Law. Some decree in the conquered lands of Creston that call for pit-fighting to decide the next to ascend. Me as a warrior again? It's pure absurdity. My old bones could barely hold a sword aloft."

He spun on his heels, his long cape flapping like a silken green banner in a sudden gale. As he met the eyes of his wife, a frown cracked his weathered lips, and he shook his head. "Although the law that banishes women from the very tables of statutes and ordinances is unmovable, you know there is no one I think wiser in the land, my love. What say you, Martha?"

The empress nodded, the creases of her years smoothing to a pearl-like femininity as she smiled. Shades of beauty still darkened her face, and although the years had passed, Truviar wouldn't trade a single line or gray hair for any pleasures of the flesh—even the shadow of her years was a fine wine itself, and he drank that cup daily.

Martha took his hand and patted his ring-encrusted fingers. "Of course they do not honor the memory of our son. Though what they say is true. We have no heir. And you cannot fight them as a soldier."

"I could have." Truviar thumped his chest. "If I were younger. 'The hearts of men are easier to sway on the end of a spear.'"

Martha lowered her gaze with a puckered grin. "And easier to see, as well. But Hunter's Law has no place in our lands. You'll need to convince the politicians to allow you to keep your position, and you cannot face them alone. However, the council will never be greater than those they represent."

The emperor's eyes flitted to the farmlands at the edges of the city. *Those they represent.* The people in the fields far below toiled like caterpillars spinning silk pods. The tart air from their fire-fallow cultivation stung his sinuses and left an ashy taste in the back of his throat—even here, high up in the keep tower.

With the setting sun, shirkers among the farmers made their way down the central cobbled street to the inns and taverns, wrapped in their own cocoons of pride from a good day's work and ready for their metamorphosis into ruffians and hooligans over entertainment and booze.

A twinge of regret grew in Truviar's throat, and he swallowed. Days with the populace and a pint had long disappeared. The gigantic stone wall around the castle was as large as the one that surrounded his heart. The emperor twisted his cape's golden clasp across his breast, watching the throng scurry about below.

"Do you know anything of your people anymore, Truviar?"

He shook his head. "Not anymore, my dear. Legions

had been at my call and command. Now I doubt any of my old soldiers would welcome my presence." He pinched the bridge of his nose and grimaced.

With gentle fingers, Martha turned his cheek away from the city. "It is never too late to gain knowledge. Go to the town—you used to love to frequent the tailor shops. Spend some time with your people. Only by gaining their favor can you face the council."

Truviar folded his arms. "I would be recognized— and Minister Dain of Denvorn would place an inquiry into actions unbefitting of an emperor. He's a sly demon. Not a mouse treads his shoes without the ledger of Internal Affairs close behind."

Martha smirked and tugged a ring off his finger.

Truviar jerked his hand away. "Just what are you doing, woman?"

She seized his fingers and slid his rings off. "Don't go into town as Truviar the Boar, go as his stable hand. Let me help you shave your beard and hair. I can arrange some clothes for you to borrow from one of our servants."

"You would have me be a pauper before the council confirms it?"

She grinned, a twinkle easing the crow's feet around her eyes. "If you win over the people, the council won't have the chance."

***

Martha had giggled as she cut his hair and dressed him. In her exuberance, she had become the girl from twenty harvests prior, when the war had come to an end and they had celebrated with far too much wine and roasted wild hogs. She even found horrible-smelling wagon grease to dye his gray hair black—but Truviar had refused to look in a mirror. He would not give her *that* victory—she had already won too many.

He hadn't sat in a tavern since before the Long War, but now here he was—surrounded by blackened oak walls, round, beaten tables encircled with rickety, sagging chairs, and a floor that sported more creaks and holes than grains of wood. He was drawn to this particular place by the distant memory of a name on his son's lips—the son who hadn't returned with him from war.

Patrons argued using language unfit for anywhere but taverns here in the Demon's Hole District, music blared from absurd wooden and tortoiseshell instruments that twanged loose and random, and the drink on tap curdled his palate and sent his tongue into hiding.

He curled his fingers around the mug in front of him; flakey grime sloughed off it and coated his palm. He wiped his hand on his shirt, resisting the urge to polish everything in sight with the silk handkerchief in his back pocket. The place was a dingy, noisy stain. No wonder his son Leofrick liked coming here. He had always hated rubbing elbows with the lofty elite. Truviar held up his mug in a silent toast to The Boar's Hole.

At the table adjacent, a gruff patron, hands caked with dirt and stinking of manure, banged his fist to raucous laughter.

"—Emperor, you say! That Truviar's a withered old man, hidin' behind his fine clothes and stash o' gold. His brains're made of rat droppin's—not a thought o' his own or fer his people in years."

Another patron with a scraggly beard down to his chest raised his glass. "Aye, I'll be drinkin' ta that, me boy. Raisin' taxes again. Fer what? 'is fine wardrobe? We ain't got any t'spare, says I. Living off me land, I am."

Truviar scraped his nail on the table to turn his mind away from the prickling shame rising to his cheeks. *I don't recall raising taxes.*

The gruff one shook his head. "I ain't trust a man what only shows his face once a year for some procession. Some fancy parade what to show off his silken underoos."

Truviar leaned over and tapped the gruff one on the shoulder.

The patron whirled, sloshing a bit of his foul drink on the emperor's beaten leather shoes. "And whadda *you* want, stranger?"

"If I may, I would like to inquire why you think such terrible things of the emperor of these lands." Truviar stuck out his chin and gritted his teeth until his jaw ached.

The man laughed. "You've got a funny accent, eh? Stranger here ain't from 'round here. Then where, old man? The hills o' Creston? Devlon?"

Truviar gripped the handle of his mug to settle a spike of nerves. "…Leo… Leofrick… from Dentshire."

The gruff patron raised an eyebrow. "Dentshire? How quaint. You inquirin' or somethin' 'bout Truviar? Here's my opinion, *good sir*. Truviar can kiss me on my rear end. He wants ta raise taxes? How 'bout a road ta Creston's lowlands so I can take my cart o' manure without breakin' an axle? I ain't never seen anything come of us throwin' money at that damned keep he farts in."

Truviar pressed his lips together then bowed his head.

The bearded patron thrust a finger toward him. "Aye! An' some sanitation!" His finger shifted toward the gruff one. "I'm tired o' yer manure damming up me irrigation!"

"Who's damming yer whatsit?" the gruff one bellowed.

Truviar hid his face in his mug of beer as the patrons at the next table sized each other up. They threw a few drunken blows then embraced, laughed, and ordered another round.

Absolute madness. What has Martha gotten me into? Truviar choked down the rest of his rotten-tasting beer and glanced toward the door. The cuts and gouges that marred its surface were like the empire—the whole thing threatened to collapse inward if they ran too deep.

"Care for another round?"

Truviar's attention snapped to the voice that flowed like the singsong cadence of bush warblers. A young woman had slipped into the empty seat at his table. A flush raised from his chest and tingled his cheeks.

An aura of sprightliness and positivity seemed to radiate from her blue-gray eyes as they darted all around. Her smile, like perfect rows of ivory harpsichord keys, focused on Truviar.

She ran a hand through her cropped hair—as dark and brown as the finest stout—and extended it across the table. "Rylia. Weaver of exotics. Peace be with you."

Truviar took her hand and shook it—she gripped like a blacksmith. Rylia was radiance, despite the frayed burlap shirt that hung loose on her collarbones. He dragged his gaze away from the fabric accenting a plunging neckline, looped together by thin strips of leather, and buried his embarrassment in the dregs and grunge of his beer mug. Her features reflected his own Martha, years before age dimmed her comeliness.

He ran a finger along the rim of his tankard and forced his eyes to meet hers. "Forgive me, good woman, but I cannot help but think that you remind me so much of my wife as a young lady."

The maiden shrugged. "You also remind me of someone. My grandfather—just before his passing. His mind wasn't all there in the end." She winked. "And like him, you seem a little lost—out of place, here in this bar."

Truviar looked down at his stained clothes. "I am in burlap, the same as you and the same as the others here, fit for the finest potatoes, if I do say so myself."

Rylia leaned over to pat his hand then coaxed it forward, drawing him closer. She lowered her voice. "Your hand is creased with the indentations of more than nine heavy rings."

Truviar hid his hands under the table as Rylia giggled like the twitter of a chickadee escaping her wine-red lips.

"I know what you need." Rylia held out her palm. "I specialize in exotic fabric. Specifically, cloth woven from gold and jewels."

Truviar peered at her outstretched hand. A square swatch of cloth rested on it. She closed her fist around it then opened it; the cloth had turned from a metallic gold to a pale green.

A charlatan, if there ever was one. Truviar glowered. Though his days browsing tailor shops for the finest fashions had become a thing of the past, his heart thumped in his chest at the promise of a new outfit. Something exquisite to face the council would leave a lasting impression. But cloth from jewels was absurd. *And what if it's true?* A smile forced its way past his dour attitude.

With a waggle of Rylia's fingers, the cloth drained of color and disappeared entirely. Truviar arched his eyebrows.

"I can see your interest is piqued, Mr....?"

"Leofrick."

Rylia laughed. "If that's how you'd like it, Mr. Leofrick."

Truviar tented his fingers and placed his elbows on the table. *A con is still a con.* "How can a fine tailor, if you do make such grand claim, don the clothes of peasants?"

"The same reason as you, I imagine." One corner of her mouth turned up in a coy grin, full of mirth.

Truviar returned her merriment. "So are you to swindle me of my ring indentations?"

Rylia waved her hand in front of her face as though

dismissing his words. "Nothing of the sort. I search out wayward souls. I thought I saw a lost man seeking answers to a question nobody is asking, fighting to keep a position that is being yanked out from under him as he sits high above the town."

Truviar blinked. *How could she…?*

"An empire of fools, am I correct, Mr. Leofrick?" Her slender fingers flowed to her mouth to cover an emerging giggle.

Truviar narrowed his eyes. *She couldn't possibly know…* "Just what is it you're asking of me, young lady?"

Rylia cracked her knuckles and produced a small notebook bound in black leather from her pocket. "Just for a moment of your attention. My services aren't cheap, and I'll require a workshop and loom. Let us discuss what special properties my wares are to hold as well—if you would prefer to keep the rings on your fingers, that is."

***

Truviar burst into his bedroom. The silk curtains swayed on their golden rails as he barreled by them, making a beeline to his heavy oak wardrobe carved with boar motifs underneath elaborate crown molding.

He whipped it open, pulling out outfit after outfit and tossing each to the ground. He fell to his hands and knees and sorted the fashions—jewel-encrusted, those woven with gold clasps, and another pile with neither. After he had three neat piles, he stepped back.

"Truviar, what has gotten into you?"

He pivoted on the balls of his feet, dancing eyes falling on his wife. With a book dangling from her fingers, Martha peered over the footboard of their canopy bed. A worried-looking frown creased her cheeks.

"My dear Martha, I have found a woman who can

spin magical fabric. This fabric will show me which of the council members are weaving plots against me. A cloth that is invisible to foolish people and liars. I'll find a way to subvert Hunter's Law, keep my head *and* my position as emperor." He beamed. "I would never get the funding for this new clothing, so I am dipping into my…" He waved an upturned palm over the piles of clothes on the floor. "Spare funds."

Martha sighed. "I asked you to find the will of the *people* in town, Truviar."

"I have found something even better." The emperor laughed and danced a jig before doubling over in a coughing fit.

Martha rolled her eyes. "Invisible clothes? Next you'll be saying you believe in dragons."

Act II

"The Emperor's Clothes"

Truviar yawned over the Minister for Internal Affairs's droning monotone and gazed up at the green silk tapestries fluttering in the stale air of the longhouse. Golden, speared boars embroidered on the hangings reminded him of his strength and youth.

Cathedral-style ceilings amplified the minister's voice, and it drilled into Truviar's ears like a sword through flesh. He hung a leg over the arm of his high-backed chair and yawned again, louder this time. The other thirteen ministers seemed to share Truviar's sentiments—glassy eyes aplenty—but none would dare speak out for fear of getting their own names ticked for internal investigations by the minister's ever-present quill.

Lord Dain of Denvorn snapped his ledger shut. "Am I boring you, Emperor Truviar?"

Truviar scratched his armpit. "Quite so. I care not of such matters regarding sick horses, the details of our previous meeting, which was only two days ago, I might add, or other petty things like royal looms missing from our dusty storehouse."

Lord Dain's hands shook as he gripped his ledger. "Trivial matters may build into urgent affairs." He glowered then cleared his throat. "And have you given more thought to your abdication? I take it by your dyed hair and shaved beard you're trying to recapture some of your glory days. Perhaps then, you are considering allowing Hunter's Law to be enacted instead? To once again fight for these lands?"

A wave of murmurs rolled throughout the longhouse.

Lord Dain tipped his chin to the other ministers then bobbed his head in a conceited bow to Truviar. "We all must consider the future of this empire." Lord Dain drummed his fingers on his ledger as he spoke. "With all due respect, Emperor Truviar, a man without an heir must step aside so we may train the next head of state. Forgive me if I am overstepping my bounds as Minister of Internal Affairs."

Truviar picked his teeth with the nail of his little finger—Lord Dain was an expert at stirring the pot, but his pot was never filled with anything more than dirty washing. "Not at all, my young Lord Dain. I have given your motion for abdication considerable thought, and I still stand by my decision. I am healthy and able, and still have much time to rule my empire."

The congregation of former kings and lords whispered amongst themselves. The whisper soon turned into a shouting match as they argued over succession, finances, and the empire's ratty and fraying borders. Truviar frowned—their pettiness prevented actual issues to grace the table, though it allowed *him* to contemplate on *his* most pressing worry: what to do with his empire. He couldn't let them split its edges, nor could he trust their pathetic sons and nephews with it. It was *his* land, and they would pry it from his stiff, dead fingers. Which was the idea, if Hunter's Law was enacted.

In the din, Truviar grimaced as Lord Dain's threats to enact the law by harvest's end rose above the angry hollers of the others. The rest of the politicians turned a blind eye to Dain's audacity—with the power he held over the council, not a one stood up in Truviar's defense.

He needed those magical clothes.

***

Truviar scratched his chest as he headed to the town. *I should stop by a tailor's and be fitted for something more comfortable.* The stained burlap shirt prickled his skin, and the itch was maddening. Even the fabrics woven from stinging nettles had a pleasant softness to them. He laughed. *Shopping for the lesser textiles.* Even in his days as a general, silken garments graced his skin under heavy plate. Where could shops be found that housed anything less grand?

He rapped on the warped and beaten door to the nondescript shack he had rented.

The sweet coo of Rylia answered. "Come in, Mr. Leofrick, I have been expecting you."

The door creaked and whined as he entered.

Inside, the loom he had "borrowed" rasped and clacked with Rylia's nimble hands. Heddles jumped and crisscrossed in shedding, followed by Rylia's deft shuttle pass and slam of the beater. Truviar blinked in disbelief. The motions were all there, and the loom functioned as normal.

But there wasn't any thread.

Truviar glowered at the heap of clothing in a dusty corner. *His* clothing. They were riddled with holes where jewels had been stripped and golden clasps had once been affixed. His hands balled into fists as the cobwebs of filth in the corners and on the ceiling swayed in time to the loom's flowing motions. *Swindled. I knew it.*

Rylia caught the shuttle in one hand and eased back in her stool, facing him. "Isn't the fabric absolutely beautiful, Mr. Leofrick?"

Truviar ground his teeth. *How* dare *she continue this deception in my presence?*

She hopped to her feet and flitted to a scarred workbench at the opposite end of the room like a fawn bounding after its mother. Pinching a bit of dust in both hands, she held her arms out as though displaying the finest bolt of fabric in all the land. "I know it's not much yet, but I hope this color is to your liking. Can you see how the pigments mix with the sapphires and emeralds? It makes for a wonderful, deep hue." She smiled—her doe eyes earnest.

Truviar glared at the empty space between her

fingers. A cloth invisible to foolish people. Sweat beaded his brow, and his anger dissipated with it. *I am a fool?* Truviar crossed the room and peered at her outstretched hands. There was no mistaking it—there was nothing there.

"Well, Mr. Leofrick? There is still time to change the pattern if the color isn't to your liking."

Truviar huffed. "A fine color, indeed." His heart hitched—to expose her would expose his own folly. To the ministers. And to Martha. "And when will this *fine* fabric be completed?" Pride choked back reason, and he sputtered.

Rylia jerked her head toward the loom, bangs flopping. "By the next crescent moon." She mimed placing the fabric back on the workbench. "I did enjoy your company the other night in the tavern and would ask you to stay, but I have so much work to do. If you come back later this week, I can show you the shawl I am preparing for your great cape."

Truviar sneered, glancing at the empty loom. *Trickster! Deceiver!* "I shall be back in the morning. If this…cape cannot be completed in the time you say, you are free to move your endeavor…elsewhere. Take what you need and speak to nobody." He had been taken for a fool. If Rylia knew what was good for the both of them, she would get the hint, claim her victory, and be out of town by morning. An invisible cape. His gut churned at the mere thought of it. *How could I be so stupid?*

He let the door close with a rusty click. Inside, the click-clack of the loom resumed. Probably to keep up her charade.

Needing to clear his head, Truviar took a brisk walk, cursing the dilapidated buildings and thatched roofs worn from ill repair. Faded shop signs swayed beneath sagging awnings, and every fourth person he passed either coughed on Truviar's shoulders or held a begging bowl to his knees. He slowed his pace.

Just what had happened to the town? This section of his empire around the Demon's Hole District had had better days. Since the war, it had slowly turned into a slum right under his gaze from the East Tower. His son wouldn't recognize it anymore. Truviar's brows hung lower with each passing hut, and his thoughts turned from his son, to his pride and the view of his great lands from the keep, to the people living in squalor. His empire was rotting.

Rylia had claimed that a fool couldn't see her woven fabric—had Truviar been blinded by his power and kept deaf by his ministers? Would they allow him to parade naked through the streets before admitting he actually wasn't wearing any clothes?

From a dirt road cluttered with jutting rocks and sinking holes on the hill leading away from town, a large man with a floppy hat set down his cart of manure and pointed. "Hey, lookit there! It's the old fella from Dentshire with the funny accent! Oi, Dentshire!"

Truviar groaned. The gruff man from the tavern. The last person he wanted to see right now.

The man waved at Truviar, bits of dung flying off his heavy gloves in all directions. "Dentshire!"

Truviar dipped his head in recognition and turned to return to the keep, but the man rushed down the hill and clapped him on the back.

"No hard feelin's 'bout the other day, eh, Dentshire? You caught me in a state, a state my poor wife says I oughta get unner control." He belted out a guffaw. "Name's Addy."

"Charmed. Leofrick, from Dentshire." Truviar looked him up and down, burying his disgust behind a twitching smirk.

Addy laughed again and put Truviar in a half hug. "I know that, Dentshire. Jus' how drunk di'jya think I was, eh?"

Truviar twisted out of his embrace. "Or *still* be, might I add?"

Addy produced a waterskin tied to his waistband. "I haul manure—you think I'd wanna make the trip ta Creston *sober?*" He took a long drag from the skin. "How 'bout you, eh? Old fella wanderin' 'round all by your lonesome in the middle o' the day looks ta me like they could use a swig o' the fine stuff."

Truviar took the waterskin and held it up to his chin. *His chapped lips touched this. I could get—*

Addy pushed the waterskin high—the foul-smelling liquid dripped into Truviar's mouth and spilled on his shirt. The drink burned like coals from the hearth with a similar earthy and ashy taste, leaving his mouth drier than before.

"Good stuff, eh?" Addy remarked with a waggle of his eyebrows. "Elric brews it himself. Jus' the right amount o' fire 'n sting."

Truviar wiped his mouth with the back of his hand. *The nerve of this—*

"Listen, mate. I gots myself thinkin' the other day, right? Fine fella like yerself, from the hills o' Dentshire no less, with a lofty way o' speakin', sittin' in The Boar's Hole for a pint with a pretty young thing."

Truviar took a step back, heart skipping a beat. *Has he seen through my disguise?*

"So, right? Old fella, young lady, Boar's Hole. Stinks like old Lord Favian wastin' our taxes at the brothels."

Truviar's eyes widened. *The Minister of Finance?*

"So I says to me, I says, 'Addy, that fella's a politician if I ever seen one,' right? Or knows one, see? So's I's wonderin'...'" Addy's gaze drifted to his cart on the hill. The cart lolled off to one side as though it could split in two at any moment. "Cart's rotting away, ya know..."

Rotting wasn't the half of it. The flow of money defined the city below the keep, and the longhouse had siphoned that flow to fill their own coffers.

As have I. Truviar stared at the creased leather shoes

on his feet then to the tattered excuses for shoes that hung loosely on Addy's. A pain, old as his bones and sharp as his wife's wit, wormed its way behind his eyes and threatened tears. If Truviar's son, Leofrick, hadn't perished beating back Creston's vanguard, he would be around Addy's age.

"So's maybe, right?" Addy wrung his hands. "So's maybe you know sommun, like a politician, and maybe, right? Maybe you could get a road built. Fer ev'ryone. Deliv'ries take twice as long, an' traders don't come this way no more…"

Truviar pressed his lips together in confusion. Even with his horrid clothes and broken manure cart, Addy was asking a favor for everyone. An altruist. His son had been the same—only thinking of the people, the low class, right until the end. Truviar wiped his damp eyes and dragged his hand through his jet black hair, greasing his palm. Dear Leofrick would have made a grand emperor.

Addy swept his hand across the farmlands. "If a road ta Creston could—"

Truviar smiled and patted Addy's shoulder. "I am a second cousin to the emperor's third most trusted advisor." He furrowed his brow. "By marriage, not by blood." *That won't arouse too much suspicion.* "I'll see what I can do."

Addy's face split into a wide grin, and he lifted his foul waterskin. "Down here, we drink ta words like that."

***

The sun broke over the town's roofline. Truviar squinted as the dawn's amber rays cut through the close-built cottages, blinking between crooked boards like a rolling fantascope. His stomach dropped as he approached Rylia's door—the clacking loom was already echoing in the morning air.

Truviar clenched his jaw and steeled himself to run

her out of town. He grasped the handle and burst in.

Rylia spun on her stool and beamed at him. "Right on time, Mr. Leofrick."

Truviar thrust his finger at the loom, ready to give a verbal thrashing the likes of which had never crossed a king's lips since the days of old, but the words fizzled in his throat.

Throughout the loom, single strands of translucent gossamer—like the web of a spider—glistened in the dawn light through the cracks in the walls. On the workbench as well, the outline of a crystalline fabric shimmered.

"I take it the color is to your liking?" Rylia giggled and propped an elbow on the loom's beater.

Truviar rushed over and reached for the cloth on the workbench.

"You mustn't touch it!" Rylia squealed and grabbed his arm. "Nobody must touch it until it is ready. It may tear. Please, look only with your eyes, Mr. Leofrick."

Truviar did. He stared at it, searching for words, and she at him—one with an expression of awe, the other of warmth.

"Are you able to see now, Mr. Leofrick?" Rylia played with a loose thread dangling from the fell. "The colors become more brilliant as one turns their thoughts outward."

Truviar backed away, pawed at the door handle, and left the workshop, breathing heavily. *Witchcraft! Of the blackest kind!* Safe outside, he patted the sweat off his brow and neck with a silk handkerchief. He slunk away from the workshop, pinching the bridge of his nose and shaking his head.

Turning down an alley, he pressed his back against the wall of the cheese maker's. *What did I just see?* He hung in the morning air, debating whether to return to Rylia and give her a piece of his mind or let it lie. Something *had been* on the loom, but what? Were his old eyes playing tricks?

Unable to work his thoughts around what he had

seen, he let out a breathy sigh and massaged his forehead. Maybe he could let her play her games for now. Another, more important task weighed on his mind and pushed Rylia and her loom out of it.

He pushed off the wall and headed toward the town's outskirts, hoping Addy had kept his end of the bargain.

Cresting a sloping hill leading to the farmlands, a group of about twenty sat on their haunches in burlap, floppy hats, and waterskins most likely filled with Elric's foul brew. Truviar scanned them for shirker-types. Addy bolted upright from where he was seated and barreled toward him. Truviar took a few panicked steps backward, but Addy wrapped his arms around Truviar in a vicious bear hug.

Truviar's breath caught, and he shoved Addy away— he stunk of manure. But not of alcohol.

"My best friend, ev'ryone! Say hello ta Dentshire!" He gripped Truviar by the shoulders and faced him toward the crowd of peasants.

The people leaped to their feet. A few shouted "oi, Dentshire!" or "dawn be the day, Dentshire!"

Addy waved to them. "So's I kept my end o' the deal. Twenty workers. You promised you'd talk to the…whatsit?"

"The emperor's third most trusted advisor," Truviar replied, shifting his gaze between the filthy riffraff and Addy's wild eyes. Was this really a good idea? They *were* common folk, after all.

Truviar glowered at the ruts and furrows crisscrossing the wide dirt path. He shook his head. Martha had asked him to "find the will of the people," and if they willed a road, that's what they were going to get. He met Addy's eyes—so much like his son's—fiddled with his belt strap, and unhooked a long metal cylinder etched with the emperor's seal.

Addy regarded the tube, and a grin worked its way to his ears. "That Truviar's personal seal? Well I'll be a hog's wife, I be."

Truviar unscrewed the ivory cap and took out a roll of vellum. He unfurled it and showed it to Addy, who leaned close as he mouthed the words on the paper.

Addy frowned. "I's learn-ed just as much as any other, but could ya do me a fair spot? All this law-speak ain't quite easy on my eyes." He tapped the wax seal affixed to the bottom of the parchment. "But I see the emperor's seal here, and that means good news, eh?"

Truviar nodded. "This is a personal request from Emperor Truviar—he has heard your call for a road, and against the wishes of the ministers in the longhouse, particularly the Minister of Finance, he has dipped into his own pocket to fund it, as long as fine workers are provided."

Addy gripped Truviar's shoulder, and Truviar steeled himself for another manure-filled embrace.

"In addition," Truviar continued, "the workers are to be paid thirty gold pieces for their time, as long as the job is well done, and further, twenty gold for materials is awarded to the foreman. That's you, Addy."

Tears welled up in Addy's eyes. "Just what didja *say* to Emperor Truviar, Dentshire? This be a miracle, if I ever—"

"He wishes to express his thanks for bringing this issue to light, as he is hounded daily by trivial matters in the council and cannot see the people as he once could. Furthermore, if the job is done well, future improvement projects are to follow."

Addy wiped his eyes with the back of his grimy hand. "Fer thirty pieces, I'd sell my own mother ta th' sailors in Portston." He grasped Truviar's hand and shook. "Dentshire, yer all right." He turned to the waiting peasants, dusting off his already filthy clothes.

Truviar grinned as Addy barked orders, divvying up responsibilities and taking to his new role like salt to meat. At a clap of his hands, the others hitched up their breeches and took off to gather materials and tools.

Addy watched them go with hands on his hips then turned to Truviar. "Thanks again, Dentshire. This road'll help ev'ryone here."

Truviar blinked at the disappearing crowds. "Forgive me if I were to question your enthusiasm, but did I see women amongst the workers? It is forbidden by law for women to stand within twenty feet of construction for their own safety."

Addy patted the emperor on his shoulder. "Who said anythin' about standin'? They here ta work jus' like ev'ryone else. Nobody'll be standin'—besides, that old law's jus' a *suggestion*, I'm sure, eh? I think there's a law 'bout 'no pigs within the castle walls,' but Truviar built a big ol' longhouse to house the lot o' them."

Truviar laughed. There *were* too many swine within the walls; the politicians would have to go. To imagine Lord Dain as a plump piglet, wallowing in filth—he laughed again. As Addy dashed off to gather his own tools, a crazy idea the ministers would outright detest swirled in Truviar's mind.

Act III
"An Empire of Fools"

"This is preposterous!" Lord Dain shouted, his voice carrying to the rafters in the longhouse. Golden goblets rattled as he pounded the table. He quieted, shoulders shaking, then thrust a finger at the emperor's wife. "She must be removed—women have no business in the affairs of the state."

Truviar stole a glance at his wife standing next to his chair. Her jaw clenched and unclenched with each comment from the minister, but her chin was high and her eyes set in steel.

She had never looked as lovely.

"I wish to address the Minister of Justice, Keeper of the Laws," Truviar said, "and ask him to read the rule in question."

The Minister of Justice stood, hefting a book as thick as an axe handle, and cleared his throat. "Paragraph seven of article nineteen states that 'no woman be allowed to sit in political gatherings, neither within castle walls nor outside.'" He dropped the heavy tome on the table with a thud, as though punctuating a small victory.

Truviar yawned. "You will note that my wife is not sitting."

The ministers' faces turned shades of color that reflected their goblets of wine as they regarded the royal pair.

Lord Dain wrenched at his high, lacy collar. "This is an affront to politics. Should we allow just anyone from their sewing circles—"

"The sewing circles are exactly why I'm here, Lord Dain." Martha curled her delicate hands into hard-packed fists. "Or do you think we actually sew and prattle on about gossip and fashion in those groups? The women have a voice, and you must hear us."

"This is not—"

"Well, we *do* gossip a little, my lords." Martha's wrinkles accentuated her smile. "Certain concubines do discuss *certain* performances, Lord Dain. And the legitimacy of those born to them. Furthermore, the wives of lords know much about their nighttime sojourns." She shot a look at Lord Favian, the Minister of Finance, who sank down in his chair. "I only wish to discuss politics. But if you would *prefer* gossip, I could—"

"Politics will do fine," Lord Dain rasped. "Though you cannot expect us to take your political natterings seriously."

Deep furrows cut into Martha's brow as she fixed an icy gaze on Lord Dain.

Truviar clapped his hands twice. "Then this matter is settled. The women are to be heard in the longhouse, so long as they are standing."

***

Small victories were to be celebrated, and Truviar couldn't think of a better celebration than a glass of a fine vintage with Martha. His wife, however, was still tied up in the longhouse—she was born from politics, and a chance to flex her muscles proved irresistible to her. Thankfully, she had dismissed Truviar when his snores became unbearable.

Instead, he had settled on a waterskin filled to bursting, an itchy burlap shirt, and a quick trip to see how his new clothes were turning out.

Rylia greeted him with her usual gusto. "Mr. Leofrick, this *is* a surprise. What's the occasion?"

Truviar poured two glasses full of wine. "I detest drinking alone, and I have something to celebrate. Also, I think I may have a plan to wrestle the land from the grip of the people in power."

Rylia took a glass from him and sniffed at it. "Oh? And what lands have you, Mr. Leofrick?"

The emperor coughed as the wine sailed down the wrong pipe. He hacked and gripped his knees, taking slow breaths, until his regalness returned. "Ah, just an old house on the other end of the town—nothing important."

Rylia grinned and gulped down her wine.

Truviar sipped, running his eyes over the loom and the workbench in the corner for the hundredth time. *Amazing.* A partially finished cape hung in neat folds. It shined in translucent blues and greens like the frothing tips of ocean waves and deep turquoise of clear lagoons, and the light streaming in through the warped holes in the walls glinted beautiful auric tones off it.

"Your work is absolutely breathtaking, Rylia." He poured wine into her proffered glass.

Rylia shrugged. "I weave as nature does. So tell me, what of your plan to win your…old house, was it? Crumbling, I assume?"

Truviar tossed his head back, emptying the cup. "I've discovered that I'm not too fond of the place, really." He blinked, heart pumping faster in his chest. "I think I've approached the house from the wrong direction all this time—and I'll gain it back by first losing everything."

***

"Oi, Addy!" Truviar, a jovial skip in his step—from the wine, or the brilliant plan he was concocting to avoid Hunter's Law, he was unsure—approached the group of workers laying down perfectly fitted cobblestones.

Addy tossed a shovel to the side and ran to Truviar. The two embraced. "Old man Dentshire! What news from good ol' Truviar ya have t'day?"

"Good news *and* good things." Truviar unhooked his

waterskin and tossed it to Addy. "Tell me what you think of *this*."

Addy pulled off the cork and took a quick swig, smacking his lips. "Sweet like children's juice—what nothin' with the bite of Elric's moonshine."

Truviar nodded. "The emperor wishes to have Elric produce his wares openly—and royally sanctioned. Tell him to come by the keep later this evening. South entrance."

Addy blinked and glanced at one of the workers.

"You introduced me to his stuff, and word got around the keep. Truviar's taken quite a liking to the dry taste." The emperor toed the cobbled road—the craftsmanship was breathtaking. "The emperor is also prepared to offer your group more work. I hear there's an irrigation system that you keep clogging with manure?"

"Old bearded Gunn'll be happy ta hear that." Addy laughed.

Truviar handed him a parchment and a fountain pen. "Make a list of everything you think the town needs. I have the emperor's ear, and now you do as well. The town's voice will be heeded."

Staring at the pen embellished with the emperor's seal of a speared boar, Addy lowered his voice. "I swear ya be th' emperor himself, somedays, Dentshire."

"Would that be so bad, my friend?"

Addy snorted back a laugh and struck his knee with his hand. "No, sir, Dentshire." He picked up the shovel he had thrown aside. "Ya workin' t'day?"

Truviar snatched the shovel from him. "Why not? I'm good and sloshed up from wine. Just tell me where to dig."

***

Truviar stood in his bedroom, preening in front of a

mirror. Earlier that morning, he had gone to inspect Rylia's work, as he did every other day since the work on the irrigation system had started. She was gone—disappeared into the wind just as she had come—but the completed cape had been left on the workbench with a simple note:

"For Truviar Black, the true emperor from Dentshire. May this cape help open your eyes."

Holding the gossamer cape, as solid as any other cloak and in vibrant greens and blues, brought energy to his old bones. "Beautiful" couldn't describe it—it was far beyond that. The creases reflected the light, and it shimmered as he turned, fabric caressing his old skin as though he had stepped into a bubbling stream.

A knock on the door was followed by Martha, who dropped her mouth open as she set eyes on him. "Where did you get…" She ran her eyes up and down her husband.

"What do you think, my dear?" Truviar spun for her, splaying his arms out wide.

The empress blinked and shook her head. "It's a nice cape, Truviar, but I think you're crazy to be staring at a mirror and admiring yourself while the meeting regarding your abdication is at hand. Lord Dain is set to declare Hunter's Law in force—you wouldn't fare well in the fighting pits with the younger lords."

"He's been going on about that law for months." Truviar shrugged. "Though I do appreciate you and your sewing circle injecting a little wisdom into the laws of our lands." He winked at her. "Keeps the lords on their toes."

Martha strode over to Truviar and picked at the cape's edges, adjusting its fit. "We've kept them fighting between each other. If you ask me, my sewing circle is on the verge of running that longhouse. But it means nothing if Lord Dain pushes you out. The Minister of Justice is already drawing up a revision of the law to keep the women out of it."

"Because they're afraid of you." Truviar crossed the room and planted a light kiss on her cheek. "I feel I have cheated the people using you as my own private advisor all these years. You must be appointed an official position."

Martha's cheeks blushed cerise.

"I'm ready to face them," Truviar declared.

Martha slid her hand into his. "You *have* chosen an absolutely brilliant cape for this meeting—more regal than anything I have ever seen."

Without the rings that used to adorn his hands, Truviar easily slipped from her grip and pulled the drawstring on his cape loose. He draped Rylia's mantle over Martha's maroon dress. She hugged it, tugging it over the lacy golden brocades trimming her dress's sharp edges and curves.

Taking a step back to admire his wife, Truviar tightened his lips over a large smile. "It's yours, then. I never was any good with politics, anyway. Wear it as you stand by my side."

They walked arm in arm to the longhouse. The earthy scent of decaying rosebushes and fallen leaves hung heavy in the air. Birds chirped their territorial songs in contrast to the heated shouts of the politicians from inside the longhouse. Or perhaps the politicians *were* like the birds, though at least *their* border disputes carried a hint of beauty.

As Truviar approached the ornately carved double doors, his wife gave his hand a quick squeeze and a worried look. Truviar straightened and drew himself up to the height he had held in his youth.

Inside, the politicians hushed as he entered and sat in the high-backed chair at one end of the long oak table. A small feast had been spread out, and the boar tapestries adorning the walls had been taken down. Truviar grinned. Nobody had even set a plate in front of his place on the council.

Fourteen politicians set eyes on him, Lord Dain's the angriest of all, complete with a wry grin of victory. Martha stood by Truviar's left, smoothing the folds of her cape.

"My fellow ministers," Truviar began, "I come before you in regards to my abdication."

"Certainly, we are aware of the situation, Emperor Truviar." Lord Dain knocked on the table with the edge of his ledger, sending a few loose grapes to the floor.

"Lord Dain has demanded I relinquish my position as emperor on the grounds that my only heir died fighting in the very wars that gave us our great lands." The stench of stale sweat painted the back of Truviar's throat as he spoke, and he coughed.

Rapping his ledger on the table again, Lord Dain scowled. "And of course, you will not, am I correct? I gave you until the harvest, but now there are more pressing matters, which is why I called this meeting. We must discuss your successor, for one, and the preparations for the fighting colosseum, should you still insist on presiding over the empire. We would appreciate you getting to the point, without any long speeches." He leaned back in his chair and stuck his hands behind his head.

"Yes, indeed." Truviar sighed. "Nobody, including myself, will need to die in combat for succession. Hunter's Law will not need to be enacted. I wish to abdicate."

A cacophony of shouts and pushing and shoving between politicians followed. Voices raised in arguments; arms and hands gesticulated violently. Martha shot her husband a look of astonishment.

Truviar waited for their silence.

"On two conditions." Truviar shot a smile at Lord Dain. "One, successors shall never again be decided by that foul Hunter's Law but by the will of the people." He glanced at Martha. Her cape rippled but seemed to firm up rather than fade. *This is the right choice. I am no fool.*

Lord Dain tapped his chin with one hand as his scowl morphed into a wry smile. "An election? So you just wish to hand the throne to my son? There is none with a greater love for the lands we stand on."

The Minister of Finance scoffed. "Surely the Minister of Justice's nephew is of higher popularity! He throws the grandest banquets in the realm."

Shouts and glasses raised, wine was thrown, and the politicians clucked like a group of chickens squabbling for the highest perch in the roost.

Truviar waited again for the clamor to subside, wondering how he had ever tolerated their infighting. "The second condition is that I wish to have one final procession throughout the town to announce my abdication and call for a general election."

Lord Dain laughed. "If you love voting so much, shall we put your call to one?" He swept his hand across the stern faces of the ministers. "Please rise, all those opposed."

Not a single man stood.

***

Preparations took two weeks, but the procession was as grand as in the days of old. From inside his curtained, horse-drawn coach, the joyous voices of celebrating people prickled Truviar's ears. They loved his festivals. This year, there was even enough drink to go around. Even the sons and nephews of the ministers had splurged to provide the people with something to remember them for when it came time to elect his successor.

Martha sighed. "Are you absolutely sure, Truviar? An election? That hasn't been done for over four hundred years."

"Ah yes, but it *has* been done." Truviar chortled and took her hands in his. "The matter is settled." He gazed into her eyes, though the splendor of Rylia's cape draped around her shoulders threatened to tear his attention to it. Each day, it seemed more brilliant than the last.

The coach came to a stop with a bump by an elevated stage with a dais.

"Are you sure you want to do it this way, Truviar?" Martha's tight-lipped frown seemed to plead with her husband to reconsider as she reached for the hundredth time to fiddle with Truviar's shirt.

Truviar patted her hand and removed it from his collar. "Go out and announce me. I will make my abdication speech with my back straight and shoulders broad."

She stepped outside to gasps and confusion from the gathering onlookers.

Glee bubbled in Truviar's stomach as the villagers outside argued colors—the red of Martha's dress or the blue of her cape—amongst themselves.

After a short speech, Martha raised her voice over the murmurs of the crowd to announce the emperor. Truviar, hands sweaty, opened the puffed velvet coach door.

The noise of the crowd died to a hush as Truviar exited the coach. He stepped to the heartwood podium emblazoned with the emperor's seal, raised his hand, and smiled.

Deep in the crowd, Addy raised his own. It trembled like a dying leaf on a maple still clinging to autumn. "Oi, Dentshire," he said in a whisper that carried throughout the populace.

Truviar locked eyes with him. "Oi, Addy." The emperor tugged at the stained burlap shirt he wore. No matter how many times he donned it, it still itched, but the itch reminded him of the people.

***

In the following weeks, Truviar carried on, his chin higher than ever before. The irrigation system was finished, and workers split to tackle smaller improvements. He frequented The Boar's Hole as well as a number of other local establishments, hearing the people's concerns and passing that information to his wife.

He had held meetings with the minister's choices for successors, each with their own swarms of attendants and conniving manners, each insisting his beautiful wife wasn't wearing a cape at all.

When election day came, the sons of the silken class gave public debates and demanded the approval of the townsfolk. They lavished the people with sweet words to match the sweet cakes and foodstuffs they handed out to buy the people to their cause.

Truviar worked, as he always did, with Addy and his group. Sometimes, he would pause mid-dig, his thoughts to Rylia. Why had she come to *him*? Would he have ever noticed his own stupidity if she hadn't?

In time, as the air turned cooler, he stopped dwelling on her and her reasons for bestowing him with such a beautiful cape. After all, the callouses that returned to his hands were greater reward than any extravagant fabrics or jeweled brooches.

***

Truviar stood at the East Tower overlooking his lands, as he had when declaring his empire full of fools, now clear that he had been the fool himself. Below, Lord Dain and the potential successors, as well as a sizable jury of townsfolk, stuffed themselves in the longhouse, counting votes and filling their faces with boar's meat and wine.

The great horn on the longhouse sounded, signifying the final counts had been tallied and a victor decided.

In contrast to the emotions in the longhouse running hot enough to steam the windows, the breeze in the tower was cool, the view of the rolling lands vast. Truviar didn't hear the soft steps of his wife until she hooked her arm into the crook of his.

"I'm going to miss this view," Truviar said with a small sigh. "Have you brought me news of the successor I'm to congratulate?"

Martha pulled on his arm and settled her cheek on his shoulder. "I have."

"Is it Lord Dain's boy?"

Martha nodded. "It is."

Truviar let out a long breath.

"But he refuses to ascend."

Truviar blinked in confusion. "And why is that?"

"Because although he won the election based on the votes of property holders, he did not win the will of the people—he is looking for the true successor, a Sir Leofrick of Dentshire." She squeezed his hand. "He will not ascend until this man sits at his right."

Truviar laughed as he looked down upon the town. Beginnings of new roads crisscrossed throughout, markets had sprung up where empty streets had lain barren, deadened farms teemed green as the lifeblood of irrigation flowed through them. He had given up his lands—but pride and a sense of accomplishment filled that loss. Much work still remained, and Truviar was going to make sure that the spirit of Leofrick lived on, both within himself and in his new successor.

He forced his lips to remain solemn under a bubbling grin—he couldn't wait to see the look on Lord Dain's face.

Story Index

"The Frog Prince" was inspired by The Frog Prince

"On the Wrong Foot" was inspired by Cinderella

"Beauty in the Beast" was inspired by Beauty and the Beast

"This Little Piggie" was inspired by The Three Little Pigs

"Out of the Tower" was inspired by Rapunzel

"True Reflections" was inspired by Snow White

"Beauty" was inspired by Sleeping Beauty

"An Empire of Fools" was inspired by The Emperor's New Clothes

Author Biographies

Heather Hayden – The Frog Prince

Fueled by chocolate and moonlight, Heather Hayden seeks to bring magic into the world through her stories. A freelance editor by day, she pours heart and soul into her novels every night, spinning tales of science fiction and fantasy that sing of friendship and hope.

Frogs are commonplace in the Maine forest where Heather lives. Peepers are especially vocal, but there are bullfrogs and other species dwelling in the marshy lands as well. Growing up listening to their calls, she often wondered if any of them were more than they seemed. That lingering spark of wonder ignited when she asked herself, "What if the frog prince left a family behind when he became human again?" She dedicates her retelling to all the peepers (and her sister) who make summer night drives so much fun.

Heather's other publications include *Augment*, a YA science fiction novel, and several short stories in the JL Anthology series. You can follow Heather's writing adventures on her blog (hhaydenwriter.com), Facebook (@HHaydenWriter), and Twitter (@HHaydenWriter).

Allie May – On the Wrong Foot

Allie May is a dog lover, mom, and Dr. Pepper addict who turns her caffeine-fueled dreams into believable fiction. She fell in love with the impossible at a young age and has been telling stories (some fiction, some mostly non-fiction) ever since. She has been published in three fairy tale retelling anthologies, *From the Stories of Old*, *Of Legend and Lore*, and *A Bit of Magic*. Currently, Allie is submitting her novel to publishers while working on many, many other fantasy projects.

She married her high school sweetheart because he takes her to Disneyland (oh, and because she loves him). Together they have a dog child and a human child who use the last of her sanity. On the weekends, you might catch a glimpse of her in the shadows as a lightsaber-wielding superhero.

Fairy tales require suspension of disbelief, but what if a character took it too far? Using that as a base, "On the Wrong Foot" was born.

You can follow Allie's writing adventures on her website (alliemayauthor.com), Facebook (@alliemayauthor), and Twitter (@alliemayauthor).

# Martia Benson – Beauty in the Beast

Martia Benson is a taciturn loner who much prefers her own company to that of others. Despite her guarded manner, she has the heart of a sentimental romantic.

"Beauty in the Beast" was largely transcribed from a dream, which began with the flood scene and included the majority of the events that followed.

Martia was born just before the turn of the century. Her only friends are books, her love of animals, and her imagination.

Alexander Thomas – This Little Piggie

Alexander Thomas is an author, a game designer, dog lover, karaoke enthusiast, and all-around nerd. You may know him from his work on roleplaying games including *Mutants & Masterminds* for Green Ronin and New Millennium Games, as well as *Quantum Black*.

His debut novel, *The Magician's Sin*, was published in March 2019, courtesy of Kyanite Publishing.

You can connect with Alexander through his website (www.alexanderwrites.com) or Twitter (@Alexanderwrite3).

Kristy Perkins – Out of the Tower

Kristy Perkins is a nanny, and a writer whenever she can find the time. Ever since she could write legibly, she has created stories. She writes fantasy and sci-fi stories to satisfy the need for more dragons and spaceships in her life.

"Out of the Tower" started as a simple tale of a boy falling in love with a girl after he rescued her from a witch. But that was too easy, so he had to lose all his memories and then try to avoid the problem. When that also proved too simple, the wonderful Rapunzel gained a secret of her own, which led to the story found here.

Short stories of Kristy's can be found in other JL Anthologies.

Visit her blog (nocluewritingplatform.wordpress.com) or follow her on Twitter (@KristyEPerkins) or Pinterest (perkinswhatif).

Matthew Dewar – True Reflections

Matthew's passion for reading and writing developed at a young age. Fascinated by all genres, enthralled by the endless creativity of imagination, and captivated by foreign worlds and intriguing characters, Matthew makes time in his busy schedule to write every day. If he's not reading or writing, you might find Matthew working as a physiotherapist, teaching group fitness classes, entertaining his dog, or dreaming of travelling to an exotic destination.

Matthew chose to write a fractured fairy tale retelling of Snow White because he wanted to reflect today's society in the evil queen and mirror. Social media—like a magic mirror—is a tool, and like anything, too much can be dangerous.

If you would like to read more from Matthew, check out his book: *Nightmare Stories*, a collection of young adult horror fiction where twelve teens discover that happily ever afters only exist in fairy tales. Other works have appeared in various JL Anthologies and Seven Deadly Sins anthologies. You can connect with Matthew on Twitter (@WriterDewar), Facebook (Matthew Dewar Author), or at his website: matthewdewarauthor.wordpress.com.

LB Garrison – Beauty

Have you ever watched the stars on a warm summer night and wondered if someone was looking back? Thoughts of dinosaurs and aliens dominated LB Garrison's childhood. Adult concerns came later, but never could quite crowd out the wonder.

A microbiologist by profession, and dreamer by choice, LB has always been an avid reader of science fiction and fantasy. As a writer, he has several short stories under his belt.

LB chose to retell "Sleeping Beauty" because he wanted to fracture a fairy tale that would be easily recognizable. Through "Beauty," he explored the twist that Sleeping Beauty was not a victim after all—but the problem.

LB has published several short stories and is currently wrestling with a first novel in southeast New Mexico.

Shannon Yukumi – An Empire of Fools

Shannon Yukumi lives and works as an interpreter and translator in Japan, writes fiction in his spare time, and parents two children in the time he doesn't have. Language tends to get away from him, but he claims that that isn't his fault.

About the Illustrator

Heidi Hayden was raised in the forests of Maine and graduated from the Maine College of Art as an Illustration major. A bookworm by nature, she reads copious amounts of questionable fiction by unpublished authors, in the few moments of spare time when she is not writing and illustrating her own books. She works in gouache, ink, pencil, and fabric, and enjoys repurposing materials for her art.

She drew inspiration for the anthology's illustrations from a variety of old fairy tale books, such as those depicting the tales of the Brothers Grimm. The medium—ink on paper—was chosen in order to capture both the essence of the retellings and the timelessness of black-and-white illustrations.

You can see more of her work on her website (haydenillustration.com).

About the Just-Us League

Hailing from all corners of the globe, the members of the Just-Us League share a common passion for words and worlds.

The League can be found on Facebook (@jlwriters), Twitter (@JL_writing), and our website (jlwriters.com). Follow us for updates, giveaways, and new releases.

Also by the Just-Us League

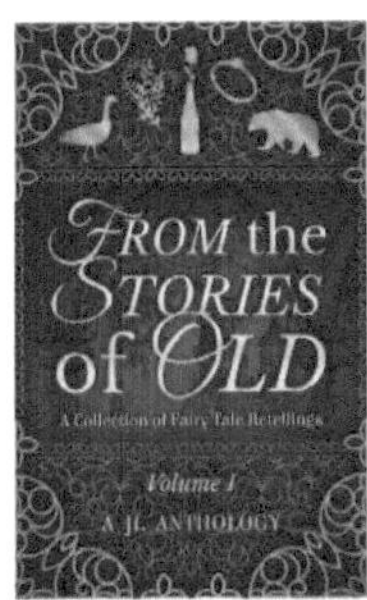

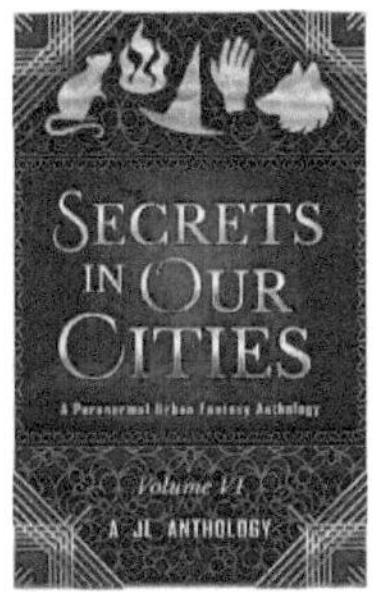